The Tales Of LaRue

By: Sydney Lyn

For my parents-
Who are my greatest friends and supporters.
Who gave me the greatest of adventures.

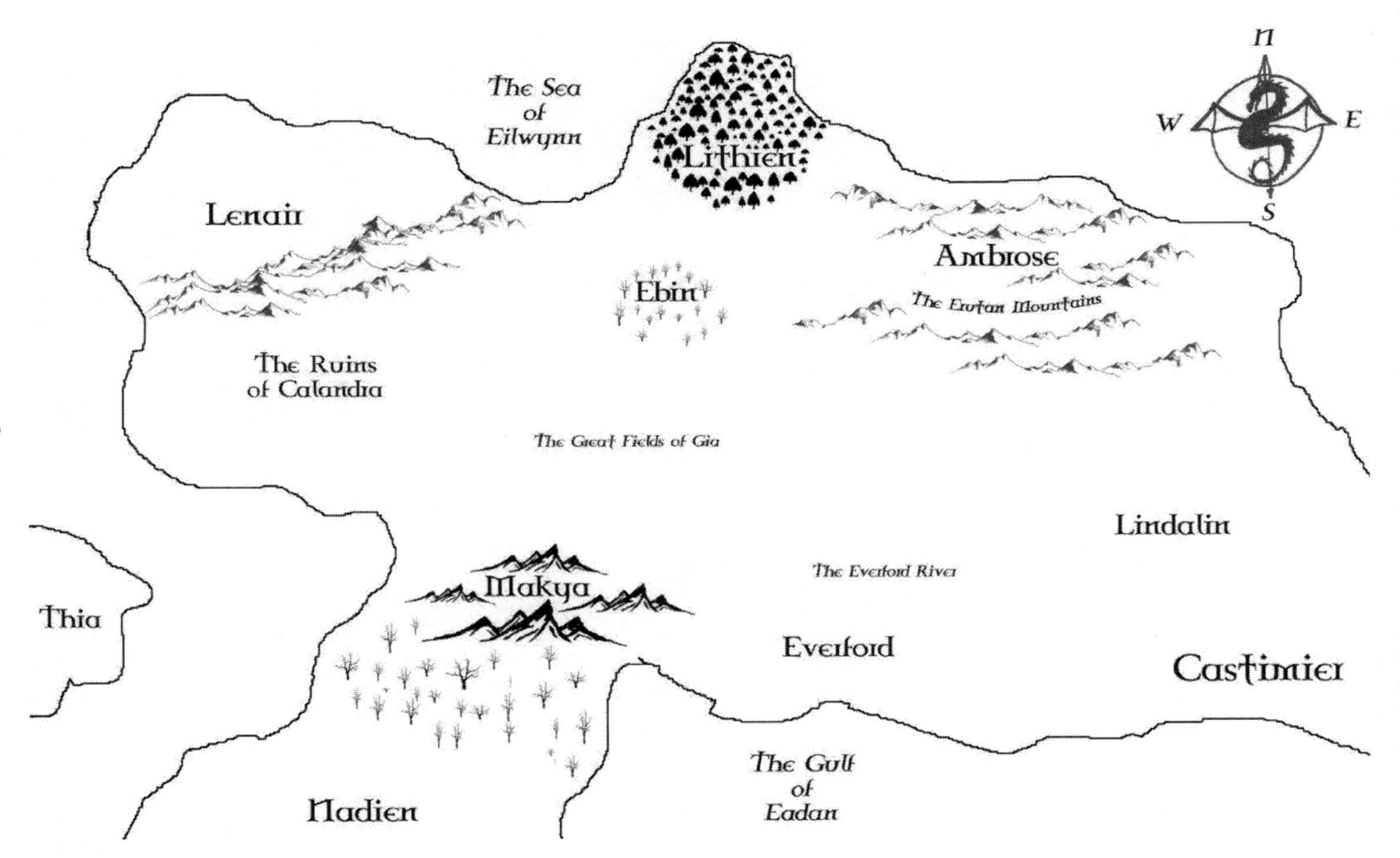
N
W
E
S
The Sea
of
Eilwynn
Lithien
Lenair
Ambrose
Ebin
The Exotan Mountains
The Ruins
of Calandria
The Great Fields of Gia
Lindalin
The Everford River
Makya
Thia
Everford
Castimier
The Gulf
of
Eadan
Hadien

When two Elves create a fourth child of
full Saleth and Narrod,
the Prophecy will begin.
Of the Silver Queen and the Golden Lord.
She shall be the Pathway.
War cannot cease until the wrong has
been righted
and the balance restored.
Princess of the stars and sun so she shall be
called.
The rightful queen to a hidden kingdom.
She would banish the evil,
bringing back the light that was once lost to us.
Last of the Fae, bearer of magic.
She shall be the Pathway.

Chapter 1

The rolling sea of meadow grass blurs by as I dig my heels into the side of my horse. I glance behind me, finding that the Orc pursuing me is closer than I thought. His spiked armor sends chills down my spine as I notice the years of blood coating the once silver iron.

I turn my head away from his mangled form to see what lies before me. The shining blue gate of Lithien is ahead of me. The gold Elven symbol of two entwining trees is just out of reach in the afternoon sun.

I wave a shaking hand to the guards and the gate slowly opens. My back arches backward in pain as the Orc slows down his Warg. He leaves his mark; a dark arrow protruding from my lower side.

I swear as I can hear the Orc snicker behind me.

The gate is silver on the other side and guards surround me to see who their visitor is. One of them grabs the reigns of my mare and attempts to tend to my restless horse.

"She needs a healer urgently," the male holding the reigns of my horse calls to no one in particular.

I am helped from my horse; the step down farther than I think it is. I give a thankful smile to the mare as I attempt to walk beside the male. The white dress I am adorning is now dripping with red and black.

I cover my mouth; trying to refrain from losing the last meal I ate. The arrow is covered with black poison and the substance is already running through my veins.

The male reassures me. "You'll be safe in the care of Lithien's healers, Lady Laerune of Ambrose."

Chapter 2

I stare up. My eyes shoot open, adjusting the new light. I sit up, but a sudden pain causes me to lower myself back down onto the bed. I quickly place a hand on my side. Its tenderness leaves tears down my face.

I look around once again; the memories of the previous morning flooding back.

I had run away from home, leaving my betrothed, but was then pursued by a pack of Orcs and their vicious Wargs.

"Good to see you are finally awake," a sweet and comforting voice speaks beside me.

I turn my head rather quickly in their direction. I find a bright, blue eyes looking back at me. His red hair shines from the sun entering the open window. He gives a sideways smirk.

"I was almost here, Luthias! I would've made it much faster if I wasn't wearing that atrocious wedding dress."

Luthias chuckles at my response. "Well, I am glad that you are safe now. I can reassure you that you will be on your way back to Ambrose in no time."

My face grows serious; my lips form a straight line. "Are you joking, Luthias Faen? I am not going back."

He turns his head to the side and I roll my eyes. "You didn't think I was actually going to marry him, did you?" I growl as he refuses to look at me. "I left for a reason," I say, following another roll of my eyes.

Luthias finally looks at me; that sideways smirk returning. "I would like to think you left for me."

My hand reaches out for his. "Of course I did. It's not like I came here to see your brother." My words are again followed by a roll of my eyes.

Luthias' eyes grow saddened; the once crystal blue turns to placid grey. "Luvon is dead."

Chapter 3

Most would be worried if they found themselves in the kingdom of Lithien. They believe the forest is evil; rumors spread across the land quickly of creatures running wild through the kingdom. The land is protected by the Salath Elves, making the city one of the biggest and strongest since the First Age.

The kingdom has always been bright; the castle adorned with bright blues and sunshine. But now the windows are covered with black curtains and maids are adorned in grey clothing. The Crown Prince is dead. No words are uttered in the halls of Lithien.

"It was during the battle of Everford," Luthias tells me. "Luvon and I left with a small legion of Lithien's army when we heard news of King Bastien and your sister wanting to take back the kingdom."

"The battle wasn't easy as you might have heard. Luvon and I lost most of our legion," his eyes gaze out a curtained window. "His body is yet to be found so my father was hesitant to announce his death. He hopes that Luvon still lives."

"Is it wrong to have hope?" I ask him, my hand linking with his.

Luthias squeezes my hand, the muscles running through his arms flexing. "It's not wrong to have hope, but I fear that this is just a fool's hope."

Luthias pauses in the hallway; his cheeks blush the same color red as his hair. "But I want to speak of other things, of good things. I want my kingdom to be happy. I want to be happy."

He shoves his hand into his pocket. "And I guess now is the best time, being that you are no longer getting married to Avon." Just the mention of Avon's name makes my heart beat with guilt. "I know we love each other," Luthias tells me. "And I want to spend eternity with you."

Luthias slips the silver band onto my finger. He then presses his forehead against mine. "Please say yes."

I grin, my eyes looking up to his. "You must first get my father's blessing. If you can face his wrath, then it shall be blessed by the Electa."

"You didn't give me your answer though," He chuckles, pushing me back slightly.

"Yes," I smirk, pushing him to the side, but he quickly wraps his arms around me. I pull away slightly; the pain in my side has yet to dissipate.

"It seems that I have been granted the chance to see our lovely Laerune again," a voice sounds down the hall.

I curtsey while ignoring the pain in my side.

King Sentier motions for me to stand. "No need for that, dear."

Sentier has always been fond of me. Luthias looks very alike to his father, their piercing blue eyes shining.

Sentier's thin face grins back at me as he places his hand against my cheek. "You have been a popular lady these past years," Sentier dismisses Luthias with a nod of his head. "Elender has gone above and beyond with your courting process," He pauses. "Do you know why he chose Avon or is that still a mystery?"

"I have yet to be told. Avon is my close friend, but not a lover."

"He could've picked his trusted assistant or loyalist guard. I know that there were options from other kingdoms, even my own. For many years we had decided that one of my sons will marry you," he looks behind him, searching for his son. "Now, it seems that you have made your own choice. A very smart choice at that."

I giggle. "I have. Your son is a very good Elf. One of the best I have ever met, other than you and my father."

"How is Elender? I do suppose he is very angry at you."

"I am not sure. I left before I could feel his wrath."

"You're a smart one. But, you will have to return to him soon. He must be worried sick."

"I plan on returning tomorrow. I just wanted to heal after my little mishap with the Orc."

"Well, I should let you return to your new beloved. I have much work to do."

Sentier's eyes turn that placid grey; his pupils filling with sadness as his eyes become glossy. So many pieces are missing in his life. His wife and son are like missing chunks from his once large heart.

Chapter 4

Ambrose lies just East of Lithien; hidden within the Erutan mountain range. The quiet, peaceful kingdom is surrounded by lush forests and large lakes. The buildings are all made from dark wood and are unique compared to the other castles in the nearby kingdoms. It was more peaceful here. More quiet and calm. War had not resided here for thousands of years.

It's been many years since Luthias has visited Ambrose. Avon had made sure that he would stay away, my father agreed. Worry fills my heart as we reach the golden gate found just outside the kingdom's borders.

The familiar smell of lavender and books fills my senses as I guide Luthias into the main building. Two guards dressed in the red and gold of Ambrose stand at attention as I pass by. I give them both a nod in greeting.

Their eyes meet each other in confusion. They know I disappeared during my wedding, but now I have returned with a different male.

I pull on Luthias' arm, leading him to my father's study. "I need my father to understand that I will not, under any circumstances, marry Avon," I shut my mouth quickly as I run into an Elf around the corner.

I fall forward, the Elf below me breaking my fall. We land with a thud on the wooden floor. I nervously laugh as I brush the hair from my eyes. "Hello Avon," Luthias rushes around the corner. "How have you been?"

My hair dangles in his face and I rise to my knees. We help each other to our feet. Avon's grey eyes look down at mine, but his face is twisted in anger. He runs his hands through his raven colored hair. It always has reminded me of real feathers cascading down his back.

Avon bites his lip. "Well, other than my betrothed leaving me right before we are to be married, pretty great," He growls, crossing his arms. I step back from his tallness. He is much taller than Luthias.

"On the other hand, we didn't have to go through the awkwardness of the wedding night," I chuckle at him.

He changes the subject. "Where have you been? Everyone has been worried sick."

"Lithien," I raise my head higher, hoping that I will gain confidence from the action.

Avon's eyes turn down in anger once again. "You went to Lithien?" He speaks slowly. I nod my head. "I am disappointed in you."

I mock his words as Avon leaves the hallway. "I am disappointed in you."

"Are you sure you both didn't elope?" Luthias comes out of his hiding. "You both sound just like a married couple."

"Oh, come on," I growl at him while pulling his arm.

I pause before reaching to open the door of my father's study; I take a deep breath. The wrath of my father will most likely be to a high extent. I question if I am even prepared to face it all.

Luthias gives me a slight push forward and I reach for the door. I attempt to close it as quietly as possible for my father hates when the door squeaks.

I stop a few steps away from his desk with my head down in respect. I kneel down, placing my hand up in front of him.

"My High Lord, Elender, my father. Please forgive me for my past mistakes."

I hear his chair back up to the floor and his rushed footsteps come towards me. "Rise, my young child, there is no need to be forgiven," I look up to his face; years seem to have sunken into his eyes. Yes, he is hundreds of years old, but age does not riddle our bodies, but our souls took more damage.

His soft hands clutch mine tightly as he helps me to my feet. He quickly searches for any harm, his hands feeling on my face in search of fever or injuries. "I'm fine, father," his shoulders drop in relief. I admire his blue eyes that are very much like my own. But his dark hair seems lighter.

My father stares at me for a moment; trying to find the lie in my eyes. "You know that I have seen what has happened already." My father can see glimpses of the future before it actually happens.

I sigh. "I just had a little mishap with an Orc. Just an arrow to my-"

"And Orc arrow!" His eyes light up. "Those can still be riddled with poison, even after treatment."

My father reaches for the door. "But father, I have come to speak of other-"

He pauses in the doorway. Luthias bows in a princely fashion. "May I speak with you, Lord Elender," Luthias straightens his back.

My father pushes me forward. "Go to the healers immediately," He bows to Luthias while guiding him towards his study. "Dehlin will escort you."

The guards in the hall stand at attention as the captain of the guard enters the hall. Luthias and my father disappear into the study and Dehlin chuckles.

I grin back at my combat trainer. He messes with his golden hair that is pulled back into a ponytail. "Back so soon?"

"Not by choice exactly," I chuckle at him as he embraces me. I place my hands on his back, feeling his sword strapped to his shoulders.

"So, I'm not the winner of The Great Laerune Courting Contest?" Dehlin holds my shoulders.

"I'm afraid not."

Dehlin has always been one of my closest friends other than Avon. My father thought it would be a good idea for us to become lovers, but Dehlin is clearly more of a brother. Maybe if I had the choice when I was younger, things would be different. Both my sister and I had a crush on the Golden Lord.

"What are you going to do about Avon?" Dehlin links his arm with mine. I lower my head; shaking with the simple answer of no. "You have many wedding gifts up in your room. Do you plan on opening them?"

"I don't want them," I growl. It just seems odd to open something when the occasion never happened.

"Everyone knows what happened, there's no hiding the fact that it happened-"

My eyes gaze forward into nothing but memories. The memory rushes through my mind.

I walk through the gardens, the hedges overgrown with roses and ivy. It's as if I am walking through a maze; I pluck a golden petal off of my bouquet of flowers, letting it drop down onto the stone path. It gets swept away with the fabric of my white dress. The train drags behind me, its weight pulling against me, telling me to turn back. To turn back and run. Run to the one I truly love. Please, winds, carry me off to the one I truly love, my mind pleads.

I stop at the rusted gate, looking up from my shoes. I look up at Avon, the smile plastered on his face slowly begins to disappear as he notices my sadness. He starts to descend the stairs and I watch as his eyes began to water at each step he takes, his hand reached out for me.

I drop my bouquet, running from the gardens. I can see Avon's heart shatter, the pain in his eyes, and the hurt look on his face. I pick up my skirts, exiting the gardens and attempting to run to the stables. There is no time to change and I try to quickly coax my horse from her stable.

I ride out of the castle gates, leaving everything behind me.

"Have you been ignoring what I have been saying?" Dehlin furrows his brow at me in confusion.

I give him a sideways grin. "I was just thinking backwards."

"Thinking backwards," He chuckles at me. Dehlin opens the door of the healers. I am then met with a rush of wind and thin arms wrapping around my neck.

"Etta, please let go," I giggle.

"Oh, I'm sorry," she brushes her skirts down.

Etta was my nursemaid when I was young for my mother died in childbirth. She's a short female with dark hair always twisted into a bun. People liked to call her an old soul because she acted much past her years, but she looked about the same age as I do.

Etta has me sit up on the table. "And what is the matter?"

"Orc arrow to the right side."

She can't help but smile that I am back even though the matter could be life-threatening. "Past or present wound, dear?"

"Past."

Etta opens up all the cabinets; rummaging through bottles of miscellaneous herbs and brews. "Ah, there it is." She pops a cap off of a small vile and forces me to drink the horrible concoction. "Drink child. Don't bother about the taste. It will start working in a moment."

I begin to cough; the taste sticking to the back of my throat. I stick my tongue out. Etta lowers her head; her pointed ears reddening. Dehlin simply stands back; his arms crossed over his chest.

"What is in that?"

Dehlin answers for Etta because she is too busy rummaging through a box of ingredient cards. "Warg piss." Etta hands me the recipe card.

"Warg piss is definitely not the worst thing in that medicine."

Etta takes back the card; placing it neatly back into its slot. "We call it Ephemeral, meaning medicine that is universal. It can help with almost any type of injury," she grinds some ingredients while placing some liquid into an empty vial. "It can help with poison, flesh wounds, and even some puncture wounds that would lead most to death."

Etta places the vial into my pocket. "Keep it. You never know when you might need it."

She gives a small wink as soon as the door opens. Luthias barges in; a smile is plastered upon his freckled face. "Elender has given us his blessing."

His smile is completely genuine and I can hear Etta squeal behind me. Dehlin rolls his eyes. "About time."

I hop down from the table. I smile at Dehlin and Etta to give them my thanks.

Luthias and I step outside. The sun shines brightly into the valley; shining against the lake below the many paths of stairs. A fountain filled with golden coins lies in the middle of the courtyard. It sprays out a steady stream of mist that fills the air with colors.

I lower myself onto the stone bench. The sides of it are carved with Elven symbols. Luthias still stands to admire the flowers growing up the latticework. A pair of Elven girls walks by, giggling at some inside joke.

Luthias seems about ready to say something, but a bell rings, cutting off his words. The bell chimes thrice, meaning that we are summoned to the hall. The two girls turn around and Luthias and I follow them to the Hall of Fire.

The Hall of Fire is where many meetings and storytellings take place. It is the people's place to gather for important information.

I stand on my tiptoes to make my way to the front. I make sure that Luthias has my hand so I don't leave him behind. He bows his head to each person he bumps into while repeating two words, "Excuse me."

I push through to the front just in enough time to watch my father stand before us all. His eyes seem sunken in more yet he stands tall and proud of the Lord he is. "I have just been informed that Adael, my trusted assistant, has been found dead along our forest borders. He has been killed by a pack of Orcs traveling down the main road," he hates giving news like this. "And with this unfortunate death, new rules have been created. Chainmail is to be worn under festival robes and clothing. And no children are allowed outside of the gates after dark unless permitted to by myself. Now, these rules are to be followed to ensure your safety."

Adeal was just about to end training for his new assistant Baylinn. I will not be surprised if he is appointed his new position much earlier than he thought.

Baylinn was also an option for my courting process. My father watched us interact, trying to find out if we were a match. Baylinn loved the art of singing and music. We both enjoyed a week together until my father deemed our match unwise.

That's as long as most of the matches lasted, only a week. It only allowed me a short time to get to know them better and to figure out their secret talents. Baylinn loved to dance, even though he is too shy to ask anyone.

That's as long as most of the matches lasted, only a week. It only allowed me a short time to get to know them better and to figure out their secret talents.

Linder's brother, Vestan, was another young man on the list. He hasn't even reached his coming of age celebration. He is a jealous type that loves to paint and draw. Then there is Dehlin who loved weapons and combat training. Lucia, who loves to tell jokes and was secretly into males. Ovaine, who is advanced in study and lore. Silvyr, from Lindalin, who loved books and reading, but we had only written letters and never met in person. Then there was Avon, my best friend, who would always get me in trouble, just to pull me right out of my punishment. And lastly, there was Luthias.

"This meeting is dismissed," my father's voice echoes in the quiet room.

I follow after him; trying to catch him before he exists the hall. His golden robes swish around the corner and I call out for him. "Father! May I speak with you?"

He wraps his arm around mine with a smile. He then leads me away from the crowd of people exiting The Hall of Fire. "You knew this was going to happen, yet you are still surprised."

My father gives me a sly smile and then begins to speak. "I like to see what you will do. The visions come in pieces. The story isn't all written out. You have to be the one to write it out."

His grin widens. "You did say you would dine with Kings." My father chuckles.

Avon enters the hall; he bows to my father. "May I speak with Laerune?" My father hands me over to Avon with a smile. I can practically see what my father says through his eyes. *Apologize and make amends. He is still your friend. You will need him in the end.*

"I am sorry for my rudeness this morning," Avon apologies before I can cough up the courage. "You are my best friend and I want what is best for you."

"Stop it with the politeness and manners," I shove his shoulder. "My father is out of earshot."

"Well then," Avon grins uncontrollably; his thin face lights up. "I am beyond pissed you didn't tell me beforehand. I could've helped you get away easier and maybe you wouldn't of ended up with an arrow in your side."

He pokes at my unhurt side. "I am already the most hated Elf in Ambrose, you could've spared me some mercy."

"You had to have known I was going to do that."

Avon rolls his eyes. "I saw it in your eyes," He blushes. "Now, you owe me." It wasn't hard to see the slight glimare of jealousy in his blue eyes.

"I know. I know," I look around for a moment. "I want you to travel back to Lithein with me. People don't know you there. You can restart and then you can get closer to Luthias and-"

"Your father needs me here."

My smile disappears. "I understand." That jealousy is going to change to anger someday.

Chapter 5

The sadness of leaving Ambrose behind seems to disappear as Luthias and I reach the gate of Lithien. On the other side, the sun blinds our vision and Luthias chuckles. He quickly dismounts his horse and strides towards a male waiting in the courtyard.

The tall Elf waits with his arms crossed over his chest and his brown hair fashioned in a messy ponytail. A scar is stretched across his face, its paleness making it quite an obvious trademark. Tasar, Luthias' best friend, lives with the Dwarves in Makya. It is still unknown to me why he would want to live in the darkness with short, stubborn Dwarves. But all I know is that it has been awhile since Luthias has spoken to Tasar.

Luthias slaps his hand on to Tasar's shoulder. A popular Elven gesture among males. I meet Tasar's earth brown eyes and he gives me a sly smile.

"That's a lovely lady you have there," he points at me.

"It is a pleasure to finally meet you Tasar. I am Laerune, Lady of Ambrose."

"Oh, all formal," he looks to Luthais with yet another smile and a wink. "It is an honor to meet you, Lady Laerune of Ambrose." He bows deeply and his dark hair falls on his face.

Tasar whispers something in Luthias' ear and they laugh. "Come, my friend, join us for a meal."

"Gladly."

I follow slightly behind them, admiring how their friendship grows stronger as they converse. I wish could have a friendship like Tasar's and Luthias'. When I was younger I had Avon, but he was never really someone I could talk to about girl things. So, I kept those things to myself, only occasionally telling Eryn, my sister.

"Back so soon?" Sentier asks; his green robes stretch a great length of the hall.

"You know how I hate to stay away," he reaches for my hand.

"I'm going to steal Laerune for a while if you don't mind Luthias."

"It's not a problem."

I smile at both of them, before entering another hall with Sentier. This hall is full of bright light, shining upon the Elven runes carved into the walls. This part of the castle has been up since the First Age. Images are carved into the oak and stone walls, creating a story and a timeline of history.

"It's about Navain and the rebellion of the Elven races," Sentier senses my curiousness. "Navain was power hungry and sought out the powers of the Electa, our Gods. Navain was then sent to the void after attempting to steal the jewels that the craftsman Maglanor created."

Sentier opens a door for me and he lets me enter his study. He immediately pours a glass of wine, the purple liquid swirling in his glass. He stands at his desk, with a smile plastered on his face.

"I would offer you some, but Luthias has told me how...what to call it?"

"I can't hold my liquor," I laugh.

"Yes, that's the word I was looking for."

He looks down at his desk, gazing at a brown box. It has a lock on it, engraved with a date. First Age, 1824. On the top of the box, mixed in with the leaves and flowers, is a name. Lauralaethee is carved onto Sentier's box. It must have been his wife's.

Sentier carefully unlocks the box and lifts the cover off. Inside the velvet box lies a golden crown. It flowers and leaves twine together mixing with blue jewels. He lifts the crown from its resting place and places it neatly on my head, fixing a loose hair in the process.

"You will be a part of our royal family soon and every princess needs a crown."

"Thank you Sentier," my face turns red.

"And maybe one day it will be a queen's crown again," he walks back over to his glass of wine, sipping only small amounts of it. "Has Luthias spoken to you about Luvon?"

"Briefly," I lower myself into a chair. "I hope you know that he will struggle with the transition to becoming the Crown Prince."

"He will not struggle," Sentier speaks sternly. "Luthias has been trained side by side with his brother. I only chose his brother because I wanted Luvon to settle down."

"There is no need to worry about him." He lifts my head up with his hand, sensing my emotions. "You're the one you should be worrying about. You're making your own choices now."

I rise from my seat. "Thank you, Sentier."

"You're so very welcome, my dear."

I start to walk away. "And Sentier, I am so sorry for the loss of your son and your wife."

Sentier simply bows his head as I leave the room.

I close the door behind me, jumping at the sight of two statues. They seem so realistic and their details are so intricate. Other statues line the hall, but they are old, worn down, and filled with cracks. These two are fairly new.

The statues are of past Elves who did not get to spend their eternity. Their immortal lives were taken away by weapons and sickness or even grief. The newest statues are of Lauralaethee and Luvon.

Lauralaethee died in battle many years ago, where Luvon just died recently. The statues each hold something different to represent how they died. Those who died in battle were given a sword. Those who were diagnosed with sickness hold a bowl and the ones that gave into grief hold a book.

But even with how detailed these statues were, they could never get them perfect. Luvon is missing his smile and the slightest scar that crosses his cheek, along with the tattoos that run up his arms. I guess some of the Elves thought it was disgraceful to have tattoos. And Lauralaethee is missing the scar that ran down her neck to her chest.

I leave the hall and the white statues behind. I walk to the house of prayer that is connected to the castle. Weddings and important ceremonies are held here and at this moment it is empty. I stand in front of the Vala tree, its tall golden branches reach the high ceiling that allows the stars and sun to shine through. The Electa had planted it here many years ago and the Elves decided to build around it, creating it a sacred building for prayer.

A cold breeze sweeps through the open windows and I shiver. I kneel down onto the steps, placing one hand over my heart and the other around my stomach. The colored glass windows allow rainbows to shine around the room and pillars of stone hold up the building, each one carved with intricate details of flowers and leaves at the top and base. Autumn leaves fall from the open ceiling, falling gracefully around me.

I don't normally pray to the Electa but I close my eyes, bowing my head. "May my prayer be answered from my Gods and Goddesses, the Electa. Please protect the ones I love and hold dear. Protect them from the ever-growing evil. Let them know that I ask for forgiveness in all that I have done wrong. And please keep my father safe from loneliness and Sentier protected from grief. Keep Avon from jealousy and Luthias protected from the hardships of our world. Please protect this forest, to let it grow. To let the green leaves shine in the sun. The Electa, please hear my prayer. Anngel."

"Anngel." I turn around quickly, searching for the voice. My eyes meet the earth colored ones of Tasar. A frown replaced his ever so common smile. "I just came to check on you. Luthias had business to take care of with his father."

Tasar kneels down next to me, placing his hands over his heart and stomach. "I know I haven't been around lately," he tells me. "But I can still tell that my best friend loves someone very much."

He looks up at the gold and silver tree. "Can you imagine the wedding you will have in here? How large it will be and how many people will travel to Lithien just to see the Lady of Ambrose and the Prince of Lithien married, uniting their kingdoms?"

A knock on the large wooden doors interrupt our conversation. Luthias stands at the door, his eyes red. "Nolan wishes for a council."

Nolan, a young king, rules the kingdom of Ebin. Ebin lies right outside of the forest of Lithien. It's a grungy place; his people are ruthless and unmerciful. It is rumored that he sent his own family into exile just to be king, along with killing his three other brothers to then become the only heir to Ebin. The kingdom is described as a nuisance to the other surrounding kingdoms.

"If you will follow me, we leave tomorrow. Be ready before the sun rises," he pauses. "And LaRue, will you follow me right now. Please?"

I walk up to his side and he takes my hand, leading me to a new destination. "I have a surprise for you," he smiles, his voice soft rather than the harness it once was when he spoke of Nolan.

We walk through the castle, stopping at a door carved with one of Lithien's symbols. Two beautiful trees intertwined together, one of gold and the other silver. Luthias opens the door and it's a beautiful room with a balcony overlooking the forest. There is a bookshelf full of novels and I know that I already wish to read them all. A table and chairs sit in the middle of the room and a desk is near the window. There is another door that leads into the bedroom.

The bedroom has a large bed, covered in blankets of green material that looks like it could put me asleep as soon as I would lie down. A couch is set up on the other end of the room and a blanket covers the top of it, looking like the perfect reading spot. Luthias then leads me to the next door. A silver tub sits in the middle of the room surrounded by brown latticework.

The next room holds all of our clothing. I barely brought any of my clothing from home and I can see the proudness in Luthias' face, saying that he was the one to pick out all of the clothes. I run my hands through the silk fabrics. Some are covered in jewels and others are simple. There are dresses for celebrations, tunics and pants for training, and a stand of armor for war if it was brought unexpectedly on the wind.

Luthias speaks proudly. "It's not quite an adventure, but I think it's the start of one," he smiles and then starts to push through the clothing. "I had a little help, you know."

He pulls open a cabinet door, revealing jewels that sparkle without the light touching them. "Luthias, this is too much."

"I hope not. You do have to spend eternity with these things, including me," he shows his sideways smirk.

"Who helped you?"

"You won't believe me if I told you."

I stare at him, telling him to give it a shot. "Tasar helped me. He has been sending boxes of clothing to Lithien for about a year."

"A year? You had this planned for a year?" My eyes open widely at the thought of it.

"I was going to ask for your hand a little sooner, but as you know, some things popped up."

He lifts up a necklace set with emeralds. "Tasar went to the High Elves of Lindalin and spoke to some of the best seamstresses. He then took the clothing and brought it to the Dwarves. They set their finest jewels into the clothing."

"I can see that. But, how did you get the Dwarves to corporate?"

"This is where Tasar was extremely helpful."

I pull on a blue skirt; tiny jewels line the bottom and around the waist. "My father is having a dinner tonight and we are important guests on the list. You should dress your best tonight. He is giving you his left-hand seat."

I give Luthias a questioning look. "I have been given his right in place of my brother."

Before I pull the ombré skirt from its hanger, I stare at Luthias and his proud smile. He only wishes to make his father proud.

The light blue silk fades to white at the top of the skirt; its silver jewels made into a belt of stars. The separate top holds the same star-like jewels. Its sleeves link up with wrist cuffs and the back laces up tightly.

Luthias leaves the room to change and I slip the skirt and bodice over my head. I call to a maid to help me lace up the back. I make a mental note to myself to invite Etta to live in Lithien. Her nimble hands lace corsets much faster than the cold hands of this maid.

My heart beats unsteadily as I stare at the armor stand next to the mirror. Rumors are spreading of Orc armies gathering and dark creatures coming from the ruins of Nadien to live within our lands. It won't take long for these creatures to become courageous and rebel against our kingdoms.

I pull my stare away from the stand of armor and back towards the mirror. I place my hand over the newly formed scar at my hip when Luthias re-enters the room.

"I hope that I don't have to explain how to act among a court."

"No, Luthias. My father made sure it was permanently stuck in my mind," I smirk.

He smiles brightly and I sit down onto the loveseat to slip on my shoes.

"My father is beyond excited for you to live here," Luthias adds as we walk down the hall to dinner. "He's hoping that your belongings will be brought over very soon. He even told me that you are more than welcome to bring a friend or two."

Two guards dressed in moss like armor stand alert at the doors of the dining room. The guests at the dining table quickly quiet down as we enter the room. Luthias takes my hand, leading me down the stairs gracefully.

I smile, taking the next step down the stairs. Luthias pulls my chair out and I sit down, politely thanking him. I watch as he sits to his father's right. Sentier takes my hand with a smile.

"Too long has it been since a woman of royal blood sat and dined at our table." A plate of food is set in front of me and maids come by to fill up the Elves' goblets. "Everyone is beyond excited about your engagement, even Nolan seemed to make a fuss about the news."

"And are you to blame for spreading this news so quickly?"

Sentier raises his glass to his lips. "I may have told a few people," he drinks.

Chapter 6

Just as Luthais asked us, Tasar and I are up before the sun. With my eyes still filled with tiredness, I stumble with my horses' saddle straps. Luthias comes around, tightening them and then helping me up into the saddle.

"Come on, wake up LaRue."

"I'm awake," I growl. The dinner lasted much longer than expected last night and I found myself unable to sleep. Tasar seems to feel the same as he mounts his own horse.

I double check to see that I have brought everything I need. Nolan will not let us in with our weapons, so we keep most of them hidden in our clothing.

The early morning sun shines through the thin branches of the fall trees. An autumn glow warms my face as the first light touches the land. Everything seemed peaceful for a moment. Silent and calming as the morning turned to day.

Tasar hums quietly to himself, his tune getting louder as the tiredness washes away from his body and the sun rises higher in the sky. He begins to add words to his tune. It's a common song; you simply have to change the names to make it more personal.

"*Three brave heroes woke with the sun,*
on a misty morning three were as one.
The forest glowed and shined bright,
warming their spirits with light.
As three great hunters we followed the sun.
We are Tasar, Luthias, and LaRue.
To the Erutan Mountains,
high and tall.
To the secret kingdom of Lenair,
with our hearts full of gold."

The kingdom of Ebin is quiet, you can only hear the cawing of a crow perched on one of the tall stone watchtowers. We leave our horses right outside of the castle doors. Immediately, as we set foot on the steps, guards come to retrieve our weapons. They don't even have to ask and we begin disarming ourselves.

The guards are tall and dark haired. And it looks and smells like they haven't bathed in months. We are escorted inside; the doors slam behind us. I look around, searching for an escape if needed.

Nolan rises from his wooden throne; he is young, but tall. His shaggy hair is in a tousled, greasy mess and a crown sits lopsided on his head. He slouches and a smug smile is curled onto his face.

"My, my. I wasn't expecting you to bring guests." Nolan caresses his hand over my cheek and then to my pointed ear. "And especially not this one. A Fae brat." He laughs along with his other guards. "Oh, nevermind. You're old enough for better words. How about a Fae bitch?"

The Fae were a race of Elves with magical abilities. "I'm not part of the Fae," I growl, looking over at Luthias who clenches his jaw in anger.

"That's not what this says," he pulls a rolled up piece of paper from his pocket. I assume its rumors sold from merchants who deal with the black market. He stuffs it away into his black jacket. "But that is not information for your eyes."

"You don't know anything of my heritage."

"I know that heritage has nothing to do with being Fae." He touches the side of my face again, moving my hair from my ears. "I wonder how much someone would pay for your head. Or just your ears alone. Your name has been escaping from many mouths. Oh, how they sing your name," he runs a hand over my pointed ear. "I would-"

"Shut up Nolan!" Luthias yells.

"Didn't I teach you you're manners the last time you came here?"

Luthias steps forward and away from the guard's hands that was holding him still. "What do you want?"

Nolan chuckles. "I simply want to know why her name is spreading far and fast over the lands. Is she a threat?" Nolan points a dirty finger in my direction. "Is she powerful? Does she know something I don't? All I want to know is if she has anything to do with the Orc armies coming closer to these lands."

"What would an Elf want with Orc armies?" Tasar spits.

"There is also rumor that Navain is gaining control of his lands and seeking out old enemies he failed to kill. It seems that Elender and Dehlin are a part of that list."

I furrow my brow in attempt to understand all the information being thrown at us. "Why would I want to kill my father?"

Nolan's arm is thrusted forward and into Luthias' side. Luthias hunches over, his hands dripping with blood. He makes a quick look to Tasar and me. "Get out."

I go to reach for him while barely slipping a vile into his hands. He clutches it tightly as Tasar pulls him away.

The wooden doors slam as Tasar and I exit them. The last thing I see is Nolan's smug grin. All I can wish for is our plan to work. A dead man hears the most information.

Tasar then grabs me around my stomach, picking me up and placing me onto my horse. He grabs the reins, turning the horse around and out of Ebin.

We stop right between Lithien's borders and Ebins. "Where do they put their dead?"

"Because Luthias is a prince they will put him on the border. It's a sign of dominance," Tasar searches across the hills. "If Luthias just simply stays still, Nolan will believe he's dead. He'll be walking over that hill in a few hours."

I duck down behind a stack of large rocks. Tasar follows behind me. I turn his head towards the forest of Lithien.

Several packs of Orcs enter the forest with weapons in hand. "Do you think what Nolan said was true."

"Nolan doesn't like lying. He simply gives you the least amount of information and then hopes that you will go out and attempt to find more. But that usually leads you into trouble."

Tasar reaches for the set of arrows at his side. "Nolan is simply a nuisance, not a real threat." He sits and makes himself comfortable on the backside of the rocks. "Don't worry, everything went as planned. Just be patient for a few hours."

I lean my back onto the rock. My eyes scan for any movement over the hill. We can no longer hear the Orcs marching into the forest. The Lithien guards will be able to handle their small group quickly and possibly have time to bring them into questioning before we even return.

***

The two hours tick by. The time drags on, almost seeming endless. But a figure comes into view over the hill and I slap Tasar awake. He tilts his head forward; his earth brown eyes blazing.

I scramble to my feet to meet Luthias half way, but Tasar pulls me down. “He will come to us.”

I tap my foot as I attempt to wait patiently. Once I can see Luthias’ sideways smirk, Tasar allows me to help him.

“Things didn’t entirely go to plan,” Luthias coughs while blood dribbles from his mouth. “They found that I was not dead and attempted to kill me again. I managed to grab this from Nolan.”

Tasar swings under Luthias’ shoulder to help him stand easier. “And that is?”

“A list of names and what their bounties cost.” We walk Luthias to a horse. “I have yet to analyze it entirely, but familiar names did stick out.”

***

“The price of your ears, Laerune, is more than your head,” Sentier throws the paper onto the desk next to his throne. “All three of your names are being spread through the black market as well as Orc camps and prisons.”

Tasar and Luthias look to each other. I reach forward for the list, but Sentier’s hand comes down quickly to stop me from taking it. I stare up at him, backing away slowly.

“Why can’t I see it?”

“Because the amount of money will shock you.”

My back goes rigid. My father would be shocked to see me argue with a King. “I wish to see it,” I growl. Sentier seems to weigh the thought in his mind. He throws the paper forward at me. “I expected more,” I joke, but the amount was far more than I ever thought was possible for a bounty.

“I want the three of you to be watchful of your surroundings. If anything seems off, report to me immediately.

My sentries have alerted me that Orcs have entered our borders. I need all three of you to help the guards this evening."

Sentier rises from his throne, his footsteps silent on the stone floor. "Tasar you will take the West Gate and for you two," he stares brightly at Luthias and I. "the Northern Gate."

Luthias sighs heavily. The Northern Gate is closest to the sea and hardly anything moves on that side of the forest. "I expect the best from all of you."

***

We stop outside as the wooden gateway is closed loudly behind us. It didn't seem like a bad idea to be volunteered to watch the gate, but being pushed out of the wall's borders and forced to stand watch until your time runs out, doesn't seem so great.

"Well, we have a few hours," Luthias leans against the stone wall. I walk backwards down the forest path to look up at the expense of the wall and gate. I turn around quickly hearing my name be called deep down from within the forest.

"Laerune," it calls again, its voice ancient.

I look to Luthias, giving him a questioning look. "What?" He asks.

"Did you hear that?"

"Hear what?"

I shake my head. "Nevermind."

***

An hour passes and Luthias quickly sits up, looking into the forest. "Luvon?" He calls. A figure stands at the end of the path. We both walk a little closer to it. "Luvon!" Luthias runs to the figure, his arms out ready to embrace his lost brother.

"Luthias!" I call after him, hope flickering in my heart. I run down the path, watching as the figure also runs into the woods. Another voice calls my name, almost like a scream for help.

"Laerune!"

I run a different way, the voice sounding exactly like my sister. I stop in a clearing, watching as my sister disappears into the thick forest. Her orange dress blends into the forest foliage.

"LaRue," she calls again, forcing me to follow her.

I run through the forest, but another voice distracts me as I almost run them over. "Laerune. It's me, it's Avon."

"Avon? You came?" My eyes search around, still searching for that screaming voice.

"How couldn't I? You are my best friend," he walks backwards, reaching his hands out for mine. "I knew the moment that you left Ambrose that you would need me."

He spins me around, making me the one to walk backwards. He stops, brushing a piece of my golden hair behind my ear. I look down at the ground, but when I look back up it's a different person.

I look up to them confused and frightened. A black cloak covers his body and his eyes are a grey blue. He lets go of my hands, pulling a sword from his belt. He points it at me, making me back away. I feel rocks crumble beneath me, and when I look behind me, the face of a cliff is at my heels, the ocean swaying beneath.

"You are the one that destroys, the queen who must die!" He raises his sword above his head, but then a sword is pushed through his stomach. "*The Killer of Innocence*," he breathes, his last words mumbling from his mouth.

I cringe, dropping down onto my knees as the creature falls at my side, inches away from the cliff. It forms into a girl with red hair, a fox tail protruding from her lower back. I breathe heavily, trying to catch my breath.

Luthias grabs my arms, helping me up and into his arms. He looks down at the cliff and then pulls me away from the darkening forest. Blood covers each of our freckled faces and he tries to wipe it away from my cheeks.

"What was that?" I feel stunned, shocked. I was not expecting this to happen.

"That was a Kitsune."

The creature's words echo in my head, still calling my name. I look behind me, but Luthias pushes my head, forcing me to look forward. I don't think I was supposed to see what was behind me, but I do anyways. About ten guards lie on the forest floor. Their bodies seem to have been here much longer than a day.

"Luthias, what happened to them?"

“What would have been our fate.” I try to look back behind me, but Luthias keeps my head forward.

The gate creaks open, a sentry waiting on the other side. “I am sorry to disturb you. But, it’s about your brother.” The guards green eyes flash over to me and then back to Luthias. “We have found something of his.”

“Show me.”

Chapter 7

The shocking experience with Kitsunes seem to leave my mind entirely as Luthias and I race down the hallway.

I look behind me quickly, sensing someone behind me. Out of the corner of my eye I see a shadow. Tall and dark. It's presence filling the air with coldness.

This is not the first time I have seen this shadow of darkness.

The memory floods my vision.

I walk down the hall. Following the shadow that turns every corner.

"Who are you?"

I look up at the tall dark figure standing before me. His eyes are grey, as if the light was taken away from them. He kneels down, meeting me at my small height.

"An old friend."

"But, I have never met you? How can I be your friend?"

"You will...someday." He places his hand on my shoulder and then disappears around the next corner.

I stand in the hallway and Luthias stops, waiting for me to continue to follow him. "LaRue are you coming?"

"Yeah, just go on without me. I will be there in a moment."

I walk the other way down the hallway. I slowly peek my head around the corner, the figure standing at an open window.

"It seems that we have met again Laerune," his grey eyes meet mine. "It's been awhile."

He lifts the hood of his cloak off his head, revealing his raven black hair and the scars that map his face. "You were only a child when we met. And now look at you," he steps close, too close to me.

I take a step back, tripping over my shoes and landing on the ground. The shadow laughs and then reaches down to help me up. I recoil from his touch, backing up against the wall.

"You do not have to be afraid of me. Not yet at least."

"Who are you?" I ask with an attitude while rising to my feet.

"I am an old friend."

And just like that he disappears from the hallway. I lean up against the wall, catching my breath that I didn't know I have been holding. I push myself off the wall and then to the room that Luthias disappeared into.

I shut the door quietly behind me. Sentier holds something close to him, his expression blank.

"What was found?" I shyly ask. Sentier tosses the sword to the ground and it clatters against the stone ground. "But a sword isn't proof that he is dead. A body is proof, but a sword, no."

I bend down to pick up what could be the last remaining thing that Luvon had before he died.

Sentier doesn't offer to take it back and I wrap my arms around the sheathed sword. "Where was it found? In Everford?"

"In the hills of Gia."

"Gia? How was it found in Gia?"

"It was brought in anonymously about an hour ago," Sentier's eyes are filled with lies.

"If you allow it Sentier, I will travel there to look for him."

"Luvon is dead-"

"I still have hope that he lives."

Sentier rises to his feet, his eyes glaring. "Then why has he not returned to Lithien?" His voice rises, shaking the glass of wine on the table. "You shall not travel to Gia!"

"I will."

I shove the sword into Luthias' arms before I run from the room. *What have I gotten myself into?* Gia, an open area of fields and then hills that lead to mountains. There is an abundance of creatures that don't care for Elves hidden in the hills. And then there is Navain, who has had his fortress in the mountains near the sea. I don't want to get too close if I don't have to.

Other than Orcs, the area is filled with ruthless Dwarves, troublesome Trolls, Kitsunes, even a few dragons here and there. There was once a rumor that the water is filled with Sirens, or as the men call them, mermaids. Their beautiful voices will lure you into the depths of the water. Their voices more beautiful than the High Elves of Castimier, which I have not had the privilege to hear yet.

I open a wooden door to my right, stepping out into the fresh air. Rain slowly trickles down, dropping from leaf to leaf. The air is filled with a layer of mist and the forest smells of rain. Little drops of rain fall from the tree tops, landing with a plop into the fresh green ivy. The leaves bounce as each drop drips down the maze of leaves, racing each other to the bottom of the forest floor.

My vision blurs, my world changing into something different, something darker. Shadows dash around, slowly turning into clear figures. *Clear and familiar.*

"Mother?"

I have never met my mother, not knowing what she looks like or what kind of person she is. I have been told that I look and act just like her though. I don't look like this woman.

"No, I am not your mother," She smirks, her whole being shining with celestial light.

"You are not here as a death greeter, are you?"

"No." She laughs. "I am no death greeter, but I do have experiences in death."

"You're not alive?"

She shakes her head no. "I used to live here. I helped rule a once great and bright kingdom, but as I can tell it has lost its once great light."

She looks around the room. "My kingdom is falling into ruin, along with my family."

I take a moment to think about where this woman is familiar. Then I remember the hall of statues and the two brightest ones.

"Lauralaethee."

"You can just call me Laura."

"You're Luthias' mother."

She smiles brightly. "Yes. I do miss them dearly."

A young Elf shows up next to her. Luvon smiles and bows.

"You must not travel to Gia. There is dangerous creatures there and they will be the death of you. Instead, travel to Everford. Go see your sister," Luvon tells me, his shoulders broad as he stands up straighter.

***

Lightning flashes and I can see Luthias jump slightly at the thunder before it. My clothes and hair are instantly soaked as I walk the cobblestone path to the stable. Venetta, my raven-black horse, whinnies at my appearance. I yank the tack off of its shelf, throwing it on top of Venetta's back. I slip the bridle over her head and I then slip a foot into the stirrup, heaving myself up onto the saddle.

"You can't go," Luthias begs. "Not in this storm."

"I have been sent a message by the Electa, I dare refuse it."

"Where will you go?"

"Everford."

I give him a smile, before Venetta begins to gallop away. The trees rock back and forth with the wind, the leaves rustling, the wind howling. The wind whips my hair out of its plait and lightning illuminates the forest, letting me see the path to Everford. Thunder shakes the ground, making Venetta run faster.

Chapter 8

I look behind me as a tree falls down onto the path and branches start to snap from the top of the trees. Venetta turns a sharp corner of the path and then rears up to stop at the closed gate. It takes a moment for her to calm down.

"I seek permission to leave Lithien." I tell the guard.

"Leave Lithien? We have orders to not let anyone out."

"It's an emergency."

"And you are going to stop that emergency?" A flash of lightning illuminates the sky and I can see the doubtfulness in his chestnut eyes. "Where are you traveling to?" The male crosses his arms.

"Everford. To see my sister."

"She has permission to leave from the King," Tasar emerges from the path, a sly smile on his face. "Open up the gate."

The gate slowly opens, creaking against the power of the wind. Tasar quickly walks over to my horse, grabbing the reins with his free hand. He straps on a quiver of arrows and my bow to my saddle.

"He is coming with you."

"Are you coming with him?"

"No, I have business to attend to in Makya. The Dwarves are in a bit of a rampage. They found a new kind of jewel, they say it is stronger than Mithril and shines even brighter than the Electa stones. But, I just think they are over exaggerating, they usually are. Those stubborn Dwarves," he laughs. "I will bring you back a chunk if you like."

"You don't have to do that. I know how much the Dwarves care for every single jewel they find."

"You need to leave. I heard talk that-" Thunder booms, making me unable to hear what he says.

He hits the back of Venetta, making her run through the gate. A sudden eeriness fills my heart. What was he trying to warn me of? Will Luthias be safe?

I should've waited for Luthias.

The wind seems to howl louder and blow stronger than before. A blanket of mist falls onto the forest, making the dark wood harder to get out of. The path opens up into a large meadow, the grass overgrown. It seems too green to be near the forest of Lithien. The forest looks so dark behind me.

A screech echoes through the meadow making Venetta rear up, nearly knocking me off. I look to my side, seeing the dark eyes of a Demet Rider. I swear out loud as they ride faster towards me and my horse. He unsheathes his sword and I kick Venetta, forcing her to run faster than what is chasing us.

Demet Riders, or demon riders, have been scarce, especially since they were practically wiped out in the Second Age. They were the spawn of darkness, sons of Navain. Their black steeds held the same aura of evil. The rider's eyes were pure gold so they could easily entrance their next victim.

While still trying to hold onto Venetta, I fumble with my bow and arrows, my hands shaking in fright. I nock an arrow into my bow, and then I turn around, letting go of the reigns. I pull back my bow, bringing the string to my cheek. I release, sending the arrow towards the Demet Rider.

I don't bother to look to see if I shot it, all I can hear is his screams echo through the plain. Venetta unexpectedly rears up, knocking me from the saddle. I land on the ground with a thud, the breath being knocked out of me. I close my eyes as I hear another horse's footsteps stop at my feet and the rider jump down near my head. I reach for my bow but I feel the coldness of their blade on my neck and they begin to laugh.

"I caught up," Luthias laughs.

I sigh. "I thought you were the Demet Rider."

"No, you killed him."

"I did?"

"Yes, you can keep the horse if you want."

I turn my head towards the horse, who stands grazing a few feet away from us. "I'd rather not."

He helps me to my feet and I brush the dirt off my skirt. He hands me the reigns of my horse and we start to walk out of the meadow. Thunder still booms and lightning illuminates our path. I look over to Luthias and I see him jump every time the thunder rumbles through the sky. It starts to rain harder than it was before, soaking our clothes.

I can see Luthias' freckled face burn red. "What?" I ask him.

Luthias looks around quickly, searching for an excuse. It seems like none comes to him and he sighs. "Adventuring with you," he sends a sideways smirk in my direction. "It's been a long wait, but at least it's finally here."

"I wouldn't call this an adventure," I grin. "More like a sideways quest."

"A sideways quest? What does that even mean?"

I search the land in front of me. My shoulders shrug in response to my answer.

The redness disappears from Luthias' face. "I know my brother is dead. I can just feel it in my heart. There is many reasons why his body hasn't been found." An invisible weight disappears from his shoulders. "His body could've been burned, taken by the enemy as bounty. The possibilities are endless. Luvon could be buried in the ground already for all I know."

I lean my head against Venetta's neck as we continue walking. It would take us about half a day to reach Everford. We will also have to convince the guards at the gate to let us in. I have heard that they have been very picky on who they have let in, especially different races. They are in a state of panic since they are still rebuilding their fallen kingdom from war that has recently reaped them of much needed supplies and troops for their army.

I open my eyes to look at him. He stares ahead, his blue eyes bright and full of color. The color of his eyes seem to change all the time. They could be a sea green to a pacific blue or even a true sapphire. And his red hair, just like his fathers, is always kept neat. Luthias usually had his hair pulled back into a ponytail, but now it's untied and unruly. I can't help but laugh.

I twist the ring around my finger, continuing to watch him. He turns his head towards me and then back up to the trail. I watch as his eyes search the shadows around us for unwanted creatures.

Something runs across our path and we both become alert. Our eyes scan the area and we listen carefully. Our keen ears can hear the heavy footsteps of a pack of Orcs. Automatically, I pull my bow off of my saddle, knocking in my arrow.

I don't think they have heard or seen us. I jump down from my horse and Luthias nocks an arrow into his own bow.

"If we just get through the gate, we can take the girl."

"Do we even know what she looks like?"

The Orcs converse with each other. I look to Luthias and he meets my eyes.

"Just look for blue eyes and blonde hair."

"All the Elves have blue eyes, you piece of scum."

"Just grab the first girl who has those qualities. Either way we will make money off of her."

Luthias steps forward, his steps soft and quiet, unlike those of the Orcs. We both pull back our bows, aiming at the few Orcs that stand in the clearing. I release my arrow and it makes its mark into the heart of the Orc.

They screech in terror, running in every which way. Luthias releases his arrow, hitting his target. He goes in first, his blue daggers in his hands. I stay behind with my bow, watching his back. I shoot another two Orcs, but I don't see the sniper up in the tree in front of me. His arrow hits my side, in the exact same spot as the last one.

I sit down, watching my blood soak my dress. The Orcs seem to be all dead and I watch as Luthias looks around for a moment, searching for me. I see the sudden worry fill his eyes and he drops his daggers, running towards me. He drops down onto his knees next to me. He places his hands around the arrow, prepared to pull it out.

"No, don't." I cry.

"LaRue, I don't know what else to do."

"Don't rip it out! That's what you do." I am making him panic, which leads to me panicking. "Luthias we need to get to Everford." I speak calmly.

"But Everford is still a half a day's journey, make it a full day because we have to find our way in the dark," he shakes his head. "You always have to get hurt at the worst times, don't you?" He growls.

I can tell that he is scared to pick me up, scared that just a single touch will shatter me.

He lifts me carefully up and onto his horse, then tying Venetta to his own saddle. She seems to whinnie in frustration, because I am not able to be by her side. "Venetta shh." She seems to instantly calm down, letting Luthias continue.

He sits behind me, looking at me to make sure that I just don't want him to rip the arrow out now. He places his hand on my side near the arrow.

"Don't you dare."

"I'm sorry."

He wraps his hand around the arrow and before I can stop him, he rips it out. I try to hold back my screams of pain by biting my lip, but it's no use. I swear at him, loud enough that probably everyone from Ambrose could've heard it.

Luthias stares at the arrow. "It seems that it came out all in one piece."

"You at least could've given me something to bite down on." My lip bleeds.

"Do you want to keep it?" He offers me the blood covered arrow.

He kicks his horse and Venetta follows. I lean my head against his shoulder, falling asleep. I don't wake up until Luthais makes sure I'm still alive by pushing my shoulder forward. I look up at the gate that stands in front of us. Five guards stand at the gate, all of them ready to discuss to let us in or not.

"Tell them who I am. They will let me in." I speak quickly to Luthias.

"Who are you and why do you wish to enter Everford?"

"I am Luthias, son of Sentier, Prince of Lithien. And this is Laerune, daughter of Elender, Lady of Ambrose. We are in need of help, she's injured and we need a healer."

"We have too many sick to take care of already, go find somewhere else."

"I don't think your queen would like that you sent her only sister away when she was dying!" I yell, gritting my teeth through the pain.

The gate slowly opens, my sister walking through the other side. "No she would not." She wears an orange gown,

Everford's colors. Her coal black hair reaches to the end of her back and her lips are always red, even without the new customs of makeup.

She places her hand over her chest, covering the simple necklace across her neck. It was a simple plated piece of gold with a nail size opal in the middle. It was my mother's and she gave it to Eryn, saying that if she always wore it she would have a piece of my heart.

She gracefully walks towards us, sadness in her cornflower eyes. She reaches for my hands and she tries not to flinch from their coldness.

"Let them pass and give them a room, send for a healer immediately."

The gate opens up to a bridge that crosses over a river, its water shining blue in the early morning light. The mist seems to wash away and the castle comes into view. My vision blurs and I try to tell Luthias that we need to hurry, that blood loss will soon be the death of me.

I begin to cry, villagers staring at me and my blood covered hands and clothes. The castle seems so far away, its expanse too much to take in. The stone towers reach high into the sky taller than the clouds.

"Luthias," the horse shifts underneath us.

"I know LaRue, I'm trying."

The villagers stare at Luthias, knowing that he helped in the war effort in Everford.

I begin to cough, I cover my mouth, but when I pull my hand away it is covered in blood. My head spins, my vision blurring more than it was before. My breaths come out in gasps, trying to bring more oxygen to my lungs. I can feel blood drip down from my lips, the irony taste in my mouth.

The doors are already open and Luthias jumps down from our horse. He reaches up to me and with no strength left, I fall into his arms. All he can do is lie me down onto the clean tiled floors. I watch as my blood slowly seeps into the tiny cracks of the floor.

"Someone please help!" He calls and someone enters the room, as if they were waiting for us.

"Luthias I need you to calm down." The man says. I look to my side, watching the tears fall from Luthias' now pacific blue eyes. I quickly take his hand, not ever wanting to let go. I don't think I have ever felt like I needed him this much in my life. I have loved him, yes, but this is more than love. He is my forever, if my forever doesn't end too soon.

I feel my mind going blank and tiredness washes over me. I stare up at the golden ceiling, a warm breeze blowing past me, turning into a colder one soon after. My eyes become heavy with tiredness and I begin to not notice the world around me.

"Why send me to Everford Laura?" I reach my hand out, searching for Luthias' mother.

Chapter 9

I don't know what happened, or how the world just faded away to darkness. But, I find myself in an unfamiliar place, with familiar hands wrapped around my waist. The sun shines through the window, revealing the floating dust specks in the air. Luthias sneezes.

"Anngel." I speak softly.

He quickly sits up. "You're awake!"

"I am awake." I tell him, unsure if he actually believes it.

I nod my head, still feeling tired as I lay my head back down on the pillow. "What now?" I ask, sitting up again and looking out the window. Birds chirped outside, a few children yelled, and horses' hooves could be heard walking down the cobblestone paths.

I rise to my feet, the pain in my side sore and unyielding. The cream colored curtains of the window billow in the wind and I look over at the glistening lake. I had only been to Everford once.

A knock echos from behind the wooden door and Luthias speaks for them to enter. Eryn stands in the doorway, a tray in her delicate hands. "I am glad to see you awake and well."

She smiles and glides to the table across from the bed. "I had received news that you both would be on your way, but who I received it from, is unknown. I would suspect from Lithien, hence the raven that brought it to Everford."

She neatly set out plates and silverware as she spoke. Her words seemed practiced, as if she was reciting from a script. "Oh." She stops for a moment and turns towards me with a smile. "Father told me of the news." Her blue eyes brightened as she continued setting the table. "Congratulations on your engagement. You have many well wishes from Everford."

Once she finishes, she sits down and then brushes her raven hair over her shoulder. She coughed, politely smiled, and then placed her hand on her stomach.

"Boy or girl?" I ask with a smile.

"Unknown," she covers her mouth as she giggles.

"How far along?"

She looks down at the floor, a bright smile etched across her snow white skin. "Three months."

"So only nine more months to go. How exciting," my voice was hinted with sarcasm.

Elves were *gifted* with carrying a child for a full year before actually giving birth, compared to the man's nine month process. But it seemed like utter Hell to be that patient. You find out the gender very quickly and the whole process moves along in a fast pace. But you are stuck in those final stages for months.

"It won't be that bad Laerune. All woman have to go through it."

"How about you ask mother? Maybe she would be able to give you some helpful advice on having children."

Eryn glares at me and then rises to her feet. "You should be glad that you hadn't died with her Laerune. She gave you the greatest gift and have you ever thanked her for what she gave up for you?"

"Don't blame me for her death Eryn."

Our arguments were common and usually lasted a while, but thankfully Luthias is there to separate us before it gets too personal.

He steps between us, his hands crossed behind his back. "Eryn, if you will excuse us. I think Lady Laerune needs some fresh air," he smiles, his skin blushing between his freckled cheeks.

"Of course Luthias," she rises to her feet and then glides to the door. "Oh. I am sure that Bainen wishes to see you Luthias. He enjoys your company." With a nod of her head, she leaves the room.

As soon as she leaves, I flop onto the bed, my hands spread above my head and my feet dangle off the bedside. "She can be a pain sometimes, can't she?" I look to Luthias who gazes out the open window. "Is something wrong?" I sit up, motioning for him to come sit next to me.

"You should be glad to still have a sibling."

"Luthias. You know I still love her." I laugh and then smile at him. "Hmpf. Children. Hopefully not anytime soon."

He begins to smirk as well and then takes my hands in his. He helps me up to my feet and we leave the stuffy, hot room. The halls are in a rush. People pass by carrying tools while other push carts of cleaning supplies up and down the corridor. Everford has been very busy with clean up since the Orcs ransacked almost everything in this kingdom.

We find ourselves walking towards the gardens, the paths becoming lined with flowers and shrubs. A metal gate shines with a copper tone and orange flowers wrap around the metal bars. The cobble path of the garden winds and twists, its walls made out of hedges and some of stone. It all had grown rather quickly since the destruction that had reaped the kingdom of its beauty.

Luthias pauses and then bows, but I am too busy admiring the daffodils that had grown along this part of the path.

"King Bainen. It has been a long time my friend."

"Why so formal Luthias?" He chuckles. "I thought we went over this last time."

"It has seemed that I have forgotten. Do remind me again how you became king and why I even have to use such formalities when greeting you." Luthias jokes.

Bainen then turns to me and clears his throat. I still stand, admiring the flowers. "Don't suspect me to use such formalities with you Bainen. I've known you for too long." I smirk, turning towards him.

Bainen traveled to Ambrose often to seek council from my father. They were very close for a human and an Elf. And it seemed that even Eryn had developed an even closer connection for the human King.

He was tall for a mortal, but with Elven blood running through his veins, it gave him some qualities of an immortal. Sadly, not the long living life. But looks and skills were greatly given to him. Bainen's hair was cut in a shaggy mess of dirt brown hair that was pulled back with a single clip of gold. It was a much better look than what his greasy hair used to look like a few years ago before he ascended the throne.

"You've cleaned up nice. Far better than what you started with when you left Ambrose."

"And you've gotten older Laerune," he jokes. "Are you still keeping track of your age?"

It wasn't a normal thing for Elves to keep track of their age after one hundred. Once you came to age, you stopped counting. There was nothing else to look forward to, except the long ages of our never ending lives. But I, the only one it seemed, still kept counting. Sometimes it was hard to keep count and years blended together, the birthdays disappeared, and life just became life I guess. I just took it day by day.

"I have come to the conclusion that I might have missed a birthday one year." I tell him, but then explain. "But I think it's safe to say that I am one hundred and twenty six years old."

"Now I see why your father had begun to court you. He never thought you were going to marry." Bainen chuckles.

Most Elven woman marry by the age of 120. After that courting begins. But I am sure that my father had it planned out for a very long time.

"So, why have you both ventured to Everford together?"

"Just because we can." We begin walking down the path, my arm wrapped around Luthias'. "A raven announced our arrival?"

"Yes. And why is that a question?"

"We did not send one out," Luthias explains. "And my father did not know that we would be riding to Everford."

Bainen shakes his head, confused. "Well someone must have known that you would be arriving in Everford." He brushes an invisible piece of dust off of his navy blue tunic. He looks towards the palace, its turrets high and tall. "How is Lithien faring?"

"Spawns of Navain are running ramped around Lithien. LaRue killed a Dement rider on the way here. Orcs are also coming down from the Hills of Gia."

I place a hand over my side, the pain still slightly there. But thankfully my Elven blood has quick healing properties. Without it, I probably wouldn't be walking around at this moment.

"And Sentier?"

"Times are rough, but I predict things will get better. We just simply have to pray to the Electa and hope that they still shine down upon us."

I never understood the Gods much. They seemed to never grant the things you actually needed.

Bainen turns towards me. "And your father has allowed you to finally travel on your own? I see no other escort."

"I travel with Luthias for I am now living in Lithien."

"And what has brought you to Lithien?"

Luthias and I look to each other. Bainen has known about my courting process and how I have disagreed with it greatly. "Engagement."

Bainen slaps his hand against Luthias' shoulder. "I knew this day would come. I was hoping it would be soon." He chuckles, but then looks over his shoulder. He calms himself.

Bainen clears his throat as a guard approaches us, his gold sword clinking at his side and his orange armour shining in the new day's sun. An owl is perched upon his shoulder. "An owl has been sent requesting that this should be given to Lady Laerune."

The letter is handed to me, the crest of Ambrose seals the paper together. My father's slanted handwriting loops across the page. *A warning.*

"My father wishes for when we return to Lithien that we avoid Nolan's borders at all costs," I hand the letter to Luthias. "We must also stay off of the main road."

Luthias growls. "I hate that he only gives us the bare minimum to whatever he sees. A little more information would be helpful."

Bainen seems saddened. "When do you plan to leave?" His eyes turn up to Luthias. "Eryn has been waiting to see you both. It would be more than appreciated if you stayed the night."

"I think that can be arranged," I smile at Bainen as his shoulders relax.

"Your sister has been begging to visit Ambrose to see you, but once we heard news of your leavetaking, we were unsure of where you went," he bows his head at each guard. "We should've guessed that you would have traveled to Lithien."

"Has Eryn been on edge?"

The young King chuckles. "She is always on edge."

"Are you speaking about me?" Eryn enters the gardens. "My ears were ringing."

She links her arm with mine. Eryn wears a bright grin upon her face as she leads us to the sitting room. She motions for each of us to take a seat as she walks across the room.

Bookshelves line the walls and the fireplace is empty of its coals. "I have found something of yours recently," she lifts open a small box, pulling a ratted book that is falling apart at the spine. "It's not in the condition I remember, but it seems as if it has been loved greatly."

The book's title is dulled in color, but the name still holds true. *Greythore's Reign.* "You must've taken it from me when we were younger."

"It seems that way," she sits next to me as I flip through the yellowed pages.

Eryn is only four years older than I am, so we were always butting heads. I wouldn't doubt it if she had taken it to get back at me when we were younger.

Eryn places her hand over her opal necklace. "I have a few more things for you."

She rises from her seat with grace, but the sophisticated attitude quickly dissipates when she reaches for my arm. "Come on," she grins.

We enter another room; one filled with wide open trunks and strewn papers across the floor. "Excuse the mess. I have been attempting to organize it and go through it all."

She bends down, placing her hand over her stomach. She places a few other books into my arms before sitting down onto the floor.

"I am a bit nervous," she looks down at her stomach. "I guess watching what mother went through is making me worried it will happen to me."

I cock my head to the side with a smirk. "It won't happen to you. Father would've let you know before."

"But he doesn't see everything, Laerune. There is things that are still unknown. There are things that can't be changed."

My father's words come to mind. *"A change in the future can change the world and changing the world can change the future."*

She continues to go on about how our father's gift works. "There are things he does not share with us. And if he did it could change our world forever. The smallest things can result in large events."

Eryn seems to ramble on. "You could kill an ant and that might result in the end of the world."

"Eryn," I place my hand on her arm. "You are worrying too much." She nods her head as I continue to talk. "We must speak of matters that might actually happen."

She looks at me with a confused frown written over her fair face. "There is a bounty on our heads. All of us. Luthias and I traveled to Ebin and we stole a document from Nolan. It was a list of bounties."

"The price of my ears alone could run a kingdom for a few years," I continue to tell her.

"But why are they searching for us? What have we done to them?"

"I don't think it's what we have done, but what we are going to do. War seems more and more likely each passing day." I let my hand settle against her arm. "I have yet to tell father, but his name is on the list as well. I am planning on sending a bird to him in a few days."

Eryn breathes in deeply. "He most likely knows already. Did you hear about Adeal? He was murdered right outside of Ambrose's borders. I heard it was by a pack of Orcs."

"It's true. He was murdered when I arrived back."

Eryn rummages through the rest of the chests. "Here," she offers me a leather sheath. "It has been passed down by the woman in our family. I have no use for it." She looks up to her own stand of armour with her sword adorning the side of the stand. "I am sure Dehlin can attest that the weapon works, he did use it once in the final battle of Lenair."

I grab the handle of the sword, unsheathing the ancient weapon. "And you don't have to worry about finding a name for it," Eryn reminds me. "Laure-eneth, the weapon of the fair and young."

The weapon was truly made for a smaller woman. The lightweight blade seemed to easily cut through air and I am sure it could cut through other, harsher, things as well.

The pommel swirled into leaves that formed at the bottom of the handle. The sides of the handle was sharp enough to slice through leather armour.

I rise to my feet while swinging the sword through the air. The handle fits perfectly in my small hand. "Thank you, Eryn." I set down the sword and then reach over to hug her.

I fall back onto the floor as the world changes and spins around me.

"Do not speak to me of loss and ruin." Sentier growls. He speaks to a mortal, worn and old, but they hold some sort of celestial light around him.

"All I want is the stone, Sentier. Now, give me what I wish for."

"I will not forsake my whole kingdom for your rock collection." He growls again, getting closer to the man's face. "That is the only thing that keeps my kingdom alive. Why would I give it to your kind?"

"Sentier. I can promise you that your kingdom will be safe from harm. Now, tell me where the damn stone is!"

"Never." Sentier unsheathes his long, silver sword. "Leave my kingdom."

"You will pay for this, Sentier. I will show you what real destruction is." The man turns to leave. "And your beautiful wife will know my wraith first. I know what she hides from me!"

My eyes shoot open quickly as Eryn stares at me, a worried look upon her face. "Is everything alright?"

"Just the past."

"Again? Are they getting longer? Clearer?" Gifts are past down from my bloodline and I have received visions of the past instead of the future. "Father said that once those get clearer the ones of the future will shine through."

It's not like a normal memory when they flash before you. It's like walking through it as a different person. Even sometimes you are a part of someone else and you see it in their point of view. It's quite an odd feeling. You could almost describe it as an out of body experience.

"What was it of?" Eryn asks as she furrows her brows.

"Of Sentier speaking with a man about a stone."

Eryn lowers her head as she thinks of the importance of a simple stone. "The only type of stone I can think of is the Saryniti. But those are lost forever."

"The Saryniti?"

Her mouth gapes open. "How do you not know? Did father ever tell you that story?" I shake my head. "Well, Maglanor, a great craftsman, was brought before the Electa. He offered each of them his greatest works as gifts. But he gave four of the Electa more powerful pieces. Maglanor gave Elbonare, Caolan, Lyrassel, and Sibylla each a stone that fit into the palm of their hand."

"But the other members of the Electa, being angered that they were not given such powerful gifts, planned to rebel and to split the stones into equal pieces."

"But Navain, son of Caolan, stole the stones from their masters and hid them within the Earth. Elbonare took charge and banished Navain from their homes. Navain's powers were taken away as well as his knowledge of where the stones were hidden. The Electa continues in the search of the missing Saryniti, but they are yet to be found; their power missing from the Electa."

I lean my back against the leg of the desk. "I think I remember hearing that, but I probably wasn't paying attention. I wasn't interested in the Electa when I was younger. I found them fake."

Eryn leans back and chuckles. "You found them fake! And you thought griffins were real?" She then grows serious. "Then what did you do during each celebration?"

"I went along with it. It was still a tradition, even if I did not believe in who we were celebrating. I first started to believe that during Beltane."

Eryn shakes her head. "I can't believe it. What would father think?"

"He is an educated Elf and I believe that he knows they aren't real either."

"You don't even know," Eryn shakes her head, sending her black hair in different directions. Her tresses slowly fall across her face.

"What are you hiding?" I growl at her as I notice her eyes flash with guilt. "Why are you guilty?"

"I'm not guilty," she snarls back.

"Then why are you getting defensive?"

Eryn rises to her feet quickly. "I am not!"

I back up with a grin on my face. "You know if you don't tell me it gives me more urge to go and find out." Usually that is enough to get the information from her, but she crosses her arms and refuses.

"We should eat," is all she says.

I can tell by how she walks that she has been told not to tell me something. I follow beside her down the hall. Eryn's arms are still crossed over her chest as if she is keeping the secret safe. "What did father not want me to know?"

"Nothing."

She is lucky that we enter the dining hall or I would've questioned her further.

"What do you have there?" Luthias questions, the sideways smirk written across his smug face. I place the sword in his hands and he admires it with keen eyes. Luthias examines the blade, checking the sharpness as he runs his thumb over the edge.

"Ancient, but powerful." Luthias hands the sword back to me and I set it on the table.

Eryn practically shouts. "No weapons on the table!" I set the sword by my side quickly. "You don't even know how much blood I cleaned off this table, Laerune Aduial. I will not be repairing blade marks from it next."

I lower my head to stifle a chuckle. "Don't think of this as a joke, sister," Eryn growls. "I've worked hard cleaning up this place." She stabs her fork into the food on her plate. She leans over to whisper in Bainen's ear.

I look to Luthias and then back to my sister. "Secrets?"

"I was just telling him the information that you told me. We are traveling to Ambrose in a week and I thought that I could warn our father."

"Have you told him you are with child?"

"That is why we are traveling," she seems to growl the words.

I lean over to Luthias. "I promise we love each other."

"My relationship with my brother was very different."

Bainen lays his hand onto Eryn's arm and the redness in her cheeks flush. She shakes her head as if she is attempting to shake away her anger. "I'm sorry," she apologizes. "My emotions seem misplaced all of a sudden."

I stare at her as she stares back at me. "You need to leave." She speaks softly.

Luthias looks puzzled by the request, but I quickly grab my things from the table before I reach for Eryn. "What did you see?" I grip the sleeves of her orange dress.

Her cornflower blue eyes stare beyond me as if she was still seeing the small glimpse of the future. "The kingdom of Lithien needs your help. The borders are being watched. The Prince is being called home."

I embrace my sister in a quick hug as I give Bainen a smile. I pull on Luthias' arm as he reaches for his own supplies.

***

I place my foot into the stirrup and then I swing my other leg over. With a nudge of my heel, Venetta bolts out of the stables and Luthias follows behind me, his cloak billowing behind him. We ride through the open gate, bypassing the guards who look at us questioningly as we pass. Such urgency is usually not common.

My mind wanders to not only my father's warning, but to the glimpse of Sentier's past. His words echo in my mind. *"Do not speak to me of loss and ruin."*

I rack my mind for any mention of powerful stones in my history books that may not be *the* Saryniti. I didn't want it to be the Saryniti. *Why would I have a part in that?"*

My father always told me that everything we see in visions is a part of our being and we should not take the information lightly. We should analyze and review it constantly.

Chapter 10

Luthias and I reach the gate of Lithien as dusk covers the land. Lights of fire glow as the gates are opened for us. I turn around in my saddle to hear the screams and yelps of Kitsunes. Their voices were like shrills of banshees, worse than those of the Demet Riders.

"Prince Luthias," the captain's eyes shine with tiredness and glow from the light of the lamp he holds in front of himself. "You are needed tonight. Many of our guards are injured and we are running out of energy."

Luthias stares at the captain with compassion as he takes the lamp from the tired Elf's hands. "Go with LaRue. Get something to eat and rest. Come back when you feel well rested."

The captain goes to resist Luthias' offer but the prince disappears into the dark before a word can be said. The captain only smiles at me.

We keep our voices down as we walk down the empty halls of Lithein. My sky blue eyes search the hall, the flames casting shadows against the stone walls. "What has been attacking the guards?" I ask the captain as he too, searches the empty halls for shadows.

"Kitsunes mostly. We had a few trolls come down from the mountains early this morning. They did devastating damage to our East Gate. You're lucky you arrived from the south road."

The captain turns the corner to the kitchen. "There has been a lot of rumors. Some seem ridiculous, but I fear they might be true. Have you heard anything about the Electa attempting to find the Saryniti before Navain does?"

The door to the kitchen squeaks open. "Navain is said to be back and searching the land for someone that can touch them, let alone find them. I guess women are escaping from Nadien and coming back with tattoos of the kingdom's symbol. It seems like something in a storybook."

The maids in the kitchen watch the windows as the captain brings up the rumors. “The kingdom is on alert even though we don’t know if these things are true,” a brown haired maid cutting up greens adds. “We make sure to walk in groups. I would hate to be by myself at dark.”

I too, look out at the window. “I am sure there is nothing to worry about. Lithien is a stronghold. Nothing has penetrated the inside of the city in years.”

I voice my goodbyes as I leave on a good note. The halls seem emptier and less inviting. Shadows dance across the walls as my boots echo on the floor.

I open the door to my room. The window is open, a swift breeze pushes the curtains away from the window and papers scatter the floor. The candle in my hands flickers and I set it down to close the window. I light a match, sparking the wicks of the other candles around the room.

The room is cold and silent. I hate the silence. I hate the way it rings in my ears like a shrill bell setting off a warning. But then the screams of the Kitsunes break the silence. I don’t know if I should be thankful for them breaking the silence with their screams or not.

While moving to the closet, I pause, listening as the hallway floor creaks outside my door. I then slip the nightgown over my head, tossing my travel worn clothes to the floor. I pull back the covers of the bed, the soft green sheets are welcoming and warm.

My eyes drift off into tiredness, my body weak and falling into the jaws of sleep so quickly. I don’t listen as the footsteps in the hallway became more pronounced.

***

I wake with a jolt, my body covered in a cold sweat that sends a shiver down my spine. The cold fall wind flows in, making my whole body shiver in protest of the cold weather. The window had been opened again, the curtains blowing slightly like a ghoul welcoming its presence.

I shove the blankets to the side, lighting a candle that had again been burnt out. Luthias had not returned yet and the stars still shone brightly, the screams of the Kitsunes still ringing through the forest.

I open the door, leaving my room behind me. The hall is empty, the candles burning at a low dim. I just wander aimlessly, feeling like I don't belong. The nightmares had been coming more often, more terrible than the last.

I find myself standing in front of Sentier's room, the door ajar. Warmth seemed to come from his room and I stepped closer. He stopped what he was doing and turned to the door.

"Come in LaRue." He commands me. "I can tell that something is wrong."

"Nightmares." Is the only thing I say as I enter the room, taking a seat in a cushioned chair. I felt like a child.

"And what are these nightmares about?" He leans in closer to me.

"Death." I meet his grey eyes. "Death of people I know and don't know. I kill them. Well, some of them at least."

"Who is it that you kill?"

I am afraid to say his name. Afraid that if I say it, it will make it come true. "Avon."

"It's just a dream LaRue. Nothing more, nothing less." He pours a cup of tea and then places it in my frigid hands. "Dreams sometimes tell us things in indirect ways. Our minds don't want us to take it literally, but to find the secret answer to it."

"Sentier? What can you tell me about *the* stone?" I am sure he will know exactly what I am talking about. And sure enough, his eyes grow brighter at my words.

He clears his throat. "How did you find out?"

"So it is important?"

"How did you find out?" He growls, demanding an answer this time.

"It was in a dream."

He sits back in his chair, crossing his hands in his lap. His eyes wander to his glass of wine next to him, deciding whether or not he needs to take a drink. "It was my wife's. It had been given to her at a young age. It was Laura's duty to protect it and use it only when it was needed."

I think about the portrait in the great hall. Laura, Sentier's wife, sits in a cushioned chair, a golden amulet around her pale neck.

"I dare not say its name out loud for I fear their spies will hear."

"Who's spies?"

He leans forward, his voice barely above a whisper. "The Electa. They roam here, cloaking themselves in human forms. They are the ones that spy upon this kingdom."

"Are they the ones that came last time for the stone?"

"Yes." He pauses for a moment. "How do you know this Laerune?"

"The gift of foresight has been passed down in my family."

"And the past has been gifted to you as well."

I nod my head, setting down the cup of tea. The Electa are our Gods and Goddesses, they protect us, and they shaped our world into what it is now. How are they allowing this once great forest to fall into ruin? Sentier sets his hand under my chin.

"Laerune. Can you see into one's past?"

"I've only been able to once or twice."

"Can you try now?"

I nod my head again. "Yes." I look at his grey eyes. "You know that I will be in your thoughts, your feelings. Everything I see will be in your perspective."

"I know."

"I will feel the pain that you felt in that moment. Are you okay with that?"

"Yes."

I knew how to do it, that wasn't a problem. It was just painful to experience what they felt in that moment. And other Elves rarely liked me going through their thoughts.

I take his hands in mine, concentrating on his eyes. "Think of the memory that you wish to show me. Only that memory, don't jump around too much." His hands grip mine as the world around me changes into a battlefield.

I moved swiftly and I couldn't feel my feet touch the ground, but it wasn't enough. I didn't get there in time. I fell to my knees when I saw the blade buried deep between her ribs. An arrow protruded through her right leg. She smiled to show me she was not afraid, even so close to the end.

Her hand reached for mine, her skin was soft and pale like clouded starlight. Her breaths were shallow, but the words came swiftly from her lips. She needed this last goodbye.

"You will keep our children safe. Promise me Sentier."

"I promise."

Laura smiled and her teeth were stained red from her blood. The sight of her made my voice shake. But I want to be strong for her.

"You should have let me go alone." I tell her.

She shook her head, and a tear fell from her eye, a way a pearl slips form a string. This single moment seems to last forever.

"You are alive. You are with me."

Her duty was done. She would have not lived without me if our places were switched. I don't know how I would live without her, but I had to protect our children. She spoke just louder than a whisper.

"I love you."

"I love you." My voice cracks.

My chest was tight, and it felt like my armor was pressing against my lungs. I bent my head and kissed her forehead one last time.

"Stay," was the last word I knew, but it was too late for begging. The moment her hand lost its grip, the earth did not split, it did not open and swallow me whole as I felt that it might. I only held on tighter, so that some part of her might still feel my warmth that she would not grow cold. She would never grow cold for she was loved.

The soldiers could have carried her home on a bed of lilies and spared me from agony, but I did not let them touch her. Alone, I cradled her body like a child away from the battlefield.

Not once did she leave my arms nor touch the ground, not once did I look at her. It comforted me to feel her head against my chest, her familiar weight in my arms. As long as I held her, I was not yet alone. We walked together in another world.

For days, I would not eat, would not speak, and would not stop. I marched ahead of the army. Some of the soldiers were wounded and fell behind, but I kept a steady pace even when they slowed.

There was no longer fear or death, no imaginable pain that would surpass this. I lost the one I loved. I missed home, my children, but what I missed most was Laura. Even though we had won the war, it did not feel like victory.

I sit back in my chair, my hands letting go of Sentier's. We are silent until Sentier breaks it with his low voice.

"She carried what held our kingdom together. An amber stone that kept the evil at bay." He began to whisper. "One of the sacred stones of the Electa."

I bite my lip. "What happened to it?"

"It is hidden. Only the dead know where it lies." Sentier takes my hands again. Mine are cold in his warm palms. "Laerune, do you know what the evil searches for today?" I shake my head no. "They search for a woman. An Elven woman. One with hair as golden as the sun and blue eyes that are too innocent to commit sin."

"There is many women like that."

"They search for you Laerune."

My stomach drops and it feels like I am falling. "Why me?"

"She would banish the evil, bringing back the light that was once lost to us. You are the Pathway LaRue. You have been born to this world for a reason. To save us all from the darkness. Elender, your father, has kept many secrets from you Laerune."

I stare up at him, not believing the words he is saying. "That can't be."

"There is a prophecy written-" Sentier is cut off when a knock echos through the now silent room. "Come in."

Luthias enters the room, his hair tousled and a cut bleeding down his face. "The forest is overrun." He walks over to me, grabbing my hand. "Three were killed, five injured. Cave trolls have come down from the mountain. Goblins have taken over the trees and there is an Orc camp three miles from the gate." He stares down at the floor. "What do you want us to do father?"

"Send out more troops. Go with them and bring Laerune. Both of you have quite a lot of skill and will be very helpful. Listen to them. Don't engage unless you absolutely have to."

"Yes father."

I rise from my seat and Luthias and I return to our room. I open the wardrobe, slipping on the dark clothes, as Luthias ties a moss colored cloak around my neck. He pulls up the hood and then places his hands on my shoulders.

"Stay with me at all times." I nod my head and then he straps my daggers in my quiver of arrows, handing me my bow right after. "Stay silent."

Luthias and I step outside and the gate is opened for us. The forest floor is covered in a layer of mist and the screeches of Kitsunes begin. There are five others behind us, their steps so silent that I forget they are behind me.

I look behind me and they're gone, already hiding somewhere in the forest. Our only job here is too listen. To listen and learn. To gain information from our enemies. Luthias and I stop at a large Oak tree. Its branches reaching high into the forest canopy. I look at him as he begins to climb up its branches. I follow after him, stopping at the largest branch at the top.

I straddle the tree, keeping myself from falling as I watch the ground below us for any unwelcome visitors in this part of the forest. The forest is still, the only thing breaking the silence is the owl perched in the tree next to us.

Luthias unsheathes his knife with a sly smile. He begins to push it into the bark of the tree, carving letters that are swift and quick. He stops, the only sound is a soft breeze that brushes away the shavings of bark. As the bark shavings float away, our names are revealed in the tree trunk. He again smiles and then sits back against the tree's trunk.

I freeze as a noise cracks below us. Luthias sits up, his hand going to an arrow. *Just listen.* The heavy footsteps of Orcs stop through the leaves. An Elf is in their grasps and she yelps, trying to get away. My eyes flash to Luthias quickly and then back to the forest floor. The woman has blonde hair and I think she has blue eyes. I look to him again.

"Will you be quiet lady Elf," the Orc growls.

"I am not a lady." The girl giggles, a tail flicking back and forth through her dress as she changes back into her original form of a Kitsune. The Orc flings her forward.

"I am tired of this creature's tricks!" He yells. "Wait!" He stops. "I smell Elf."

Luthias freezes and he pulls up his hood, shielding his pale skin from the eyes of the Orc.

"The smell is strong here." He walks around in a circle, his grey skin barely visible. "A male and female." He snickers. "Royal blood."

Before the Orc can say another word, arrows go through all three of the Orcs there. Two from Luthias and one from my bow. The Kitsune just simply walks away with a slight flick of her tail. She stops, her red ears pinning back. She turns back around, circling under the tree.

"I know what you seek," her voice is sweet, but with a hint of aggression and taunting. "Come out little Elf. I know you are here." She teases, her tail flicking behind her. I look up at Luthias and then back down to the Kitsune. "Owls send important messages."

She flicks her tail as she returns to her fox form.

***

Sentier runs his hand over a brown spotted Owl that sits perched at his desk. Elender's, my father's owl. It ruffles its wings.

"What does he want now?" I fall gracefully onto the loveseat behind me.

"He is travelling to Lithien for...a celebration."

"A celebration is for good times, this is not a good time," Luthias says, agreeing with me. He crosses his arms, standing taller.

"This celebration will be a new start for our people Luthias. It will give them hope when the darkness has been so near them lately. And I am sure that once you hear of the excitement, then you both will happily join in." He smiles widely.

I sigh. "You both planned something. Will you spare us of this waiting and just tell us." I look up at the ceiling and the story painted upon it. Elves fighting against a dark shadow, weapons in hand.

"A Danen." Danen meant forever celebration in Elvish and a forever celebration was marriage. "You and Luthias will finally have your Danen."

I sit up, looking to Luthias with a smile and he returns it. I then replace my smile into a frown. "But is now a good time? I suppose you have heard the rumors." Luthias' eyes turned grey, the color vanishing in them for only a mere moment, but then returning to their sky blue color.

"Now is the best time. Now go on. You both need the rest." He rushes us out the door, closing it behind us. I intertwine my fingers with Luthias' as we walk down the hall to our room. I can't keep my eyes off of his bright blue ones. Oh how they shined and sparkled and held so much hope.

He laughs at me. "You look so tired."

"You look very tired too. When was the last time you got a full night's sleep?"

"Not for a while. You have been too busy running off to different kingdoms and getting yourself hurt and almost killed." He laughs.

"Oh, shush it."

"You know I'm right."

"Yeah, I know." I push his shoulder with mine, both of us almost falling over. "Why is it so dark here?"

"I don't need the sun when I have you."

I glare at him. "I'll just ignore that you said that."

"What? Am I sounding like Avon?" He smirks.

"You sound just like him. It's uncanny. Please don't ever do that again." I roll my eyes.

"But it's true."

"I can't tell if you are being serious or not."

"Maybe I am. Maybe I'm not."

Luthias opens the door to our room and I step inside, moving towards the closet. I strip off my clothes and then slip on my nightgown. My footsteps are silent as I glide over to the bed. Luthias lifts up the blankets and I slip under them. Within minutes my mind wanders, dreams appearing. The darkness becomes colorful and bright.

I am standing alone, an empty field before me. The tall grass rolls like waves along the sea. My plait is unbound and tangled, my sword dripping with blood. I look around, searching for someone, anyone. I spin around, searching in every direction, but the sea of grass goes on and on. A never ending ocean of green and gold.

Cloaked in shadows of black, a figure draws near. Its hand is reached out, summoning me to come closer, to come closer to its shadow. "Laerune." It calls. It stands in front of me, towering over me. Like a tree to a flower. "I have a task for you to complete. An important one."

He flicks his hand and Avon stands in the field, his arms gripped by invisible chains. He struggles to rip free.

"Please LaRue. Please let me go. Please." He begs, tears running down his face.

I lift my hands to help him, but with the magic of the shadow, a bow and a single arrow appear in my hands.

"You know what you must do Laerune." The shadow speaks, his voice low as if it was being sung through the echoes of a cave.

I knock in my single arrow and then pull on the string of my bow. It creaks and I try to stop my hands, but invisible phantoms hold them in place. Voices inside my head chant. *Release. Release.* My hand slips from the bow string and I watch as the arrow makes my unwanted mark. Avon staggers backwards, his eyes reaching for the sky. Not a single word escapes his mouth.

The world seemed silent, not a word uttered at the crime I have committed. But then the world changed. Changed into rock and cliffs. A mountain range rose around me. A girl stands before me. Her violet eyes gleamed in fright and she tried to untie the rope that bound her hands. Her white hair was tangled and her dress ripped.

"Why LaRue? Please. I am begging you." She steps backwards towards the edge of the cliff. Her voice is sweet and innocent. "I thought we were friends?" My hands are shoved forward, impacting with her shoulders as her foot slips, causing those violet eyes to disappear off the edge of the mountain side.

I wake with a jolt, my head spinning. The room is still dark, the sun not peaking over the forest yet. The stars still shined, the moonlight shining through the open doorway. I rise to my feet, the floor cold as I walk to the doorway. The screams of the Kitsunes had ceased and the world seemed silent even for a moment.

Silence. It seemed to make the air cold and chilled. Like the world was filled with nothing and it was only me. Only me, lost in a world full of disaster and destruction. Where fire burned brighter than the stars. A world is nothing without light, because even at night, the stars still shine. In the dawn the sun will still rise.

I look up at the stars. They all shined. They seemed to gaze back at me as if they knew my every thought and secret. Like I spilled my words to them, causing them to light up and shine. To dance with color as my words brought life to them.

I grip the railing of the balcony, my hands rubbing against the wood. The stars were like diamond dust had been blown from the hands of a god or fragments of the moon, scattered around the sky.

"Laerune." I jump, startled as Luthias walks closer to me, candle in his hand. "What are you doing up? Is everything alright?"

"Just nightmares."

"Again?"

I place my hands around the candle in his hands, blowing it out. "You're ruining it."

"Ruining what?"

"The starlight. They get very jealous over other lights, you know that?"

"How do you know this LaRue?"

"I just do." I whisper.

He sighs. "Come back to bed LaRue."

I look up at the stars one last time before following Luthias back to our bedroom. I would've stayed up the rest of the night if he hadn't of gotten me to go back to bed. He was always my calm against the raging storm that kept me awake almost every night.

Chapter 11

I wake up again, the sun shining and glistening through the doorway that we had left open last night. A cool breeze of autumn air brushed against my face, waking me up with its crisp coldness. Luthias was nowhere to be found, his only hint of leaving was the slip of paper he had left on the bed stand.

It read: *I am with my father. You can find us both in the library.*

I lean my head back onto the bed, ignoring the sun that shines directly in my face. The leaves were falling from the great trees and the sun shined through the now bare branches. Fall was ending and winter was on its way. I think it worried everyone in Lithien. Winters were harsh here.

It had been years since Lithien had last held a celebration in its halls. It had been months since a large group of people had travelled to Lithien's borders.

I swing my legs over to the side of the bed, the cold floor sending shivers down my spine. The seasons were changing rather quickly. Autumn is turning into winter. The cold air becoming crisper and colder each day.

I close the window, locking its clasp. The cold air ceased and the warm fire filled the room with dry air. Without even changing from my night clothes, I make my way to the library. Each of the Elven kingdoms has their own set of unique books at each of their libraries, but Lithien's had to be my favorite.

The bookshelves were made from the trees themselves that grew through that very building. The ceiling was made of glass, usually covered in leaves during the autumn season. But it changed the colors of the room, matching with the seasons.

I creak open the door, slipping through. Luthias looks out the window as Sentier sits, a glass of wine in his hand.

"Wine so early in the morning?" I ask him.

He quickly turns towards me. "Good morning Laerune. Come, take a seat. We have much to discuss."

"What is there to discuss?" I ask Sentier, but I smile at Luthias. He returns it and then walks over to the table set with plates and glasses.

"Your Danen of course." Sentier replies as Luthias pours a glass of tea and places it in my hands. "It is a very special day and it will only happen once in your life. I allowed my wife to plan the whole thing by herself. I trusted her with the decisions." He chuckles. "But I want you both to plan it together. As a couple."

"Well, what do we start with?" I cross my legs, sipping the tea from my cup. I know that there is many traditions to follow from both sides of our kingdoms. The Leithia Elves were stricter with their traditions compared to the Saleth.

In Ambrose, the Danens were small, while in Lithien following the Leithia traditions they were large and extravagant.

"Start with colors."

I look to Luthias, admiring the green in his tunic. I then turn to a man standing next to Sentier. He writes across a notepad with a feathered quill.

"I would love green, maybe some ivy? And purple would be a lovely color."

"That was simple." Sentier smirks.

"What about traditions? What do they consist of here in Lithien?"

"Ah. My wife asked the same thing when this time came around for us. She was very curious." Sentier was beginning to bring her up often. He pushed back his dark blonde hair. "The couple must be separated for at least two days."

The Elf stops his quill. "Don't forget the Brielle, my King."

"Oh yes. I almost forgot. Thank you." He stands from his seat. "Do you know what the Brielle is LaRue?" I shake my head. "The Brielle is a dance where your hands are bound together and if the ribbon touches the ground, the marriage is not blessed and doomed forever."

"In Ambrose we have Melde, which is handfasting."

"Yes, I know. But do Salath Elves create their own handfasting ribbons?"

"The soon to be wife will make them."

"Then it seems that our traditions are set in stone. Now, to what must be your favorite part LaRue." He walks towards the window. "Your dress." He chuckles.

"I have one already." I speak quietly.

Sentier turns around quickly, his face in a grim, straight line. "You do?"

"I was engaged to Avon, but that one got practically destroyed. But I had another picked out."

"Oh yes. I remember now." He clears his throat. "Well, that is one less thing we must take care of." Sentier's eyes widen brightly. "Up, up, up." He motions with his hands.

He opens a wooden box up and pulls out a long ribbon. "I will be the one to teach you the Brielle."

He takes the colored ribbon and wraps it tightly around my hand and his. He steps away, leaving a space in between us. "Keep your hand up and don't let go of the ribbon." He takes a few steps and I follow. "Don't get tangled either, we don't want you breaking a wrist."

He continues to show me how the Brielle works. A complicated, but simple dance to learn with lots of spins and steps. Apparently Luthias won't have to learn it with me because when he was young his mother taught him. I can slightly see the vision in my head of them dancing together. It makes me smile knowing that they did at least get to spend some time with each other unlike my mother and I.

I never met her. I never got to meet the Silver Lady of Ambrose, the one they call Andwin. I heard stories of how great she was, how she made Ambrose the way it is now, with the help of my father of course. She was great and beautiful, so I have been told. My father tells me that I look much like her and everyday he looks at me he sees a woman growing up to be something great, just like my mother.

She fought in wars, ended conflicts, and even brought peace to our lands. But her death wasn't glorious and righteous. She didn't die in battle or fought valiantly for something she loved like her land and people. She died while having me. She died for me. She gave me life while I gave her death.

It was tragic. Her passing brought sadness to many people including my father. I was blamed and punished by the Gods. I was very sick for many years and I struggled to grow and get stronger. Many of the healers thought I would die as well, but I didn't give up so easily.

I watch as Sentier puts the ribbons back into their box and then sets the box upon a shelf. Luthias had already left to do more productive things other than watch me learn how to dance. Supposedly, he was going to go find Tasar who had just returned from Makya.

I glide over to the window, the leaves slowly falling from the trees. I watch Elves that pass by, carrying things that needed to be brought in before the winter snow fell over the forest. Sentier stands at my side.

"Where is that savage, little mutt of yours? I haven't seen her around in a while."

"Oh, Oka." I giggle. "She's at home, probably lounging with anyone that's willing to pet her."

"I am surprised she hasn't followed you here yet. She's a protective pup."

Oka, a silver dog, who I swear is more wolf than anything else, had been welcomed into my home as a pet. I've had her for only a couple of years and she is barely over three. She is rambunctious and will steal your food if no one is looking. Hence why Sentier calls her a savage mutt. But she's sweet and loving. She would've followed me here if I hadn't occupied her with food before I sneaked off.

"If you allow it, I wish for her to be brought here."

You had to be careful when asking for things around Sentier. His temper usually got the best of him and having a pet in his house hasn't happened since Luthias and Luvon were little.

"Of course Laerune." He leans over to whisper to me. "I secretly like Oka."

"Oh really, not like I noticed you feeding her biscuits the last time you visited."

I walk towards the door, winking as I walked into the hallway. The days were dwindling down to my Danen, even though it was only the first day of planning it. Sentier was wasting no time in planning the rest of it. He wanted it to happen quickly. He wanted it to happen and most likely plan for the next phase of the forest.

There are many things that this Danen will bring. And through Sentier's eyes I see two kingdoms united, a future heir, and a world renewed. A world where his forest and home can be safe. I see a new life, a new home, and the freedom that I have wished for my whole life. And maybe even some answers to my past and future that seems to becoming more of a mystery to me each day.

I don't know what Luthias sees. Maybe a new beginning. I haven't had much time to speak with him, he seems so far away and busy all the time. I am hoping that once our Danen happens then we will have more time together.

I feel lonely in a way. Without Luthias I have no other friends, no one has even tried to make conversation. It seems that the young elves of Lithien are no more. Like they don't exist anymore. Like they have gone extinct.

Which they have in a way. A lot of them have died. They have been taken, stolen from their homes, killed, and died of unknown illnesses or grief. I think it had something to do with the prophecy and when they were born. Evil races have been searching for Elves for years since the prophecy has been written. And I am one that they probably seek.

I am of the right age and my birthdate is near when it was written. Sentier was speaking a couple of days ago about this prophecy. He spoke about returning the light that was once lost to us which he thinks is the Electa's hidden stones or even the light of his dear forest.

It makes sense, but I don't know why he thinks it's about me. I am nothing, I have done nothing to amount to any prophecy. I have done nothing to help anyone. So, how could it be me?

I open the black, Iron Gate, it creaking loudly. The wind blows, brushing my hair over my shoulder. Dark clouds cover the sun and snow lightly falls from the sky. Just flurries, like small jewels falling from the hands of a God, gifting us with the light of jewels unknown to us.

I move forward to the stone courtyard, the wind becoming stronger and I watch as both snow and leaves fall from the forest canopy. Winter has finally met autumn.

I stand at the bridge, the water rushing below it. Cold and unforgiving as it splashes over the rocks. I can't explain how I am feeling at this certain moment. Like I know that something bad is going to happen. That the weight of grief that will be put on us lies all in my heart in this one moment.

It's like the sound of weapons ring in my ears even though I have never heard the sounds of war and battle. But it seems like a memory or a vision. A secret glimpse of something not yet written in history books.

I look around quickly, the world changing rapidly. The trees disappear and grass is under my feet. The air is cold, the clouds dark and grey. I look around, Elves and men fighting around me. Fighting against an evil race of creatures. But behind me is *him.* His black cloak billowing in the wind, his face hidden by darkness and shadow.

"Kill him." Is all he says as I look down at the spear in my hand. He repeats it until I raise my hand, aiming at the Elf standing in front of me. Luthias stands in front of me and I try to hold my hand back, but the phantoms begin to move it for me.

I have no control. None at all. I cry, trying to force myself to stop, but my hand releases. I shut my eyes, hoping that there was some chance that I missed and that he would come running to calm me. But nothing happened and I dared to open my eyes.

Another man stood there. Tall, strong, his eyes blank as he searched for the sun. "I bow to no queen but you." Is all he says before the brown disappears from his large eyes. I close my eyes again, forcing myself to wake up or get myself out of this vision.

Once I open my blue eyes again, I find myself back on the bridge, my hands gripping the railing. I am no queen. A hand is placed on my shoulder and I turn around quickly. "I am no queen."

"What are you talking about Laerune?" Luthias asks and Tasar ponders behind him.

"Nothing. It's nothing."

"A queen? Who's a queen? There is no queen here anymore."

"Luthias-" Tasar begins to speak, but Luthias interrupts him.

"We do not speak of that Tasar." He growls, quickly turning back to me.

"Well I am going to tell her anyways."

"Don't you dare." Luthias swears at Tasar.

Under Tasar's breath he coughs. "Queen of the Hidden Kingdom."

That was it. Whatever that meant pushed Luthias over the edge. Luthias pushes Tasar into the railing of the bridge, pushing his head close to the water. Luthias' dagger is in his hand near Tasar's throat. I stand there unsure of what to do. I quickly try to push Luthias away from Tasar, but he grabs my wrist instead.

"Luthias Faen! How dare you touch me!" I growl, pushing him away. "You should be ashamed of yourself!" I cross my arms, seeking an apology to both Tasar and me. Tasar sits on the floor looking up at us.

"He had no reason to tell you. We both vowed to be silent."

"Why am I not allowed to know?"

"Because it will put you in danger."

Tasar stands up. "She needs to know. It will help her in the long run."

"Just wait for her father to tell her. That was what we were waiting for."

"Fine, but it's not my fault if she goes snooping around to find more information."

"Maybe if you didn't tell her any information. I was informed by her father specially to keep it a secret and to only tell her if he died before he was able to."

"You both are confusing me. I am going to take the information I got and I am going to find more. You can find me downstairs."

I push my hair over my shoulder and walk away from the bridge leaving Tasar and Luthias to figure out the mess they have created. I push on a wall, following a narrow stone staircase. Not many people know that there is a downstairs to the castle, but Sentier allowed me to know some secrets about his kingdom. The basement was filled with scrolls and old, important documents.

The lights were dim and dust filled the air. I turn the corner, finding an Elf leaning against the stone wall, a smirk plastered onto her face. Her bangs dangled in her eyes and her red hair shined auburn under the light of the lamps. She tossed an apple in her hand and then bit into its crispness.

"You must be Laerune." She rises to her feet, tossing the half eaten apple to her side. She then bows deeply. "It is an honor to meet with you."

"Please no formalities."

She grins, her smirk sly like a fox. The young Elf's hair looks like it was kissed with dragon fire, the bright red color like flames against the black of night. And her eyes were green like tumbled sea glass, polished from the waves. She sticks her hand out to shake mine.

"I am Chalsarda Eilis." Her green eyes seem friendly as she smiles.

"Could you help me?" I ask her, looking at the pile of papers sitting upon the dusty desk.

"That's why I am here. It's all I ever do." I look at her clothes as she walks towards a wall of books. "What is it that you are looking for?"

"Queens who have ruled."

She searches. "Such a vague topic, huh?" I look at the emblem on her uniform. A guard's uniform.

"Why are you down here when you should be with the rest of the guard?"

"Because I am a woman and I am young and know nothing." She speaks in a thick accent. "Because I'm a stubborn bitch as they like to call me. I'm not one to take that name lightly. I am not a dog." She smirks. "They didn't like it when I beat the men in training I guess."

"So they brought you here?"

"As punishment I guess. Which isn't much of a punishment other than I really want to be up there learning things other than books. But this is my new job and supposedly I am quite good at it. Which I know I am." She smirks again, her sly smile becoming more and more like a fox.

She stops at a shelf overflowing with loose papers and broken bindings of books. "Ah. This seems promising." She hands me a stack of papers binded together with string, the pages barely staying together. "It's a bit old, but that usually means it gives the best information."

She sits down onto a dusty chair. "Isn't it just great down here?" She leans back in the chair, spreading her arms behind and over her head. "Just damn great."

"It sure is," I say, while returning my focus to the stack of yellowed papers.

"Hey, don't you know any combat skills?"

"Yes, yes I do."

"Could ya maybe refresh my memory? I know it all, but it's been awhile since one on one training."

"I could possibly get you back in training if you would like." I flip the old book closed.

"You would really do that for me?" I nod my head. "Thank you and the Gods and Goddesses that brought you here LaRue."

She follows me out of the basement and back into the hallway. With a few turns down the hall and out into the open courtyard we find ourselves where they are holding training. It's all males. No women. Chalsarda smirks as the other males notice her bright red hair. One man sighs and turns to Chalsarda.

"What did I tell you girl? Don't come back unless you have leave from you punishment from a royal. Do you not get that?" He raises his hand to hit her across the side of the head, but I grab his wrist.

"I would not do that in front of someone with a royal title." He drops his hand.

"You're just a Lady, nothing else."

"Soon her title will change, Arvellas." Luthais stands behind me. "Who declares you to give punishment?"

"Your father." He growls.

"My father would not see this punishment as wise, especially if you are punishing her because she is a woman." Luthias stares at Arvellas. "I don't think my father would want to hear that you are breaking the rules that his deceased wife had made especially for this reason."

Luthias grabs the man's spear and knocks him over with a swift smack. "And that is for disrespecting my bride."

Luthias bows and then places a hand on Chalsarda's back, motioning for her to follow him. "What are you doing?" I question Luthias whose hair is pulled back in a ponytail. He must have been helping with training today.

"Giving her a trainer that will do her good. I'm taking her to Alastar."

Chalsarda pauses. "Alastar? You can't do that."

"He will help you the most. Trust me."

"You're giving me too much." She shakes her head, her fire kissed hair escaping from her plait.

"We are giving you what you need. And you don't need Arvellas."

Luthias takes us to a room and shoves the door open. Alastar, a tall, broad Elf, leans on his desk. His black hair is like raven feathers and his eyes are clouded over in white. Not many people would think Alastar would amount to such important things, especially being a great warrior whose stories have been told all around Laiqulasse.

His blind eyes search around the room as he walks around his desk. "Yes Luthias?" He knew exactly who was in the room and what they were doing, but he was unable to see. He surprised me every time I saw him. He could see things that we couldn't, yet he is blind to our world.

"I need you to train Chalsarda."

"Oh yes. Chalsarda. Red haired, quite a large spirit. Stubborn!" Alastar chuckles. "I've been waiting for her for quite some time."

He seemed old in mind and spirit, but he still looks like a young adult. Alastar walks over to Chalsarda and he takes her hand in his. "Strong but caring. Perfect." He then turns back to his desk. "I will train her. We start tomorrow morning. Good day." He goes back to sitting at his desk. "Laerune." He points a finger in my direction. "I have something for you."

I reach out to accept the paper he is holding forward. A simple sketch of a raven covers most of the page. "Thank you?"

Alastar simply nods his head. "You see what others can't."

We leave Alastar's room and Chalsarda stands there in silence. She then turns to Luthias, her sly eyes dimmed. "Thank you Luthias. It is much appreciated and I will return the favor someday." She leaves, allowing Luthias and I to be alone.

"Laerune." He turns to me. "Have I told you how beautiful you are lately?" I just smile, looking up at his cornflower blue eyes. They sparkle with a hint of gold as he looks down at me. "Your hair is just absolutely beautiful. I wish you would let it down once and awhile. It's always up."

He pulls the pins from my hair, letting my golden tresses fall to my knees. "And your eyes. Your smile." Luthias steps closer to me, the paper shaking in my hands.

"Laerune Aduial!" My father's voice booms in the hallway, followed by Etta, who was my nursemaid when I was younger. "Why have you not come to greet your Lord father?" He chuckles, embracing me in his arms.

A bark echos through the hallway and I watch as a blur of white and grey slides across the stone floor. Oka's paws slip and slide across the floor as she tries to reach me. I kneel down, petting her head as she wags her tail. She licks my face as she continues to whip her tail wildly.

"Why have you come father?"

"For your Danen of course. It is in a couple of days you know."

"Has anyone else arrived?" I am hoping that maybe Avon had decided to come, but he would've been following closely behind my father if he had.

My father takes my hand and I walk with him down the hall. Luthias stands at my father's side and Etta and Oka follow closely behind us. "Many have arrived my sweet Laerune." My father takes us to the balcony, a bench is set up close to the railing of the ivy covered stone. "There are many things we must take care of." He motions for us to sit. His blue eyes look tired and grey. His hands look aged, but his maroon robes bring color to his hair and fair face.

"If my life is to come to an end I shall give you both the crown until two others shall return. When they will return is unknown. All I ask of you is to wait for Eldar and Eldrin. Do not seek them, just wait."

"And who is Eldar and Eldrin?" I question my father.

"You will find out someday, but now is not the right time."

The names seemed familiar, but clouded at the same time. As if I read them in a book many years ago, but somehow forgot what the characters' names were. My father sees that spark in my eyes, knowing that I am going through every memory trying to figure out where those names came from. But, I draw a blank.

"Luthias, I wish to speak to Laerune alone." Luthias leaves and I am left alone with my father. He sits next to me. "Do you know why your mother and I picked Laerune to be your name?" I shake my head, meeting my father's eyes. "Your name means beautiful warrior. You are strong and you are beautiful. Your mind works in wonderful ways and your heart can see what some cannot. But LaRue means pathway. And you have created your path to the future yourself. You have pushed through and have taken control of your future."

He takes my hands in his. "And Aduial means daughter of the starry twilight. You are a gift from Sibylla herself. A daughter of the stars and the sun. A piece of Sibylla and Lyraesel. A piece from the Gods and Goddesses."

"I am nothing special father."

"Then you know nothing daughter. For you are much more important than you think you are LaRue. You may even change the whole world someday my Aduail." He winks.

"Like that will happen anytime soon." I pause for a moment, my giggle slowly fades away. "Has Avon traveled with you?"

I can already hear the no escaping from his mouth.

"He will be arriving soon. There was a few things I needed him to take care of along the way."

I can feel my eyes light up with excitement. "I was afraid he wasn't going to come."

"You think he would miss this?" My father chuckles. "Now, go get changed. You're still in your nightgown."

I blush while giving a slight cursey to my father before rushing away from the balcony.

***

I open the door and then quickly close it. I lean my back against the door, but my face turns a ruby color.

"I am sorry," I quickly say with a stutter as I look at Luthias who has his shirt off. I turn around, leaning my head against the wooden door. "I'm sorry." I giggle, smiling brightly.

I hear him slip his shirt over his head and I turn around to meet his blue eyes. "What did Elender have to say?"

"Just to say that I am special and I am going to change the world someday. That kind of nonsense." I roll my eyes.

"Maybe it isn't nonsense." He caresses my face, but quickly pulls his hand away.

"You don't believe him do you? What father doesn't tell his daughter that?" I move towards the closet, opening the doors and pushing through the dresses. "It's just another way to make me feel better about myself. To make me feel more a part of this world."

I slip on a plain yellow dress and walk back into the room. "He has his reasons LaRue. You are going to be a part of something big, something great very soon."

"Oh really." I sit down in a cushioned chair, crossing my legs and my arms. "All hail Queen Laerune, the warrior of all warriors, shield maiden of Lithien! The conqueror of lands!" I roll my eyes. "More like hail Laerune, the bearer of Luthias' heroic children."

I lean forward. "I know your father's plan. I know what you want as well." I murmur the dreadful word. The word that ends all adventures. "Children."

"You speak of them as if they are goblins."

"Maybe they are." I turn my head towards the window. "I want to show everyone that I am much more than a mother bearing sons. I want to show them that I am able to fight and change the future."

"I've heard rumors of war." Luthias mumbles with that sideways smirk of his.

I stand up from my seat. "War? Against who?" Luthias shrugs his shoulders. "Ah come on. You know who it is."

"I am joking LaRue."

"No you aren't." I laugh. "You wouldn't have told me otherwise. And plus I have heard my fair share of rumors."

"Your sister is here," Luthias changes the subject.

"She is?"

"She wishes to speak with you. The last time I saw her she was in the art hall."

I smile at Luthias as I leave our room. That sneaky lynx. He knows exactly how to knock me out of a subject. And I falled for it, even with that smirk of his.

***

The art hall was a great, long corridor, filled with paintings and tapestries. It has portraits of the royal families all the way up to when Lithien was created.

I enter the hall, the light shining against the art that covered the walls. Stained glass windows reflect the sunlight, letting it shine upon the hall. I look up, the tapestries were clear as if they were made just today, but they have been up for hundreds of years.

I look at the painting of Luthias' mother, her blue eyes full of light and happiness. Her silver hair catching the light of the sun shining upon her painting. My eyes fall onto the amber stone around her neck. It too caught the sunlight.

The one next to her is of her family. Sentier and Luvon stand behind a chair that their mother, Lauralaethee, sits in. Luthias sits on the floor at his mother's feet. They seem happy, their smiles not yet frowned from war and death.

As I continue down the hall there is one of Sentier and his father. They are both sterned face and their eyes look cold hearted. There is no women in the painting, no younger children. The time that Sentier's father ruled was one of the hardest years Elves had ever had since the First Age.

Our kind had almost gone extinct. Thousands died in war, a sickness was spread over our lands and grief struck through thousands. The kingdoms were in destruction and treachery was convicted through the land. Secrets were shared for food and money. Lives were taken for information on war. And love was taken from everyone in the kingdom. It seemed like no light had shined for years. And the war continued until Sentier's ruling changed everything.

He sent more and more troops to enemy lines and took out their camps one by one. But many lives were lost along with

Lauralaethee's. After that they needed to start building up their kingdoms again.

There were three rulers of the Elves during that time. Sentier, Elender, and Faolan. The each mourned their sorrows in different ways, some good and others bad. Faolan chose to put himself closer with nature, immersing himself in the glory of his home. Even though his kingdom is now surrounded by a great wall, the creatures are kept inside and are cared for.

Elender, my father, found comfort in his work. His study was his sanctuary and was always covered in stacks of important papers and documents. He would write and read the damaged and torn papers, placing them in neat piles so they could be stored in safety. During the war many books and papers had been burned or stolen.

Sentier, on the other hand, created the worse habit for himself. He found that the more he drank, the more numb the feelings of loss and pain felt. They were still there, like shadows in the darkness, so he drank more to keep the feelings at bay. His habit has seemed to calm down and he has been drinking less and less as he realizes that his kingdom needs him to be fully functional if anything were to happen.

Families were large many years ago but now they are small. Only one or two children compared to the seven that the other families had years and years ago. I am only one of two. I look to Eryn, who stares up at a painting of a handsome Elf with red hair.

"Do you ever wonder what happens to them after death?" She asks me.

"Well they go to the Void. And if they pass a test of acceptance then they can be brought to Elenda where their souls will never die."

"I know that LaRue. I wanted to know if they still watched us or cared for us."

"I'm sure they do. How couldn't they?"

She pauses and then turns towards me, her red gown matching some of the tapestries. She shows me a kind, simple grin. "Someone told you, didn't they? About the Pathway." I nod my head and she turns back to the wall, admiring the red haired

Elf. "You are in danger LaRue. Once they find your name they will search the whole world for you."

"They already are Eryn. They just don't know exactly who they are looking for at this moment. Sentier brought it up to me briefly. And I saw my price of bounty. I know how high the stakes are."

"You are going to be the biggest target in this world Laerune. Not just because you are the pathway."

"And why is that?"

"You are becoming princess of Lithien. That means that Ambrose and Lithien will have the chance of having an heir. And that hasn't happened in hundreds of years. Luthias is the last of his family, without you, there will be no future for this bloodline. And your titles. You tie the kingdoms together."

I am not just a lady of Ambrose, but of also Lindalin. My mother was born in Lindalin and my sister and I have earned the title of ladies in their kingdom. That means that I tie three kingdoms together. And Luthias would tie Thai to Lithien. But Thai was destroyed years ago. And with having my sister in Everford, that automatically makes us allies.

"I know. I can sense that something is going to happen. The snow is coming and the smell of war drifts with it."

"Stay out of war sister." Eryn warns.

"I will fight alongside my friends. I have trained for it, prepared for it."

"War is no place for a woman. Especially one that can turn the tides of the future as we know it."

I turn towards her shocked. "You fought alongside Bainen when he needed you."

"That was not full out war Laerune. You are to fight if it is your only choice."

"I am not going to let them go off and fight alone. I too want to stop this evil and I will do everything in my power to stop it."

"War?" Tasar walks down the hall, his daggers strapped on his boot. "When, where, and who?"

We stand there silently, turning to face the paintings. "We were just talking about the war during Sentier's father's ruling."

"Oh." He seems disappointed. "That was a depressing time. I was only three when it all began. But you were both much older. You must remember it."

We nod our heads. "We spent a lot of time in Lindalin then. I was only five and my sister nine."

"That was when my parents gave me to a Dwarf. Apparently they couldn't afford me, so they sold me as a slave when I was only three." Tasar explained. "I bought my way out after years and years of working, but they begged me to stay and work for them." He looked up at the painting. "I could've had a life like that. Filled with riches and jewels, fancy clothes. But I was sold and when I left the dark caves of the Dwarves I went to look for my parents. But found nothing but a kingdom burned down to ashes."

The kingdom of Calandra was burned to nothing but dust that had already blown away into the wind. If you went to its remains, there is nothing to be seen. Many travelers pass by it without even knowing that they are stepping on the ruins of Calandra. That they are walking along the ashes of Elves burned in the raging fires of Tion the Fire Drake. Tasar was the last of the Calandrians.

"It's just me. Only me."

"You have us Tasar. We're your family now and forever."

He smiles, his brown eyes becoming brighter. "You are all too kind. You have been too kind to me." His face turns smug. "What happened to the sassy Laerune that everyone knows?"

"She comes and goes." I smirk.

"Sentier sent me to tell you that the maids were bringing in boxes to your room from home. Apparently your father had packed your things for you and brought them here." Eryn dismisses herself and I watch as she leaves the art hall alone.

Tasar turns towards me. "Huh. Only a few more days and you won't have to worry about that damn courting process anymore. That must be a relief."

"Only two more days? Sentier made it so early."

"There is many things that he wants to get done Laerune."

"An heir," I scoff.

"He will be patient with that. I think he just wants what is best for his son. He wants him to have a future before it's too late. And Sentier himself wants a family. It has been years since his has been complete."

"Does this mean that tomorrow I am to be kept separate from Luthias?"

Tasar nods his head. "You will be kept hidden until the Danen." He then whispers. "I'll keep an eye out for Luthias, we don't want him getting into any trouble before the Danen, do we?" He winks, his brown eyes filled with laughter.

The sun's rays suddenly disappear from the hall. And clouds take in the light, sending snow to the ground.

"It looks like a storm is coming."

"Hopefully it won't last long."

Tasar walks me down to the dining room, the evening activities starting early for the sun has been covered. That's how the Elves worked. They worked with the sun and if not the sun than the stars and its moon. Winter and autumn was the season of the sun and spring and summer was the season of the moon and stars. It seemed like we hardly slept in the warm months for we were up all day and night.

Elves began to pour into the room, taking their seats and waiting for Sentier, their King, to be seated. He was usually the last to sit during the evening meals. I take my seat left of the King and Luthias enters, taking the right.

My father and sister sit close by and I look behind me at the blazing fireplace. Oka lays calmly near the warmth of the fire. Her nose moves slightly to sniff the air around her. I can imagine her dreaming about biscuits and and the fried potatoes that sit upon Sentier's plate.

The doors open across the room and Sentier finally takes his seat. I look around the room, the ceiling carved with tiny flowers and ivy. The room was dark and lit with candles that are placed against the dark wooden walls. The curtains are closed on the windows, allowing no light to shine in.

My father's eyes look calm and kind as he spoke with Eryn. She laughs as she tells him about how Everford has been fairing. His eyes say that he is proud of what she has done. He has never looked at me that way. He has never had anything to be proud of from me.

You could call me the troublemaker of the family. The one that knew from right or wrong but still managed to do the worst. Avon didn't help with that. He asked me to do things and I listened. He was my friend and I did what he asked of me. But I was always the one to get punished. I was the one that was sat down and taught a lesson.

A lot of the things I didn't think were wrong. I wasn't allowed to do a lot of things. I wasn't allowed to go outside by myself, I wasn't allowed to step out of the borders, and an escort followed me around constantly. And I always had a lot more studies than what my sister had.

"Laerune? How have you been?" Someone asks me, but I don't remember who they are. They place a delicate hand on my shoulder. The male looks down at me, his eyes sad and sunken.

"I'm sorry. I don't know who you are." I turn around in my chair to face him.

"I am Thatcher. I live in Ambrose."

"Oh yes. I am sorry. I remember now."

Thatcher is a blacksmith, his work worthy of the greatest knight. "You're father has asked me to come along with him so I could help you here."

"And what help has he suggested?"

"Well, I've been looking for work and I know that you have done some drawings for weapons. I wanted to help make them for you."

"Oh yes. Of course."

He bows his head and then slowly walks away.

"That poor Elf." Sentier speaks. "He's going crazy.'"

"Why is that?"

"He watched his whole family die. He was forced to kill his sister and eat her or his daughter's life would be taken." Sentier leans back to speak with another person that stands behind him.

I listen to their conversation. "Congratulations on your son's upcoming marriage to the Lady Laerune. She will make a good match for your son. Very beautiful too."

"Her sword arm is a pretty equal match for her beauty."

"Oh is it?"

"The great Dehlin taught her himself."

"She must be very honored."

I smile, searching down the table for more familiar faces. I still listen to Sentier speak to the Lord beside him. "I have yet to spare against her, but I am sure she can out beat me."

"Your Majesty, I would highly doubt that. You are skilled beyond years and she is only a young female. One who has not yet experienced the sorrows of the world."

"I would not downgrade her for being a woman. The only Elf who ever challenged me in a duel was my wife."

The Elf leaves to take his seat at the table and Sentier leans over towards me. His blonde, reddish hair shines in the firelight. "Ignore them. They do not know the strength of women." He laughs, his ocean eyes glistening. His smile draws back to a tight frown.

"Is tomorrow hard?" I ask him. "Being apart for a whole day?"

"It's not hard. But quite boring." I roll my eyes at him. "You sadly can't even go outside, let alone look out your window."

"What will Luthias do tomorrow?"

"He will do things involving tradition. The son usually spends the day with his mother, but we have different circumstances. I will take up what his mother was supposed to do." Sentier again whispers. "But what the women do not know is that he has a party."

"That's extremely unfair." I lift my fork to my mouth. Oka's nose twitches more.

"It really is. I would change it if it wasn't a tradition over a thousand years old."

He begins eating his meal, stopping every once and awhile to speak with someone who bowed before him. I look to Luthias who speaks to Tasar. Tasar's hand goes under the table as he tosses a biscuit in Oka's direction. She quickly gobbles it down without even opening her eyes.

"Lady Laerune?" Etta pulls me out of my trance of boredom. "It is time to be dismissed to your room."

I rise from my seat, bowing to Sentier and Luthias before leaving the dining room. Luthias pulls on my arm. “Don’t worry about tomorrow. I won’t get in any trouble.” That sideways smirk appears again.

“Should I trust that? A lot of people have been reminding me not to worry. That usually means that I should be worrying.”

Oka stretches and quickly trots to my side. Tasar gives her another biscuit in the process. Etta politely pulls on my arm. “It’s time to go.” She sings.

Etta would be staying in a room connected to mine so it is impossible for me to break any rules and traditions. Oka follows at my heels. She will be my only company for the day tomorrow.

Chapter 12

Etta opens the door for me as I enter my room. "Your clothes can be found in the drawers and everything you need for bathing is in the bathroom. If you need anything I will be the next door down."

She bows and then closes the door behind me. Oka jumps up onto the bed, spinning in circles until she finds the most comfortable spot. "You silly dog." I pat her head. Candles are lit around the room and I stoke the fireplace to add more light and warmth to the room.

I fill up the bathtub with water that had been heating up over the fire. I slip my dress over my head and I sit down into the bath. Oka comes running in just to lay at the bathtubs edge. She places her head on the metal edge, licking my nose. She then runs off, but quickly returns with a leather pouch in her mouth.

I take it from her, opening it up and handing her a biscuit. "I've missed you." I look into her shiny blue eyes. Oka looks at me like I am the only thing in her world. I laugh as she turns her head to the right and then the left.

She then lays down on the tiled floor, resting her head upon her paws. I rinse my hair with water, letting the soap soak in. It took a lot of time to wash my hair, for its tresses reached my knees.

I step out of the bathtub, reaching for my towel. Oka immediately gets up to her feet, stretching out her back. She follows me to my dresser as I continue to get ready for bed. I slip on my nightclothes and then move over to my vanity. Oka then decides to lay back onto the bed, finding her perfect spot once again.

I brush my golden hair, braiding it once I get all the tangles out. I run my hand over the vanity, the silver wood polished and clean. I rise, moving quietly over to the bed. I lift the blankets, trying my best not to disturb Oka, who is already sound asleep.

I run my hand over Oka's fur coat, the familiarness comforting and warm. She places her nose on my hand and then moves closer to me. I would do anything to make her live forever. Her years are days compared to mine. Seconds to my hours.

In only a couple of days, I will be the biggest target in all of Laquilasse. Everyone will be watching me, waiting for me to do something wrong. A crown will begin my new life, one I have no clue of what will happen. My mind wanders as I slowly drift off into dreams.

***

I wake up early, Oka's nose in my face, as if saying that I waited for you, aren't you glad? She jumps off the bed and then back on. And as if Etta knew when I was to get up she knocks on the door, coming in with a tray in her hands.

"Good morning." She sings. Etta looks young, but her personality was old. Old and caring. Like how the men would describe their elders but without the looks. Her dark hair is held up and out of her face with a jeweled, pointed stick. She sets the tray upon the table and pulls up the sheets and blankets around me. "Up, up," She commands, making motions with her hands.

I sit up, gliding over to the table. She pours tea into a blue glass cup and she then begins to place food onto my plate. "You better eat up. You have a big day tomorrow."

"That's tomorrow Etta. I can eat then and now."

"Oh no you can't. It's another tradition. You don't eat until the actual Danen happens."

"These traditions are outrageous."

"I know. I know," She grins. "But they must be followed."

I nod my head, beginning to eat the food that has been placed in front of me. I feed little bits to Oka who rests her head on my thigh. She whines whenever she sees a piece of food that she likes in my hand.

"Am I just supposed to stay here all day?"

"Yes. But I'll bring you anything that you want to do." She too sits down to eat. "You can paint, draw, and play music, read. Anything you desire."

"I'm sure that you won't be able to fit a pianoforte in here. Let alone find one."

"I am sorry Laerune. The only one left was in Ambrose, but your father got rid of it."

"I still haven't forgiven him for that."

She sips her tea. "It's in the past."

"Yes, the past." I turn to look out the window, but there are none. "What is it like outside right now?"

"The snow has fallen. A lot of it actually."

I nod my head. I suddenly feel trapped. The thought of staying in here all day without even being allowed to look outside hurts. Oka again begs for the food on my plate. She whines, her tail wagging back and forth.

"Will you take her outside? She looks like she's just begging to go out and play in the snow."

"Oka," She calls, opening the door. Oka follows but stops in the doorway, waiting for me to follow her.

"Not today Oka." I wave my hand, signaling for her to go with Etta. She listens, running out the door with Etta in tow.

I lean my elbows onto the table, resting my face in my hands. I am already wanting this day to be over. I can imagine all the fun Luthias is having and then I am stuck here. Stuck in this miserable room, nothing but the light of candles to keep me company. The day has only begun.

I pace back and forth, trying to decide what I want to do with my time alone. There is no character to the room, nothing interesting but a shelf of books that I have already read before. I lay down onto the bed, staring at the ceiling above me. It's plain and boring.

My eyes then are drawn to the paint that Etta had brought. I sit up, reaching for it and the paint brushes. I dip the brush in, painting the stars and moon onto the ceiling. I can barely reach from the bed. And I find myself standing upon the table to reach the rest of the room. I move over to the walls, painting them with a sun and blue sky. And near the bottom of the walls my hand paints grass and trees. I make the room come to life, adding an artificial light to it.

Etta walks in, Oka covered in melted snow. "I am sorry that I've been gone for-" She seems stunned for a moment as she sees me standing on the table covered in paint as I try to reach the last spots. "You painted...everything."

"Just the walls and ceiling."

She begins to smile, her face becoming warm. "I like it."

"I hope it wasn't the wrong thing to do." I did have some skill with art, but I wasn't sure if it was right to paint over every wall.

"No, I am sure that Sentier will just love it. He loves everything you do." Etta smirks. "But you are covered in a mess." She tries to wipe the paint off of my face.

She was and always has been the motherly figure in my life. She loved me and taught me many things. And always, *always,* treated me like her child. She loved me unconditionally.

She runs water over a washcloth. "You are always getting in a mess. How are you going to take care of yourself?"

"Etta," I whine. "I can take care of myself perfectly fine." I push her hand away.

She stands back for a moment. "You have grown up so much."

"No tears Etta. No tears," I raise my voice.

She fans her face. "No tears." She paces the room, Oka looking oddly at her. "Okay, go wash up, I can't stand to see you in a mess."

I do as Etta says and I watch as she prepares the bath. She pulls a vial from her dress pocket and places a few drops into the bath. "Just in case." She winks. "We wouldn't want you getting sick during your Danen."

I clip up my hair and Etta leaves the bathroom. I lay down into the tub, the water warm, washing away the paint on my hands. I hear Etta across the room playing a music box, the tune calming. She begins to sing, her voice echoing through the dark room. I close my eyes, sending my mind into a dream.

I'm walking through a large gate, guarded by many. Crowds of people stand, moving out of my way as I walk by. They stare at me, their faces scared and frightened. Their eyes searching mine as if pleading for help. A small child pushes through the crowd, stopping by me, just to watch me pass by.

I look in front of me, rushing to the front of the crowd. Gallows stand tall in the courtyard and six people stand tall with blindfolds on over their heads. I unsheathe my sword as they begin to take their blindfolds off. They shove the people forward to the ropes. Dehlin stands tall while the dark haired Elf next to him reaches for a female. Chalsarda struggles against her restraints and Tasar laughs hysterically like he has gone crazy. Then there is poor Etta who shakes uncontrollably.

I catch the eyes of Dehlin as he stares up at the steps to the unknown kingdom. A throne is set outside and a male Elf sits in it. “My, my. The Queen has finally arrived. I’ve been waiting quite some time.” He jumps down the steps, waving his hand to signal the men to pull the lever of the gallows.

I throw my sword at the rope around Dehlin’s neck and he cuts his bonds, doing the same to the two Elves next to him. Luthias shoots his bow over my head, aiming at the ropes that are around Chalsarda’s and Tasar’s necks. I reach for my dagger to cut down Etta but it’s too late. I scream as her eyes gloss over, her neck broken in an odd angle.

I wake up, searching the room. I focus on my surroundings, the water cold and Etta still singing and playing her music box. I grab my towel, leaving the bathing room.

I pull the first thing I see out of the dresser and I slip it on. I tie my pants and slip the shirt over my head. “Etta?” I search for her around the room, finding her sitting on the couch. “How much longer till nightfall?”

“Maybe two hours.”

“Could you deliver something for me?”

“Of course.”

I find paper and a quill, scratching a note in gibberish that only I and one other can read. “Give this to Eryn,” I tell Etta. “She’ll understand.”

Etta bows and then leaves the room. Oka looks at me, knowing that I scheming something. “Don’t give me that look.” She seems to shake her head and then continues to rest, setting her head back down on her paws.

Etta doesn’t return and I believe that my father had given her something to do, or my plan worked with Eryn. I pace back and forth for what seems like hours, which was most likely right. For my mind told me that it was time for sleep, but I forced myself to stay awake.

I turn around quickly when I see a piece of paper slip under the door. I quickly go to it, picking it up from the cold floor. *I am here.*

I lean up against the door. “I miss you.” Luthias voice is soft from across the door.

“I miss you so much. I didn’t think that you would be able to come here.”

“I worked some things out with Tasar and your sister.” I think he smiles. “Tomorrow we will be together.”

“We will,” I whisper. Oka raises her head and I look at her and then back at the door. “How’s the party?”

“Quite boring. I’m surprised you can’t hear it from down here.” He chuckles.

“Are there any pretty young females there?” I smile, but then frown.

“Absolutely not. Your beauty outshines them all.” He laughs but then sighs. “Sing for me LaRue.”

Before the sun came up,
Before the birds came to sing,
A young girl proposed to her love.
Will you be betrothed to me?
I offer you gifts of my love,
You can answer yes or no
If you wish to or not.
I will surely give you my gift of love
If your answer is yes.

“My answer would always be yes. You wouldn’t even have to offer me gifts Laerune.” I can imagine him smirking. “I miss you.” He whispers.

“I wish I could see you.”

“Soon Laerune. Soon.” I smile at his words. “At least we aren’t thousands of miles apart. There is only a wooden door between us.” He is silent. “Someone is coming.” I hear him stand up. “I love you Laerune.”

“I love you.”

He disappears and I move to cuddle with Oka. Eryn walks in and I see a glimpse of Luthias' cloak as he disappears down the hall. She sits down onto the bed, petting Oka's head.

"I am sorry," She confesses. "I would've given you more time, but Sentier was looking for him."

I grin at her, staring at her cornflower eyes. "Thank you Eryn."

"How are you feeling?" He places a hand on my forehead, brushing away a piece of my hair from my face.

"I am tired."

"You haven't been sleeping have you?"

I shake my head. "Those nightmares, or whatever they are, have been becoming more and more common."

"They're just dreams." Eryn was like my mother. When Etta could not tend to me, it was my sister who was always there. Yes, we have our fights and arguments, but she has always been here for me. "You must rest. I don't want you being tired all day tomorrow."

She blows out the candles. "I'll see you tomorrow morning." She leaves and I quickly find myself falling back into dreams with Oka snuggled close to me.

Chapter 13

I wake up to Eryn in my face, telling me to wake up. I sit up and she holds my hand as I follow her out of the room and into the lighted hall. The sun is low in the sky, hidden by trees as it begins to rise.

The windows are open to the room I am led to and a cool breeze brushes through the curtains. "Wake up LaRue. Look more alive."

"I'm getting there." I growl.

Two maids wait in the room, standing where my dress is hung against the window. It billows in the breeze. I look out over the balcony, snow covers the courtyard and the trees. The river is iced over.

Eryn sets me down into the chair, brushing my hair. Etta rushes in and begins to get my dress ready. "Your Danen is early for there is much to do today." Etta places jewels in my hair, braiding pieces of my tresses.

I am brought to my feet and Etta quickly slips the dress over my head and then pushes me forward into a pair of shoes. I walk over to the mirror and Eryn fixes a stray piece of hair. She holds my shoulders as she too looks at me through the mirror.

"You look stunning."

"I can't believe I am doing this again." I smirk.

"But this time it's right."

"It is."

She stands in front of me. "Sentier is awaiting you outside." Eryn continues to tell where to meet Sentier.

I step out into the woods, snow had fallen at great amounts last night and frost covered the trees and shrubs. Beyond the trees a faint pink sun rose, summoning the beginning of a new day.

Sentier enters the wood, his silver cloak dragging across the newly fallen snow. "Are you not cold?" He asks, placing his hooded cloak over my shoulders. "A Danen dress isn't the warmest." He chuckles, pulling the hood over my head.

"You will soon be a part of this family." Sentier states the fact proudly. "I must say that I have waited for this for a very long time. A royal woman in this kingdom should do us all good.

I see many changes in our future," He turns towards the rising sun. "Ones that we all will have to make together. Remember that loyalty is needed in a kingdom. If you need anything you must speak up."

I stand taller as he continues to speak. "I value your opinion although there are some within this kingdom that will not. Don't lose your temper over those people. Simply prove them wrong."

He takes my hand, leading me to the tall Oak tree. "Put your back against the tree and reach your hand around." He smiles and my hand is quickly grabbed by Luthias' familiar grip.

"Luthias," I breathe, then laugh.

"I know you look gorgeous." He chuckles, gripping my hand tighter. "I must go." He let's go of my hand and then disappears. Sentier takes my hand. "We should get you back." He tries to rub warmth into my hands.

Sentier walks me towards the courtyard. The doors to the celebration room guarded by two captains. I look up at the trees and icicles hang from their branches. The crisp air fills my lungs and I smile at two young boys who throw snowballs at each other. They quickly return to the middle of the courtyard, following two girls who drop flowers as they walk.

And the soft sounds of harps began and the guards allow me to walk down the frosted path. I pay no attention to the smiling faces around me, I can only hear the sound of my heart pounding in my chest.

I only see Luthais as he stands with his hands at his side and a smile upon his face. The sight of him in his silver robes made me blush. His hair is down, which is an unusual style for him.

Sentier had talked me through what was going to happen and what I am was going to say a couple of days ago. It was just Luthias and I speaking to each other without any help from the others.

I hold the Brielle ribbons in my hands as I walk towards the great tree in the front of the room. The colored glass allows the light to shine brightly and the red leaves from the tree fall gracefully to the ground around Luthias.

I smile brightly as I near him and he takes the Brielle ribbons from my hands, binding ours together. I look around me, meeting the eyes of my father and then Sentier. They both nod their heads, telling me to go on.

Luthias breathes in as he thinks of the right words to say. “It is as if I was lost. The only time I was found was when I was with you. I’ve been a wanderer, going only where I was told and needed. It is now that I feel like I can’t wander, I have a purpose, and that purpose is to devote my life to you. When I make a promise that promise is held true and so, Laerune Aduial, I promise to love you with every second of this immortal life. I promise to always be there when you need me. I promise to protect you with my life, to keep you safe, no longer do I want you to fear. I do not know the reason why you have chosen me to share all your years with, but I will thank the stars every day, that you have.”

I hang onto every sweet and calming word that comes from Luthias’ mouth. I grin widely and Luthias’ grip on my hands become tighter. His sideways smirk shines.

“Through all my years, every day I have wondered and questioned my destiny. I have always feared I would not do anything that would amount to great importance or that I would have to go through something terrible alone. I have learned my destiny and I know what I am meant for. My destiny is to be with you. That is something of the greatest importance. I am meant for you Luthias Faen and I couldn't be happier. Through everything I have endured, you were always there. Always. My only wish is to always be there for you, the way you are for me. Words cannot describe the love I have for you Luthias Faen.”

Luthias places his hand onto the back of my neck and quickly pulls me in for our first kiss. I have no words, for Luthias has taken them away. I have nothing to describe the feeling. And I don’t think I ever will have the words to describe it.

We have known each other for many years and we have known our love since then. And now, finally we can show it. He takes my hand as we step down the stairs of the hall. Flowers are thrown around us by women in the crowd and I smile brightly. I am now the princess of Lithien. *The biggest target in the world.*

A Danen has not happened in a very long time in Lithien so the people are very grateful for this celebration. They are all practically dancing to where the rest of the celebration will be held.

The hall where the festivities will begin is very different. It's like a whole different world placed inside. An indoor forest is the best way to explain it. Trees still grow to great heights and grass is soft under your feet. It was an odd sensation being in a season of summer when outside it was winter.

But we all kick off our shoes, feeling the soft grass under our feet as music begins to play. The guests move to the edges of the forest, allowing Luthias and I room to dance for the Brielle. Our hands are once again tied with different ribbons, ones longer and stronger.

The music slows to a stop as Luthias and I prepare for the Brielle. My heart pounds with nervousness and I pray to the Gods and Goddesses that our Danen will be blessed and our ribbons will not break or leave our hands.

Sentier warned me that the music was going to be fast pace, but I never thought it would be like this. I count my steps, following Luthias and still managing a smile. He begins to laugh and I keep a tight grip on the ribbons. Only one more set of counts and the dance will be over.

I am pulled close to Luthias and we both smile as we try and catch our breath. "That wasn't so bad, was it?" He grins.

"You had a lot more practice than me."

"But you did so much better than I did." Luthias whispers as we become surrounded by other dancers, their gowns flowing by.

Sentier pauses the dancing before everyone gets too wild. He holds a goat under his arms and it attempts to wiggle free. "Is that for us?" I ask Luthias.

Before Luthias can open his mouth, Sentier places the goat onto a platform and then brings an axe upon the small creature. I jump as the axe digs itself into the platform.

The blood from the goat streams down into a bowl and Sentier calls us forward. "Our sacrifice has been made to the Electa! Ashendel and Catoneras have come together to witness this great day! Let us drink in their honor."

I am hesitant as Sentier hands me the bowl. I hold it away from my dress in fear that the blood will stain the beautiful, white fabric.

"Go on, sweet Laerune."

I see my father and sister grimace out of the corner of my eye. Eryn holds her stomach. I bring the bowl to my lips. The warm, iron taste meets my tongue and I quickly pass the bowl to Luthias.

Luthias wipes his mouth after the large drink he has consumed from the bowl. "That wasn't only for a blessed marriage," Luthias chuckles. "It's to make sure our child will have red hair."

"You really believe that?" I reach for a glass of water to wash down the metal taste.

"There hasn't been a single child in my bloodline that doesn't have red hair."

Luthias takes my hand to lead me to the next part of the Danen. Even though we gave our original vows with the Brielle ribbons, there is still the Melde. The Melde ribbons are a part of my father's ancestry.

"Please join hands," My father approaches us. "As your hands are joined, so your lives, holding each other, caressing each other, supporting each other, loving each other." My father ties the ribbon around our hands.

"I, Luthias Faen, promise you, Laerune Aduial, that I will be your husband, from this day forward. To love and respect you. To support and hold you. To make you laugh and to be there when you cry. To softly kiss you when you are hurting and to be your companion and your friend. On this journey that we will now make together."

I repeat the same words as Luthias.

"Luthias and Laerune are now bound to each other." My father announces with a grin upon his face. He then has Luthias take the sword from his sheath. "Luthias will you give your honor and loyalty to Laerune."

"I will." Luthias places the sword in my hand.

"And will you, Laerune, Give your honor and loyalty to Luthias?"

I return the sword to his hands. "I will."

Sentier links his arm with mine. "Come with me Laerune, the bride-race will begin soon."

The bride-race was another tradition from my home kingdom. The husband, the brothers of the husband, and the wife's brothers race each other to see who will carry the bride to the dining table. It is a great honor to be the one to carry the new wife. It showed that the wife was not alone and that both families are there to carry her through life.

I don't have any brothers and Luthias' brother, Luvon, has passed so our closest male relations and friends will be chosen to attempt the bride-race.

Dehlin rolls up his sleeves along with Bainen. They would be representing my brothers. I would've chosen Avon as well, but he has yet to arrive.

Tasar and one of Luthias' second cousin's steps up to represent Lithien. Luthias joins them.

Sentier continuous to lead me away from the room and most of the guests follow in step.

I shiver as Sentier opens the door into the woods near the kingdom. He places his cloak around my shoulders and attempts to rub warmth into my hands. "Who do you think will arrive first?"

"I do believe it will be very close between Dehlin and Luthias."

"Of course Dehlin will want to be the first to carry you. But I think Tasar will get pretty far if it is carrying you to the dining table. He has been starving all day." The King chuckles. A horn echoes through the area. "Your father has added a twist though."

I raise my eyebrow in curiosity. "And that is?"

"Fighting is encouraged, but all the males will be blindfolded."

"My father came up with that?" My father usually opted out for fighting and competitions.

"We have a bet." Sentier chuckles. "He doesn't think that Luthias can beat Dehlin."

The crowd begins to cheer. I stand on my tiptoes to see the first of the males enter the straight path of the forest. Luthias attempts to shove Dehlin to the side, but the Golden Lord keeps his ground. My husband shoves his competitor once again, sending Dehlin to the ground. Tasar and Luthias' cousin turn the corner.

Dehlin grabs a hold of Luthias' arm so he is unable to continue running. Bainen pulls on Tasar's hair, sending both of them backwards. They topple over each other.

Luthias rises to his feet followed closely by Danen. They continue to shove each other as they reach their hands out for me. Sentier holds my shoulders to keep me upright. Luthias and Dehlin both reach me at the same time.

The lift up their blindfolds as sweat drips down their foreheads. Luthias bows to Dehlin. "I am giving you the honor of carrying Laerune to the dining table."

Dehlin chuckles. "Good, because you get to carry her into the bedroom."

I stifle a giggle as I turn my head behind me. I turn around quickly, noticing red against white out of the corner of my eye.

The pathway is here is written in the snow with blood. The dead guard lies close by to the message. A woman screams in the crowd.

We all pause. Luthias swears.

Luthias pulls me away from the blood covered snow. I feel the contentsof my stomach churn. I reach my hand up to my mouth. I lean myself closer to Luthias side and he quickly places a protective hand around my waist.

Luthias unsheathes the sword at his side, but his father raises his hand in protest. "This is not our problem at the moment. The guards have everything under control."

Dehlin reaches under my legs and my back, lifting me up into his arms. Luthias and Dehlin both give me a reassuring smile. I look over Dehlin's shoulder at the dead guard and the blood covered snow. *I am the biggest target in the world.*

I wrap my arms tighter around Dehlin's neck while burying my head in his shoulder. I keep my eyes on Luthias instead of the dead Elf behind me.

Luthias keeps his eyes on the ground but he quickly glances up at me. His sideways smirk brightens up his face. I reach out for his hand. I run a finger over the ring.

"You are my husband." I smirk, my voice filled with joyfulness, but it still breaks from fear. I shiver at the fact that whoever is hunting me will figure out who I am eventually.

"And you are my wife."

Tasar fixes his hair as he runs up to Luthias. "Don't worry LaRue, we will keep you safe."

It wasn't the fact that I was worried about others not protecting me. It was the idea on not being able to protect myself. I had no access to weapons if someone did decided to raid my Danen. I would have to entrust my new family in protecting me.

The crowd begins to clap as Dehlin carries me to the dining table. He kisses my cheek as he sets me back down onto my feet. "You will always have your brothers no matter what." He reaches his hand towards Bainen, Tasar, and Luthias' cousin.

Luthias takes his seat next to mine. I look to Luthias and I smile. "I am so happy to finally be with you."

He leans in to kiss me. "As am I Laerune. As am I."

Gifts were to be given to us by the guests. When I was to be married to Avon I was given many gifts that are still yet to be opened. The neatly wrapped presents still sit in my closet back in Ambrose, waiting to be open. Yes, I am curious at what is in them, but I feel bad if I open them because the marriage was never finished.

My father and Sentier move to the front of the table, offering us a gift from both of them. Luthias allows me to open the box, revealing a simple ribbon that seemed like it was wrapped in the essence of silver and stars. Its only use would be to adorn a dress, nothing else.

"It goes by the name Gleipnir." My father tell us.

"Let it be your hope if all else fails." Sentier concludes adding to the mystery.

Luthias and I bow our heads, thanking them for the gift. I look around the room, Elves watch us, waiting for their turn to greet us with congratulations. My sister bows before us with a smirk across her red lips.

Without a word she places her gift onto our table, leaving without a trace. There is a little note tied with a ribbon. *Open in a few years.* I look to Luthias and he shrugs his shoulders. I move it to the side of the table and continue to speak to the rest of the guests who come to visit with us.

I stare at the box, my curiosity rising. Luthias laughs. "Just be patient LaRue. You will find out soon." He takes my hand and then sits back in his chair. "Patience my sweet Laerune." He leans in to kiss me again. "Patience." He closes his eyes.

He turns to a young female with onyx hair. "Congratulations." She giggles, bowing before us and meeting the eyes of Luthias.

"Thank you," I tell her and she dances off.

"The first signs of jealousy," A soft voice speaks to me in my head. I look around for the sweet familiar face.

"Will you not show yourself Grandmother?"

"Not yet. Maybe soon. Now is just not the time."

"More secrets?"

"Congratulations on your new title and marriage."

The voice disappears and I smile. My grandmother was very powerful and had reigned over land in the East. Her power was more than just governing her land and people, she was one gifted with magical abilities unlike our own.

I keep a watchful eye on the guest at the party. My eyes scan for any unwelcome visitors. I cross my legs and Luthias stares at me. "What?" I ask him.

"Oh, nothing." He continues to smile.

"Well, you surely know something." I clear my throat. "More secrets?"

He nods his head. "You know someone is here for you. I see it in your eyes."

I search around the room. "Him. His eyes keep on darting around the room. The stitching of his Lithien uniform is off, stating that he tried to replicate it himself." Luthias follows the direction of my eyes, stopping at the young Elf with brownish hair and grey eyes. "He's too short to be a part of Lithien, so why would he be wearing a guard's uniform?"

He walks around a large group of people, his eyes darting to us and then to another female walking towards us. She bows and gives her congratulations, moving swiftly away in shyness.

"Watch him," I tell Luthias. "He is coming nearer."

"He's not a part of any of the Elven kingdoms. Look at his eyes."

His eyes are coal black, not a single line of white in them. "He is not one of us."

The male reaches our table, bowing. He lunges forward across the table but I hold a dinner knife to his throat. He swears loudly, causing the guests to stare at us.

"Who are you? Who is your master?"

"That is none of your business female," He spits, his voice almost like a hiss.

"It surely is my business if you want to live." I push the blade closer to his throat.

He struggles for a moment, but then he becomes more relaxed. "Across the fields of Gia. I am one of many."

"Enough with riddles."

"I am only just a shadow. Apart of the night."

Luthias has a sword in his hand, aimed at the male. "A Night Elf of Naden." Luthias sheaths his sword back to his side, allowing the guards to take the Night Elf away.

Night Elves were not common. They hardly ever left their forest since they were scared of the light. But if they truly wanted something, truly needed something, they would venture into the light to find it. If they were here for the pathway then he was either out for the glory or the money that my head would surely bring. Or just my ears as Nolan said would come for a lofty price if he were to sell them.

"We know she's here!" The Night Elf hisses as he is dragged away.

I run my hand over my pointed ear. I would much rather keep my ears and head intact than for them to be sold off. People are starting to know who and where I am. Nolan knows. But I don't think he would tell people the information he has. Why would he want someone else to find me and earn the money themselves? So, I have faith that only Nolan knows and he will keep the secret until my death.

"Is Avon arriving tonight?" Luthias questions. I think he can see my eyes searching for our missing guest.

"My father said he was going to be late."

My husband fills my glass with water. "How about we plan on traveling to the lake with Avon and Tasar tomorrow afternoon? We can bring skates if you would like?"

I nod my head as I sip from my glass. The guests dance across the grass covered floor. I envy them as Luthias and I are still stuck accepting congratulations from long distant family members and young, giggly girls waiting to catch a glimpse of the prince.

"When did you know Laerune was the one?" A young girl with golden braids questions. She holds the skirt of her dress and swings from side to side.

"When she approached my father with such confidence. LaRue announced her titles with such pride that my father spoke to her as if she was a Queen, not a young Lady still learning her studies."

The girl straightened her spine as if she was trying to stand taller. "And you Princess Laerune?"

"It was when I kicked his ass in a sparring contest." My comment causes the whole table to erupt in laughter.

The girl blushes and prances away to join the other's in dancing. The last of the congratulations dissipated and I tap my foot in eagerness. The music beats in my heart and I watch as Tasar picks up a violin. He dances around a female dressed in a blue gown.

My father rises, placing his hand under Eryn's as they join the rest of the guests. A little girl who is barley four feet tall smiles up at Sentier.

The King politely takes the little girl's hand, leading her towards the dancing and the music.

I cock my head at Luthias. My eyes plead for him to let us join everyone else. He quickly takes my hand and pulls me from my seat. Luthias spins me around, his hands reaching for my waist.

The world spins around me, but Luthias stays centered in my sight. I grin as my adrenaline rushes. *Oh, how perfect this moment is.*

My hair is let loose and my heart wild. I have never felt so free or so in charge.

But the feeling soon ends as I accidentally bump into a male. I ignore his scowl as Luthias pulls me closer. But the man grabs my arm and leans closer to my face. "A woman like you shouldn't be here."

I pull away from his grip, ignoring his words as I join Luthias. My father takes my hand instead.

"May I have this dance?" His eyes light up as I accept his invitation.

It has been years since I have danced with my father. I used to stand on his feet and he would occasionally lift me to his shoulders so I could see the whole room. But now, we are face to face, close to even height, and age hiding behind our open eyes.

"I am proud of you." My father's face is contorted in seriousness.

I lower my head away from his sight. "You've never said that to me."

"I should've said it long ago. But your future was split into so many different paths and I was worried the one you selected wouldn't end well." He chuckles. "But it seems that you have chosen the path that would make your life the most adventurous."

"Who should I look out for, father?" I know he knows their identities and who I should avoid.

"Just avoid Nadien at all costs. The ruins of that kingdom will only give you death." He spins me around. "And I don't think Makya would be an enjoyable stay."

"Is that from your own opinion or did you actually see what will happen."

"I simply see war and the kingdoms that will fight against us."

"I have seen the casualties." I shiver runs down my spine. My father raises an eyebrow. "Most of them are people I have not met before. I kill them in my nightmares, but I don't feel like I am the one doing it. A stronger power is forcing me."

"That's how the people with gifts like ours see the future. They see it through their own eyes. You are not the one to kill them Laerune, someone else, someone more powerful is causing this chaos. Or it could be the Electa guiding you."

"Do you believe in the Electa?" My father is an educated man and I expect him to know better than to believe in silly Gods.

"I have met some of them. And so have you. I would show more support to the Electa if I were you Laerune. Follow the Lithien traditions and you will see how they will favor you."

The music stops abruptly and Tasar pulls at a broken string on his violin. He plucks at it as if he could magically put it back together.

"The sun is setting," a woman calls from the doorway. "It is time to make a sacrifice to Elbonare."

I look to my father with a nervous glance. "It's not going to be a small goat this time is it?"

My father shakes his head with a saddened look. "Elbonare seeks the biggest offering. He will be the one to truly bless your marriage."

Luthias and Sentier lead me back into the forest. An altar of the Electa stands solid amongst the oak trees. Even Luthias looks a bit nervous.

I am handed a match stick to light the candles around the altar. Three women dressed in cream colors step up onto the altar. A knife is set into my hands. I hesitate.

"This is something you must do." Sentier tells me, even my father pushes me forward.

The first woman gladly steps forward and grabs my hand. My wrist shakes as she takes the blade to her throat. "May the Electa grant you a strong voice." She slumps forward on the steps. My eyes wander to the blood flowing from her body.

The second woman places the blade on her stomach. "May the Electa grant you fertility."

The third whispers. "May the Electa grant you power," as she stabs herself through the heart.

I step back, their blood seeps around my shoes. Luthias pulls me into his arms quickly.

"We should retire for the night." Luthias suggests.

"I agree." My stomach still turns as I attempt to not look at the women upon the altar.

Oka sprints behind us and rubs against the side of Luthias. He pets her head as we continue back inside.

***

Luthias opens the door and Oka jumps onto the bed, her tail wagging. She then rushes over to her food dish.

Luthias grins and he places his hands around my waist, spinning me around. “We won’t have to say goodbye anymore. We are one now. We are the prince and princess of Lithien. How perfect does that sound?” He asks.

“I killed them.” I shake uncontrollably.

“You didn’t kill them. They offered themselves to the Electa. It was their choice.”

Oka barks and then scratches at the balcony doors. The sun sets, turning the snow an orange color. “I need air.” Luthias confesses.

“Can I come with?” He points at my dress. “I can always change.” I stare at him.

I glide over to the closet, trying to reach the many buttons on the back of my dress. I growl in frustration as I push those women out of my mind. “Do you need any help?” Luthias asks. I nod my head as he walks in. His hands are cold, sending shivers down my back as he unbuttons my dress.

He runs his fingers over my spine and then backs away. He bows his head and then leaves the closet. I push through the clothes, finding the warmest pants and shirt.

When I walk in, Luthias is in the midst of taking off his shirt. I blush. He zips up my jacket.

“Why are you blushing?” He runs a hand over my cheek.

“Because you don’t have a shirt on.” I look down.

“You are so modest it’s cute.”

I throw a warmer shirt at his face and I reach for my cloak, strapping it around my neck. Luthias does the same, handing me a pair of gloves in the process. Oka trots towards the door, waiting for us to follow her.

We step out the door, the sun almost blocked by the trees and the sky now turning a dark pink. Snow continues to fall and the sky slowly begins to turn a deep purple color. Oka runs around in a circle, her nose pressed up against the snow.

I walk into the forest, the sky becoming suddenly dark. I lose track of Luthias as he goes another way, following Oka. “LaRue?” He calls. I stand behind a tree, a ball of snow in my gloved hands. The thought of that sacrifice is long gone from my mind. Almost as if someone had taken away the guilt. I thank the Electa.

He walks closer to me and I stifle a small laugh. I aim the snowball at him, hitting him right in the chest. He looks down and then back up at me. He quickly picks up snow and runs towards me. I rush away, Oka at my heels as I dodge trees. My steps are light, barley sinking into the snow. I hide behind another tree, watching as Luthias runs by me, but then stops suddenly.

He spins around, searching. Oka gives me away and he throws the snowball, only missing my head by an inch.

"It seems that my aim is better than yours."

He throws the snow at my face. "Most definitely." He laughs, falling onto the ground. I brush the snow from my face and I reach down for more snow. I go to throw it at him, but he reaches for my arm, pulling me down to the ground.

His hair dangles in his face and he reaches his hand in front of me to help me up. I stare at him for a moment, admiring the smile on his pale, fair face. And his bright blue eyes that shine even in the darkest of places.

I place my hand on the side of his face, but before I can kiss him, Oka runs by, kicking snow up with her feet. I whine her name and she licks my face. I stand up, but I quickly duck my head as an arrow comes whizzing by. It hits the bark of the tree behind me and then shatters.

Oka growls, her voice low and deep. I hear the Black speech of Orcs as they send more arrows through the woods. I tug on Luthias' arm as we rush out of the dark forest. I stop behind a tree, my heart beating rapidly.

"Orcs are here. What do we do?" Luthias searches the bark of the trees and then continues to run ahead. "What are you doing?"

He then sticks his hand into the bark of the tree and pulls out a horn. It bellows and Oka howls with it and within seconds guards come rushing near us with weapons in hand, already shooting at the Orcs who had been following us.

Chalsarda's one of them, her red hair lighting up the night as she disappears into the forest. Luthias goes with them and a guard hands him a pair of daggers. And I am left behind with Oka at my heels and nothing but my dog's teeth to keep me safe.

There are no more steps crunching across the snow, only the wind howling through the trees. I swear as a dagger embeds itself into my arm. Oka whimpers and then barks. I walk towards a birch tree, trying to keep my balance. I breathe through the pain. It's not even half as bad as when I was shot with the arrow in my side. So I keep an eye behind me as I exit out of the forest and to the gate of the castle.

My name is called behind me and I swear, looking at the carvings of the blade in my arm.

"You hit me with a dagger Avon." I pull it from my arm, throwing it on the ground. "I didn't think that I looked that alike to an Orc."

Avon begins to panic and he presses his hand against my arm. "That hurts!" I yell at him and he looks up at me, his blue eyes full of guilt, but they seemed to be laughing at the same time.

"I am sorry," He chuckles, brushing his raven hair from his thin face. "I can't believe I hit you with a dagger." He continues to laugh as he walks me inside.

"I can't believe it either. Can you let me sit?"

He leads me to a bench in the hallway. Luthias comes running in and Avon takes his hand away from my arm.

"What did you do to her?" Luthias yells while wiping blood away from his cheek.

"I didn't mean to-"

"Didn't mean to? She's not a practice target!"

I stand up, using my other arm to lean against the wall. "Would you two stop bickering?" My hand slips, sending a bloody handprint down the wall. "Please. I just want to lay down." Luthias sighs and then picks me up, bringing me to our room. Avon follows us for a while until he disappears and then reappears with a healer.

The healer does her job and then quickly leaves, telling me to rest and that it will be healed in the morning thanks to my Elven gifts.

I close my eyes and Avon and Luthias sit down in the living room. I can hear them talking.

"I didn't mean to. I saw Oka growling and I thought it was at an enemy, but I didn't see that it was LaRue." Avon pauses. "I am so stressed. What if she doesn't get better? I am already late for one of the most important things and now I threw a knife at her-"

"Stop, you're stressing me out."

"But you are a Prince. You are used to stress."

Luthias laughs. "You think I handle stress well?" I hear him rise from his seat. "One does not simply handle stress when LaRue is around." He chuckles more. "Gosh, she's so stubborn."

"Tell me about it," Avon laughs. I haven't heard him laugh in a long time. "When we were just kids, it took me from dawn till the sun set just to get her down from the waterfall. She spent all day climbing that thing. I thought she was going to die. She ended up breaking her ankle instead."

"There was one time that she shot an arrow over my head. I take extra caution when I see a bow in her hand."

"Oh!" He laughs once again. "There was this one time when she-" Avon stops. "Wait. You have books here right?"

"Yes we do. Open that door."

I hear Avon walk over to a small room and opens the door and then returns. "This is something that I have forgotten for a long time. But you must know as well." He says as he flips through the pages of an old, worn book. "When LaRue and I were closer, she would tell me that she saw certain Elves. Elves that had passed. They would tell her things, warn her of situations that were arising."

"So LaRue can walk in and out of the Shadow world? Power like that hasn't existed since the First Age."

"Her father has kept LaRue hidden from other kingdoms just in case they find out about her powers. There is a prophecy and it has been going around for many years. The race of men have stolen it and are now looking for this girl. They do not know that it is LaRue."

Luthias sighs. "They do know. This evening in the forest, a guard was killed and the pathway is here was written out in his blood. They know she's here."

Their conversation becomes choppy as I begin to fall asleep and Oka curls up closer to me.

Chapter 14

"LaRue?" A voice calls, waking me up. Luthias shakes my shoulders. "My father wishes to speak with you." I am barely awake as clothes are thrown at me and when my mind truly does wake up, Luthias and I are already on our way down the hall to meet with Sentier.

Sentier pours me a glass of tea and then commands me to sit down. "Orcs have declared war." He shows me a blood stained piece of paper saying only a few words. *Let war commence.*

"Wow. I didn't know they knew that many words." I say sarcastically while dropping my whole body upon a cushioned couch. "What do we do next? Do we even have enough people to begin a war?"

"That is what I need you to do LaRue."

I sit up, leaning my elbows on my knees. "Where do you want me to go?" I was good at convincing people, good at showing what was best for them even though it might be the worst.

"Makya." Makya, the dark caves and mountains of the Dwarves. "Tasar will not be going with you. We will not allow him to go against the people that took care of him for so many years."

"When do we leave?" I roll my sore shoulder as I think about what my father said about Makya.

"Now. It takes a few days to get there. Start while the day is still young." Sentier turns to the window. "And bring very few possessions, the Dwarves like to steal anything with value."

I nod my head as Sentier rushes Luthias and I from the room. My heart races as I think about being in the dark caves of the Dwarves. I had never seen a Dwarf before, let alone been in their mountain. I hear that it was filled with riches for they were greedy, stubborn creatures.

As we enter back into our room, I grab my travelling bag from the closet, shoving clothes into it. "Are you nervous?" Luthias asks.

I roll my eyes. “Am I nervous? I’ve never seen a Dwarf before!”

“Our relations with them were once great and they would come here often, but they turned stubborn.”

“They didn’t join the last war effort. Right?”

Luthias’ eyes say yes, but he doesn’t say anything.

“Right.” I answer for him as he shoves food into another bag. “Do you plan to go through Ebin?”

“I plan to go around it. I am not risking it with Nolan again.”

I stand behind him, placing my arms around his waist. “I am going to go saddle Venetta.” Luthias nods his head and I leave our room with my bags in hand.

Venetta snorts as I enter the stable. I run a hand over her silky, black coat. I slip the bridle over her head and I then reach for her saddle. Tasar enters the stable, petting the horses he passes by. He leans over the gate to feed Venetta a handful of grains.

“Do you know what you are going to say?”

I shake my head as I throw the saddle over Venetta.

“You will be integrated by a guard. Don’t be afraid if you spend a few days in the dungeon. Yes, it will be rough, but it’s what you need to do. Don’t show weakness, they hate that and it will just make them want to keep you longer.” He leans up against the wooden post. “If you manage to upset them to the point of no return, speak to Dâykan and tell him that I sent you. He will get you out.”

“Got it. Don’t upset them. Show no sign of weakness.”

Tasar lowers his voice to a whisper. “And don’t tell them anything of the Pathway.”

Luthias enters the barn, his bags and saddle already in hand. I watch as he saddles up his horse and pulls her from her stall.

“Are you ready?”

The nervousness definitely showed. I didn’t like the thought of being held captive by a race I have never met. Tasar helps me onto Venetta, giving her one more handful of grain before we exist out of the Mithril gates.

As we follow the main trail through the forest we keep our senses alert, our eyes search the forest. The snow blankets over the woods, but the sun still shines through the bare trees. I slip on my gloves and I pull up the hood of my cloak.

"Once we get out of the forest we will be able to get there by nightfall. My father said two days, but Venetta is fast. She can make it in one." Luthias tells me. "I don't want to risk making too much noise through the forest. Spies are still here, hidden in the trees."

***

The day turns to night, the stars showing our path to Makya. The torches of the mountain glows and we can see the entrances to the caves. Luthias and I had hid our mares a few miles away and we sit on a stone ledge, watching and waiting.

"Are you ready?"

"I think so."

Luthias just simply walks towards the entrances, not even bothering to look like he was a danger to the Dwarves. And within minutes our hands are bound and we are taken to the dungeons. I thought that maybe that they would question our reason of being there first.

I am shoved into a cell, being separated from Luthias. They take our weapons and armor, setting them on a table just right out of the cell.

I lean my back up against the wall of the dungeon cell, crossing my arms. Water drips from the ceilings, which is a normal thing for a Dwarven kingdom. The floor is covered in a layer of water and the whole place smells of mildew and rats, which you can hear rustling by. I doubt that any prisoner would've sat on this floor unless they absolutely had to.

The guard returns, the keys clinking is his large, grimy hands. I wonder how easy it would be to attack the Dwarf, but my odds against him are not in my favor at the moment. I stare at Luthias and I's armor and weapons that are under lock and key across my cell. They seemed dull against the pile of jewels that were most likely stolen from another prisoner.

Luthias and I both rise to our feet quickly and the Dwarf moves towards out separate cells. If it wasn't for the few lit candles across the room, I wouldn't have even been able to see the freckles of Luthias' pale face.

The key clicks into place and the Dwarf grabs my sleeve, pulling me from the dank cell. He shoves me forward, pointing a dull stick in my back.

"I don't like being herded like cattle." I growl at the Dwarf behind me.

"Shut up She-Elf."

The lights become brighter as we entered the throne room. Being interrogated by the King was not my plan. The throne room's walls are covered with every jewel imaginable, and the floor is made of solid diamond that had been hewed out of the mountain. The amount of money that the Dwarves had earned must be outrageous.

I look up from the floor, the King in front of me. He sits on a throne of blue metal. He sits relaxed, not tense like most Kings these days. He holds an egg shaped jewel in his hands, that he seems very protective over. His fur coat surrounds his throne and he rises, just to sit back down a minute later.

"Greet the King in front of you Elfling. Bow before me." His voice echoes through the caves. His brown hair is braided in intricate patterns that start at his head and end at his beard. I give a slight bow.

"Thank you for gracing me with the sight of you, King Mim of Makya." My voice sarcastic.

"What is your name Elfling?"

"Laerune Aduial, daughter of Elender, Lady of Ambrose and Princess of Lithien."

"Lithien?" His voice is raised. "You are pledged to Sentier's son?"

"Yes, I am Luthias' wife."

"Did they buy you? How much did they pay for you?"

"I do not come with a price Mim. I am not an object to be bought." I stand taller. "Now, Luthias and I have come here to talk strategy with you. War is upon Lithien. And we have similar enemies."

"Similar enemies. This is true. Orcs have raided our kingdom for many years."

"Not just Orcs Mim." He sits up taller in his throne, seeming more intrigued in what I am saying. "Navain."

"That can't be. He was sent to the Void. He is powerless."

"He has returned and his power is growing, the darkness coming closer." I look to him. "We need you Mim. We need your soldiers. Without them this war is over in a matter of minutes."

"What do I get out of this?"

"Does peace not matter to you?"

"Jewels and treasure matters most to me Laerune." He rises from his throne, walking closer to me. "And you are a treasure Aduial. A jewel I would like to keep."

"I am not an object Mim."

"I will have my most prized jewel one day Laerune, but for now, let me think about this war compromise and I will send a bird with my message in a few days. Go, leave my sight." I simply bow. "Wait." I turn back around. "I ask of you one thing for now."

I raise an eyebrow, waiting for his request.

"What do you know of this Pathway?"

I pause, the breath hitching in my throat. "I know nothing of the Pathway. It is a rumor. A false hope. A myth."

He slightly bows his head and I am led out of the throne room and back to the dungeons. I am worried that they will throw me back in, but they unlock Luthias' cell and proceed to return our possession back to us.

"That was quick." Luthias whispers as we walk back the few miles where we had hid our horses. "What did he say?"

"That he will send a bird with his answer." I look down at the ground. "It's a no. He didn't think that any of this would be helpful in his part."

"It's okay Laerune. Don't beat yourself up just because a Dwarf was being stubborn." He looks towards the ground and then back up to me. "Did he say anything about the pathway?"

"He asked, but I told him it was a myth. An Elven fairy tale for children."

"Good. Hopefully that will spread across the land and we won't have a problem with it."

"Nolan has to be the only one to know anything of value that can be harmful." I look back to the mountains. "I can just tell that war is coming."

"It's already here."

We reach our horses and they turn their heads to the right. Luthias and I duck down. Orcs are marching along the trail to Nadien. "Like I said. It's already here."

Chapter 15

We reach Lithien at nightfall of the next day and we make our way to bed, exhausted from our trip. I don't remember falling asleep or waking up the next day but Luthias drags me out of our room and down the hall.

"Are you sure this is a good idea?" I ask Luthias as we run through the palace halls, dodging maids and other Elves that quickly scramble out of the way.

"No," He smirks.

We turn several corners until we find ourselves at the silver doors of the throne room. Luthias pushes them open and runs inside. "Luthias? What are you doing? If your father finds out that you were snooping in his stuff again he would surely have your head."

"Oh, Laerune. He's gone. Some weird business in Lindalin. He won't be back for a couple of days."

"You're acting like a child."

"Can't I be whatever I want to be?"

I shake my head, following him into the throne room. I watch as he sits upon the throne, relaxing against its stone seat. He throws his cloak over his shoulders and unsheathes a sword from an armor stand at his side.

He clears his throat and points the sword in my direction. "Are my lands clear of enemies?" His voice is deeper and echoes around the empty throne room.

"Yes, your Majesty." I bow.

"Are my chambers clean?"

I giggle. "Yes, your Majesty."

He stifles a laugh. "Is my son the most handsome Elf in the land?"

"That's a bit dramatic isn't it?"

Luthias nods his head and places the sword back in its sheath. "But, if I was King, would you be my Queen?" He reaches my hand for his and I begin to walk towards him, but the doors begin to open and we quickly find a place to hide. Luthias hides behind the stone throne and I quickly move towards the blue curtains that oddly matched my dress today.

Sentier enters, his council men behind him. Sentier's voice booms as a maid quickly appears behind him with a glass of wine. "A gift from the Electa? The Gods think of her like a jewel that can be sold or bartered! She's just a girl."

"We could barter information to the Dwarves about her. They have been looking for her for years. They would surely replace the fee of expenses after this war is over."

"Never! Not for all the jewels in Makya would I trade information to them. Like I said. She is just a girl. She is like a daughter to me." His voice gets soft for a moment, but then rises. "And to anyone that gives me counsel like that should be dismissed from my sight."

Sentier sits down onto his throne, crossing his legs. The other two councilmen stand before him. One with light, silver hair speaks quietly.

"She has strayed far from that path the Electa wanted her to go down."

Sentier places his head in his hands. "So she is in danger? More danger than she already is?"

The councilmen nod their heads and the other one speaks. "Ironic that she is the Pathway, but it seems that she has created that herself. The Electa has been oblivious that this would happen, that she would create her own future."

"The Electa has already tried to warn her. One of these days they may decide to take her life. Would it be wise to set her back on the path the Electa had originally intended?"

"What God or Goddess has taken to the liking of her? One that could possibly be on her side?" Sentier asks.

"Sibylla. The Goddess of the Stars. She seems to watch over Laerune. This is just a guess. The Gods seem to have less of a liking to her. But the Goddess have been more lenient."

"We do predict that Lyraesel may also have a great liking to Laerune."

"Our council is trying to base Laerune's unique gifts on what member of the Electa is trying to protect her."

"There is one God that is trying to help her." They are silent for a moment. "A God who is not the nicest."

"The God of Death?" Sentier questions.

The councilmen nod their heads. "He wants her to find the stones. Apparently she is able to find them with the gifts the Goddesses of the Electa have granted her."

"And what gifts has he granted her?" Sentier uncrosses his legs and leans forward.

"The ability to be enter the Shadow World."

"Why would this be helpful to her?"

"To speak with the dead of course. To be able to speak to the ones who last held the stones. She will be the one to find them. We are positive about this."

Luthias stands up from his hiding spot, grabbing my hand and pulling me from the throne room.

"Why did we leave?" I ask him, wanting to know more.

"My father would be furious if he knew that we were listening to his council meetings."

I continue to argue with him. "This information should be shared with me. I shouldn't have to find these things out like this."

Sentier enters the room followed by three other Elves. They are dressed like captains and by the symbol on their upper arms, they are at the highest rank of the Elven military. They do not introduce themselves, they need no introduction for anyone in their kingdom will know of their great deeds in war.

One of them carries a map in his scarred hands, ruined by years of battles and wars. Another Elf carried a box. He too had scars and his stretched across his pale face all the way to his chest and shoulder. The other was young, few marks written across his skin.

The Elf with the scarred hands lays out the map and the other opens the box, setting up where we have our armies, soldiers, camps, and scouts. The map was new and it spread all the way to Lindalin and then to the islands of the Gods.

"We have calculated that we will meet with their armies near the fields between Lithien and Ebin. Few of us are worried about the men of Ebin joining in the enemy's ranks." The youngest speaks.

The eldest clears his throat. "We have defeated much worse in the past ages, if Ebin decided to join with our enemies, then it is another evil that is vanquished from our land."

"Winning the lands of Ebin would surely put a target on our backs." The one with a scar across his face speaks.

"We already have a target on us and we will until this evil is defeated. We will decide what to do when the time comes. Now, I have summoned you here to tell me what armies have decided to join with us." Sentier's voice booms in the quiet, empty hall.

"We have eighty three from Everford, fifty from Ambrose, twelve from Lindalin, and two thousand from Makya."

We all stand back in silence. "Two thousand from Makya? How can that be?"

"It seems that they had just the right person to convince them." Sentier smirks and then winks. "I know you heard." He whispers. "Good thing you did." He places his hand onto my shoulder. "You have a guest wanting to join you for tea. It's best not to keep the Lady waiting." His golden robes swish as he turns for the door.

I exit behind him and he points towards the gardens that hold the stone courtyard. It has flowers that are still growing since the First age and they're probably one of the oldest things in Lithien other than the forest.

Part of me is glad that whoever this guest is, has chosen to be outside. With planning this war, many of the long meetings are held indoors. A table and chairs is neatly set up in the courtyard overlooking the river. A tall Elven woman stands admiring the flowing river. Her golden hair, much like mine, catches the light and falls to her knees. She turns around gracefully, a smile upon her fair face. Lady Azariah.

"Welcome to Lithien Grandmother." She was from my mother's side of the family. Tall, fair, blue eyed, and exactly like my mother. And I seemed like another replica of them. The Lindalin genes were passed on to me, while my sister got those of my father's ancestors.

"My Aduial." She embraces me. "You look more and more like your mother every day." She releases me and looks at how much I have grown. I was still growing, still ageing, unlike other Elves. I was still a child to them.

"On what occasion have you traveled to Lithien?"

"I have come to contribute to this...Peace War. I have heard many call it that. My Lindalin guards have come with me and I assure you that their all of the greatest warriors I can spare you." She turns towards Luthias. "Now I must say that I have missed visiting Lithien. I can still see its beauty even past those deadly gates."

"Thank you for your kindness, Lady Azariah." Luthias bows, his light red hair bright in the sun.

"You still must have hope Luthias. Without it, our world will fall. Yes, evil runs rampant here, but they will leave." She turns back to the iced over river. "Now, if you'll excuse me Luthias, I would like to speak with my granddaughter alone."

"Of course Azariah." Luthias bows and I watch him as he walks away, his movements graceful compared to my clumsiness.

"I have something for you Laerune." Her warm smile brightens the air around us. It was almost like magic. Her eyes glide over to the large travelling chest to her right. Leaves and flowers are embroidered across the leather covering of the chest. "Go ahead. Open it."

I unclamp the lock, opening the chest.

"It's just a few of your mother's things that she left in Lindalin. I thought you would like to have them." My hand touches something sharp. "Be careful of that, it's quite sharp."

I carefully lift the armour out of the chest, the gold scales sharp and still shining from being unused. The metal is almost blinding.

"What is it made of?"

"Scales from Braithwaite the Dragon, slayed by our kin in the First Age." She grins. "I had them sharpened so they would look a bit more...rebellious."

"Thank you Grandmother." I turn to look for her and thank her more, but in an instant she was gone. Disappeared like the wind. She did this often for she hated goodbyes.

Luthias returns, helping me carry the chest back inside.

"My father is planning to leave in a few days." He seems saddened. "I don't want you to go."

"Don't want me to go? Why not?"

"Well, you know what happened to my mother."

“Yes, but what use will it do for me to stay here.”

He is silent, but then speaks up. “You are a woman-”

“Do not say that!” I growl at him, gritting my teeth in the process. “My skills shouldn’t be judged on if I am a woman or not.”

He leaves, grabbing his cloak off of the door and slamming it shut behind him. I growl in frustration. I hit my fist against the wall. I open the door, watching as he walks down the empty hall.

“This is my war and I will fight!” I scream at him, but he doesn’t turn around. I follow him down the hall, but I lose track of Luthais as he disappears around a corner. I turn a few corners of the hall and to Sentiers study. The door is slightly ajar and I see him writing. He lifts his head as the door squeaks open.

“Is something wrong Laerune?”

This is the first time I have ever yelled at Luthias and I feel extremely guilty. Tears start to fall from my face. "I yelled at him," I say just above a whisper. He comes over, enveloping me in a hug and giving me reassuring words like a parent would do to a child. He leads me to an oak chair with a red cushion.

"Being in love, you will have your arguments. This will not be the first one. My wife and I had many...she usually won, but still, it makes the relationship stronger." He smiles and grabs my hands, giving me a reassuring squeeze. "If you want you can stay in here tonight." He points to a small loveseat.

“You loved her very much, didn't you?"

His smile disappears. "Of course I did. And when she died...a piece of me died with her."

He hands me a book from his shelf as he had read my mind, knowing that I had been admiring them for a very long time. He leaves, closing the door behind him and I move the candle closer to the book. It’s wrapped in a green leather binding with gold lettering. *Extinct creatures of Laquilasse.*

The sweet smell of leather and parchment calms me. I lay down onto the loveseat, holding the book up in the air to read it.

***

I don’t remember setting the book down or falling asleep, but I am woken up to the squeaky door and a shocked elf. "I am so sorry my Lady, I didn't know you were in here."

"It's okay.” I rub my eyes, the book falls onto the floor. “I needed to get up anyways."

When I return to my room to apologize to Luthias, the room is empty. There is absolutely no sign of his presence. I change into a blue dress, slipping on my shoes before exiting the door. The dining hall is also empty except for a few maids. *Where is everybody?* Angrily, I walk to the kitchen.

"Do you know where the Prince or King is?" I ask a young maid.

"They just left to the armory, they are readying for war."

"Why have I not been told?"

"Women like you don't fight in wars."

I stay silent, biting my tongue. *Just simply prove them wrong.*

I run out of the kitchen towards the armory. They can't leave without me, I refuse. I swing the armory doors open with all my force. I simply walk to the stands of armor that had been brought to the armory. I reach for my sword, but Sentier grabs my wrist.

“What do you think you are doing?”

I ignore him and I continue to reach for my sword. “You did place my armor in the armory. So I had to come here to put it on.”

“I put it in here so you couldn’t find it!” His voice growls, much louder than the banging of metal against metal. The blacksmiths pause their work to listen.

I meet him face to face. “You are the first I will prove wrong, Sentier.” I rip my hand from his and I sheath my sword to my side. I shrug on my armor.

Sentier’s lips are set in a thin, angry line and his eyes glare in front of him as he scans the armory. He simply nods his head and continuous to examine his sharpened weapons.

Chapter 16

Before exiting the dark forest, Sentier stops, jumping off his grey horse. A tall statue stands before the gate leading out of Lithien. Vines and flowers are twisted around the tall figure. And yellow flowers grow at the bottom of the statue's skirts.

Sentier carefully pulls away the vines, revealing a beautiful Elven maiden. The crown upon her head draws my attention. How the metal twists and bends into shapes of leaves and flowers. She was the Queen of Lithien, Sentier's wife and Luthias' mother.

Sentier's face grew bright but then quickly turned grey, his emotions like waves, always changing. Someone taps my shoulder and familiar bright red hair catches my eye.

"Chalsarda." I bow my head.

"LaRue." He reaches for my hand, almost slipping from her mare. "How have you been? It's nice to see another female here. I was starting to get a bit lonely." Her accent is strong today.

"And it's nice to see that someone else has gotten past that roadblock these men keep thinking."

She laughs, brushing back her fire licked hair. Her green eyes brighten up. "There aren't a lot of us. Only a few shield maidens."

"Just us."

"Just us." She laughs again. "I hear much from the blind guy." She looks over her shoulder at her trainer.

"I see you have created nicknames."

She nods her head. "He tells me about you. And that you are the Pathway." She whispers, looking over her shoulder again. "But you already know that, don't ya?"

"Yes I do."

"Hopefully a pathway to peace or something nice, like food." She giggles again, running her hand over her sword at her side.

Alastar calls. "Chalsarda. Stay close to me."

"Yes Alastar." She slows her horse down, meeting back up to Alastar.

***

When we reach the canvas tents of the camp, all is silent. Soldiers stare at us as we pass by. I try not to make eye contact, too scared to see the fear in their eyes. You can practically feel the fear surrounding the area.

I sit up straighter as the beat of drums sound our welcome. The soldiers rise to bow to their royal court. I nod my head to three woman with needle work in their hands. The emblem of healers is stitched onto the sleeve of their dresses.

Three large tents are set up in the middle and Luthias helps me down from my horse. He opens the flap of the tent's doorway as our trunks of weapons and armour is carried in.

Banners of the allying kingdoms cover the inside of the tents canvas walls. Candles are placed around a table already littered with papers. I run a hand over the parchment to examine its information.

"Two hundred from Everford? Eryn has been too gracious."

"This is their fight too." Luthias sits down into a chair and I begin to help him tie up his red hair. "And plus, we need every male we can get."

"And woman," I scoff while tugging on his hair slightly. "We would be nowhere without those healers out there."

"Maybe you should've become one of them?" Luthias shows off his sideways smirk.

"Me? A healer?" I shake my head. "I am not very sympathetic."

Luthias points towards the doorway of the tent. "And you think they are?" He turns around in his chair. "They rip arrows from warriors' bodies!"

"Maybe you should be a healer. You like to rip arrows from people's bodies too."

Luthias' sideways smirk disappears. "I wanted to be a healer." I brush through his hair as he continues to speak. "After my mother died, I wanted nothing to do with fighting. I simply wanted to heal. But battle is in my blood and I must protect my kingdom."

I run my hand over his pointed ear. I grab at his ear as I notice a hole where a piercing had been. "Explain."

Luthias simply moves away from my reach and smirks. A healer steps in, a stack of papers in her hands. "What is your report?" Luthias questions the female.

"There is twenty of us, Prince Luthias."

Luthias nods his head and leans his face to rest in his hands. "How many are you prepared to bring to the front lines?"

"As many as you want, Your Highness."

Luthias rises from his seat. His attitude quickly turns king-like. "I am leaving that decision to you," He paces the space of the tent. "You know your group better than I do."

As she bows, her eyes glance at my stomach. "I am sorry if this is out of line, Princess, but should you be here fighting? Especially after the wedding celebration?"

"I can assure you that an heir will not be brought into this world until this evil has been defeated," I growl.

The woman only nods her head and exits the tent.

"They are only looking for something to have hope for, Laerune."

I begin to braid my hair. "What happened to calling me LaRue?" Luthias shrugs his shoulders. "I like LaRue better."

The wind shifts, sending a cold breeze through the tent. The weather was getting worse and frost was coming down from the mountains instead of the steady snowfall.

I step outside, the breeze slipping through my plait. Metal sounds ring through the field. Luthias places his hand on my shoulder. "All of these people are fighting in Lithien's name. Fighting for the Pathway." He places his head on my shoulder. "I haven't heard of many Princesses that stand with their people during times of war."

"I am not just a Princess. I will be a Queen someday."

I step forward, pulling my cloak closer to my ears. The soldiers shiver as they place their banners into the snow. I search the area for the red banners of Ambrose, but a group of Lithien warriors dance around a fire catch my eye.

I grin at them as I one of them grab my arms. The male's face is covered by the hood of his cloak as his steps become dangerously close to the fire's heat.

A second male steps in, spinning around me quickly. I recognize the Earth brown eyes as Tasar places his hand over the fire. Tasar sends me over to the next male.

This dance was often used in the courting process. When there are multiple males fighting for the love of one female, they all dance with her until she becomes dizzy. The Electa's fate comes in and sends her falling into her true love's arms.

The young male grins at me with bright, ocean eyes. I giggle at the playfulness in his face as he pushes me back, sending me to the next man's arms.

I stumble, finding those familiar arms wrapping around me. Shadows dance over Luthias' face as he helps me to my shaking legs.

Tasar places an arm around one of the Elves, the young one, with ocean eyes, disappears to the next group of warriors.

"I would like you to meet Amar."

Amar pulls off his hood, revealing a tanned face and golden eyes.

"Prince Luthias, Princess Laerune. It is an honor." Amar turns to face me. "I want to give an oath of my allegiance to you Laerune. An oath of friendship." He grips my hand tightly. "Friends till death. And hopefully after," He chuckles.

"May it never be broken."

Amar makes the same oath with Luthias. "I want you to know that your friends aren't far. This world is in need of more friends." He speaks roughly, bowing his head. "Good evening."

Tasar and Amar disappear to go find their younger companion.

"Allegiances made in the beginning will last forever," Sentier breaths. "Those are the people you will need in the end. They will be the ones that keep your kingdom together."

Sentier hesitates, but hands over a paper to Luthias. "I want you both to stand watch at the hill in the morning. You can bring your friends with you." The King leans in close to me. "This may be your last chance to get to know them, to get to know their stories." In other words, *they may die.*

***

The sun rises in the morning, red shining over the melting snow. It seemed like winter had hardly come here and the snow melted by morning, only leaving a layer of delicate frost. Luthias and I search for Tasar as he promised earlier that he would bring the best warriors with him.

We ride up a few miles to the top of the hill, meeting the rest of our group near an outcropping of trees. One of us would sound the horn if our enemies were near.

I offer them a sparring match to make the time go by. Two others stood watch at the top of the hill.

Vestan, the most skilled with a blade, lifted his sword above his head, a grin spread across his face. "Do I really get the honor of spending another week with you LaRue?" He was one of my courting options. Vestan brushed a piece of loose hair from his ponytail. My sword quickly collided with his. He is too young. Too young to be fighting in this war and if I had a say in it, I would have sent him back quicker than he could protest.

He wasn't even to his full height yet. He hasn't even had his coming of age celebration. In my eyes he was still a child. But his eyes shine with so much spirit that you thought you were looking into the ocean. An ocean whose tides had not collided with pain and destruction.

"Mum fell in love with a Dwarf, da's dead. What else am I to do with my life? Waist away in grief?" He shakes his head. "Nah. I spend my time having fun, going to parties and seeing all the pretty Elves while I can. You never know, I might be the next one to just drop dead."

"That's a way to look at it," I smirk, my sword barely stopping his from colliding with my side. He manages to get the sword out of my hands and me onto the ground. He then bows, reaching for my hand to help me up.

"Now, I have never met a Dwarf, but from what I see in pictures is that they sure are an ugly creature. Not as ugly as them Orcs though." Vestan looks to Tasar. "I don't know how you stand to look at them creatures every day."

Tasar pokes around the fire with a stick. "It is dark you know. Not much to see if you can't see in the dark." He shrugs his shoulders. "And you get a good works pay out of it." He steps away from the fire and then pulls his hair up into a bun so it's out of his face. Tasar then continues to mess with the fire, placing his hands above the flames.

Luthias ties up his boots next to Tasar, the flames rising higher as the sun begins to set. Silvyr, the golden haired captain from Lindalin, sits near the fire. A sword in one hand and a rock in the other, sharpening his blade. He reminded me of Dehlin, but with sad grey eyes.

"Are you in the Elven military?" I ask him while watching Amar and Chalsarda hike down the hill and back to our small camp.

"No. I protect my Lady and my Lord."

"Then how did you end up here?"

"My mother thought it would be a good way to make me leave." There is a harshness in his low voice. "As she said, this is my punishment for disgracing them with an unroyal marriage."

"Unroyal marriage? Why should it matter?"

"Money. Fame. Status. Everything that a parent wants for their child." Silvyr's eyes dart to the quiet Elf to my right. His back is leaned up against a tree and he carves the bark off of a stick of wood. He is strong, but his face held no emotion. Not even his eyes shined with the light of a story.

He's from Ambrose, one of the fifty that was given the choice to go to war and fight in Lithien's name.

I saw him many times with Avon, just the two of them. I hardly ever saw them speak to each other so most of their conversation are probably done in private. Avon was a secretive person and it seemed like his friend was as well.

"Thank you for joining us Caldon."

"Thank you for starting this war. It's not like I had anything better to do." Caldon frowns, his brown eyes seemed lifeless, fearless.

"This war is not my fault."

"You are the one they talk about, aren't they? The one that the enemy wants?" I keep silent. "They expect me to bow down to a woman. A queen." Caldon says the words in disgust, like they were rotting food in his mouth.

I leave him be, letting him mope in his rudeness. "What does it matter if I am a woman or not?" I tell Luthias.

"A Queen hasn't ruled in ages." He explains.

"Come on LaRue. One more match." Vestan whines, his sword in his hand ready to fight again. But I look past him and up towards the hill. "What is that?" Vestan questions.

"Elves by the look of it." Tasar answers. "Two of them. No symbol of a kingdom. Looks like their brothers." He looks to me and then to Luthias. "Twin brothers."

Luthias grabs my arm. "LaRue, it's best for you and me to leave right now."

"Leave?"

"Yes. Now."

I pull away from his grip. "No. We have to figure out who these Elves are."

"I know who they are."

I cross my arms. "Then who are they?"

He is silent, looking to Tasar for help. "You will find out in a moment." Tasar answers for him. They unmount their horses, their moves in unison as if they were one. They both bow.

"I am Eldar."

"And I am Eldrin."

I am speechless. These are the Elves my father was talking about. "You are Laerune Aduial, right?" I nod my head. "The daughter of Elender?" I nod again. "We are your brothers."

They both smile widely, embracing me in a tight hug. "My brothers?"

"Yes. Brothers. You are our sister, as well as Eryn." They place their hands on Luthias shoulder. "Luthias." They bow. "It is nice to see you again."

I place a hand on my head. "How are you my brothers?"

Their smiles disappear. "Well you do know what people do when they want kids, right?"

"No, no. I don't mean it like that. I mean why have I not met you before?"

"Father kept it secret."

"To protect you." The other answers.

A loud boom sounds and we see the Orcs cross over the hill.

I yell. "Tasar sound the horn!"

The horn bellows through the open air. Quickly, we pack up our camp. Our stuff is shoved into saddlebags, not caring whose supplies it is.

Chapter 17

I mount Venetta and with a small nudge from my legs she runs towards the front lines. Her black coat almost looks purple under the afternoon sun. I look to Luthias, his sea blue eyes filled with fear. Another horn bellows, making me jump. Real battles do not feel like ones I have read in my books.

"Always remember that I always love you LaRue." His horse shifts its feet.

He looks back at the Elves and men. The Dwarves cannot be seen, only occasional axes towering over the other races. My armor shines in the sunlight, like a beacon of courage and hope. My red cloak billows behind me, my hair loose from its usual braid. My heart beats in my head, the pounding echoing in my ears like a drum. My adrenaline skyrockets, mixing with my ever changing nerves. Everything seems too fast, yet so slow.

War chants are yelled around me, each in a different tongue. Prayers are said to the Electa, our gods and goddesses, to high kings of the past, to dwarven warriors of old. They wish to live, but if death takes them, to travel to the Halls of Lost Souls, to live out the endless years of the dead.

I will not fail to bring peace to this land, I tell myself. *This is the Peace War and it is only the beginning. Be prepared to fight another day, to fight for what I love. To fight for the things that mean the world to me. To fight for Luthias, my family, my friends. Fight for the ones that have died at the wrath of this evil. Fight. Fight.* The words chant in my head.

I unsheathe my sword, Laure-eneth the weapon of the fair and young. A weapon only fit for a woman my size. The light handle covered in leaves of silver seems to hum with energy to fight. My armored hands grip the handle, preparing to defend myself.

The combined voice of the races rumble through the green hills, the horses' feet stomping in rhythm. *Fight.* Arrows fire overhead, each making its mark. *Fight.* Spears clash into the unfortunate. *Fight.* Horses gallop towards the commotion. *Fight.* Laure-eneth makes its mark into an ill-starred Orc.

My first bloodshed in battle. The noise and the commotion overwhelms us all and I lose track of Luthias. Panic builds and I spin myself around, searching the battlefield quickly. My sword reaches out for another enemy, but this one actually wants to fight. His body towers over mine, the mud covers his arms and blood drips down his mouth when a smile comes across his face. He tries pulling my sword away, his hands seemed unfazed by the blade dragging against his palm.

With much needed force, I pull the blade away, swinging for his head. He ducks, waving his mace towards my stomach. I side step, my blade moving around my body, and making its mark into the Orc's side. He falls to his knees, in failure.

"I will not be so easily killed."

Each step I take sends me to another enemy. Each different, some with swords and others with axes or maces. Screams of terror and battle cries set the backdrop for this Peace War. The ground is slick with an unearthly mix of red and black blood.

The familiar color of red hair catches my eye. Three boulders stand tall, blocking Chalsarda's path to retreat. With a swift motion of skilled hands, I nock an arrow, pulling back the string, aiming and then releasing. Her yellow cloak moves away quickly, and the Orc lands right in front of her feet. With a smile of gratitude, she continues on her way, her steel sword swishing and swinging.

Another familiar face catches my eye, the pulled up cloak and the spear strapped across his back is a clear indicator. With brutal force Amar takes down a Goblin, not caring as it falls to the ground in a heap at his shoes. He wipes his blade clean with the end of his black cloak, blood flicking onto the dead Goblin.

"You know you could see well if you took off your cloak."

"You may be right, but I like it this way."

"Alright then, it's your death." I joke. Death didn't even seem to be a question to me. I didn't even think about it.

"Then death it will be."

He unstraps the spear from his back, throwing it up into the air and catching it in his fist. His arm goes back and the spear launches from his hand and into a running Orc. The commotion continues as Amar disappears into the crowd of deadly competitors. I follow, my sword ready for my next enemy.

Up the hill, I notice Sentier fighting with deadly efficiency. Thousands of years of training made him strong and unyielding. Yet it seemed that something caused his mind to wander far from the battlefield. An Orc swings his mace, catching him off guard. The splinter of bones rose above the noise and commotion. Sentier staggers back, clutching his arm, but still, he rises, prepared to fight. His swords swing around his body like a whirlwind of steel and metal. In moments the Orc had fallen, its black blood staining the green grass.

"Sentier!" I call.

"LaRue watch out!" His sword work is sloppy, yet he still kills the Orc aiming for my head.

"You need to leave."

"I can't," He growls.

I move in front of him, blocking him from a too bold Goblin. My knife protrudes from his neck. "If you cannot defend yourself from your enemies, you cannot fight. I am not asking you to leave, I am commanding you!"

"You do not command your King!" He yells back.

"I can do as I please! Now leave!" I whistle and Venetta gallops around the corner of a large boulder.

"You will feel my wraith-"

"I will feel it when I return to Lithien!"

Stubbornly, he jumps onto the horse, trotting away from the battle. He disappears in a wisp of blue and silver as the battle continues to rage on. Familiar faces come closer to me, surrounding me in a circle of hope. They're all safe, every single one of them, yet spirits are low at the sight of the neverending army of Orcs and Goblins.

Everything seemed slow as a collection of arrows was aimed at our group. Shields seemed to cover us all, except for one. "Vestan!" I scream, thinking that I could stop time and move him out of the way. He only turned to me, smiling, as the arrow shot into his chest. He turns, looking at the sky as he falls into the soft grass. Noises echo through my ears as I run to him. His eyes stare up at the sky, as if searching for a lost hope. They flicker towards mine as I lift his head up and into my lap.

"Vestan, stay."

"I can't." He smiles. "It just doesn't seem right to stay. I would love to...but...I can't." He starts to cry.

"No, you can stay. You can stay." The tears seem to endlessly fall.

"Thank you...for the hope you gave me. And in such a short time." He seems to start to panic. "Such a short time. I'm only seventy! I haven't even had my coming of age celebration." He cries louder. "Why does everything have to be taken away from me?"

"There is always an adventure after death. We don't even know it yet. The Electa had a plan for you and they still do." I move his long black hair from his bright blue eyes. "It is an honor to fight with you Vestan. And more of a true honor to be your friend."

"A friend." He pauses. "That's what I have been looking for." His breath catches and then stutters. "You're my friend." His hand reaches for my face, as he smiles for one last time. His hand drops, going limp, as his ocean eyes fade into a placid grey.

My body seems numb and unable to move, grief stricken. I am forced to my feet by the strong familiar hands of Luthias. My anger rages and revenge rushes out of me. Every archer of the enemy is shot down with a golden arrow from my bow. The string twags as each arrow makes its mark into yet another enemy.

A gleam of gold shines across the battlefield, my father still stands fighting next to many others from Ambrose. The gold and red colors mix together, the colors of my home. I don't think my father would think that he would fight in another war. He wasn't aggressive and took kindly to everyone.

A spear is thrown towards Luthias and my hand reaches out to save him, but my body doesn't move. I stand frozen in place as Caldon steps in, taking the blow. Luthias quickly kills the Orc with a death blow to the head. Caldon falls into Luthias and he struggles to keep the large Elf up. Slowly, he sets Caldon onto the ground.

"I said that I wasn't going to be killed so easily. And now look at me, I am dying saving you." He swears colorfully. "I really didn't mean all those things I said to you LaRue. You would be the only woman I would bow to. I would even take a blood oath for you."

"Thank you Caldon." I lay his sword on his chest, but he pushes it away, with a still strong arm.

"You will be a great King and Queen, I do wish I could see that happen. But I ask you for one thing. Give it to Avon, he needs it more than I will." His eyes wandered around the battlefield, stopping at the sun setting over the hills. His eyes turn blank, and lightly, I close them. I take his sword, strapping it across my back.

It's more than exhaustion that tires me. The tears blur my vision as I stumble across the battlefield. It starts to rain, the ground slick with mud and mixed with blood. Through the deluge, Amar and Chalsarda carry Silvyr, his arms wrapped around their shoulders. His silver hair is dripping with blood and it hangs down in front of his face, hiding the pain in his eyes.

"He won't lay down until you talk to him." Amar breaths, his voice breaking.

"I only trust you with this message." Silvyr says as we lay him down into the mud. "There is no way I am getting back to Lindalin. I need you to tell my Elora that she needs to be strong. She needs to be strong for our child. And tell her that she cannot be afraid to love again."

"I will help her as much as I can."

"And give my parents hell! They deserve it."

He coughs, blood dripping down the side of his mouth. His eyes search mine as if for help. His head falls to the side and his last breath stutters out. I pull my knees to my chest, finally letting myself cry. I stand up, screaming across the battlefield. With determination for revenge, I lose myself in the battle. My sword waits for its next bloodshed, hungry for more.

Exhaustion takes over my revenge and I fall to the ground, my weapons dropping around me. The rain falls, like the tears of the fallen, washing away the blood. The mist hides the sun as an enemy circles around me, binding my hands as they drag me away from the battlefield.

"We got lucky she is still alive," An Orc says.

"Master will be very happy." The other laughs.

There is no energy to fight or to call for help. A single tear drips down my face as they drag my body to a cart, pulling me far away from the land I know. My life is over, promises broken, and lovers lost.

I searched around the empty battlefield for LaRue. "LaRue!" I called. "Laerune!" All that returned to me was echoes of my own voice. I start to run, slowing down when I pass Vestan's body. He was too young. His sword lays in his open palm and I grab it. It would be all I could give to the ones who lost him. I force myself to continue to move.

Panic builds as the space that I have searched gets smaller. Her silver dagger points me in a new direction to search. A pile of her weapons seems to be all that is left. Orcs sometimes take bodies away from the battlefield to show their masters that they have been killed.

I fall down onto my knees, cradling her bow and sheath of arrows. I don't know what to do.

I rise to my feet. *There is still hope.*

Chapter 18

I open my eyes, lifting myself up from the cold, stone floor. Hammering of metal echoes through the cavern and Orcs pass by, patrolling the cells. But it seems that the only cell occupied is mine. I am in the ruins of Nadian.

All the kingdoms thought that Nadian was empty, just a pile of rubble in the South. But now, the truth has been exposed. They're rebuilding their ruined city in the canyons of the Black Land. I stand up quickly, grabbing onto the metal bars of the cell as an Orc passes by.

"Where is your master," I growl at the disgusting creature in front of me.

"You will see him soon enough," He spits in my face, the black liquid oozing down his chin. He leaves, limping down the dark hallway. I lean up against the wall, my arms crossed, scanning the hallways for other creatures to pass.

If I was to be here awhile I better at least get more of an understanding of the place.

Not even five minutes passed when a dark, cloaked figure slips down the hallway. He reaches my cell and shoves his hand forward, grabbing my ripped cloak in his pale hands. I slam against the sharp metal bars, winching at his force. Under his dark cloak, his eyes glow with a pale evil that I have only seen in nightmares. But at the same time his eyes are familiar.

"Where is it?" He snarls. "You have come to me just like the prophecy said. Now, where is it!"

"I don't know what you are talking about. You searched me and I have nothing."

I try to squirm away, but his grip moves up to my neck, squeezing tighter. His other hand moves to my necklace, lightly placing a pale, scarred hand onto its shining jewel.

"You are no use to me. Not yet."

He pushes me away from the cell door, sending me towards the stone wall.

"How much can you survive Aduial? How much pain can you go through?"

"More than you think," I breathe heavily, rising to my feet.

He disappears back down the corridor. I feel my neck, the bruises already forming from his hands. *I don't know how much pain I can take.*

Lithien seems silent. I played the act of a grieving Prince, but I know in my heart that LaRue is still alive. I just pray it's not a lost hope.

The kingdom was set up with golden flowers and handkerchiefs seemed to be in everyone's hands.

"You are coming today, right?"

"I can't believe you actually think she is dead," I snap at Chalsarda.

"Do you think we have the warriors to send to Nadien if she is alive?"

She leaves, her red hair let loose and her armor shining. She had been promoted to the guard since she played such a great part in the battle. I move to the desk, looking at the array of shining swords. The golden handle of Silvyr's was longer than the others and Vestan's small, but swift. Caldon's wide blade was handled with red, the colors of Ambrose. LaRue's sword, Laura-enth, shined brighter than the others.

I pick it up, the metal leaves entwined around my hands. The lightweight was odd to hold, but I knew that it felt so normal for LaRue.

I walk out of the door and down the empty hallway. The amber lights shine down the corridor, the stone walls cold and unforgiving. Chalsarda pushed some flowers in my hand as she braced her arm on my shoulder.

"Everything is going to be alright." she assured me.

"My father left my mother as a prisoner once and she was tortured. I don't want that happening to LaRue," I snap.

"I don't either."

We are silent for the rest of the walk. The courtyard was opened up, the daffodils and bluebells shining bright around the garden.

I move to all the beautiful yellow flowers blooming in the summer sun. I pluck a handful of daffodils, flicking a bug off one of the petals. I carry her sword and the handful of flowers to the table of her memories.

The sword clatters to the ground and the courtyard changes into the forest. LaRue's bright smile glows in the forest light.

"LaRue?"

"I cannot speak for long, I do not have enough energy. Do not believe that I am dead. I am alive, but not for soon. The Black Land holds more evil than we thought. Hurry, there isn't much time."

The woods change back into the silver courtyard, people stare as I bend down to pick up her sword. I strap it behind my back, turning to the staring crowd.

"She's alive." Is all I say, before running out of the courtyard and into the stables. I tack up the horse's saddle, riding through the gates. The trees blur past me, the slightest green glowing through the black and brown. The snow had gone away so soon and now the forest seemed to be turning back to spring.

Chapter 19

They had beaten me almost every day. I tried counting the days, but I lost track in the darkness of the dungeon. The cloaked man came every day, his eyes gleaming behind his dark cloak. The bruises he left on my neck have ceased to disappear, including the ones he adds to my body every other day.

The cloaked figure returns for the second time today, I look up to him, my eye bruised at the last meeting with him. Scars were etched across his face, his eyes not only holding evil, but sorrow.

"Who are you?"

"It doesn't matter."

"It does. I would like to know who is killing me."

"I am not killing you, I need you. Then I will kill you."

I cross my arms. "So nice of you to keep me alive for so long." I was growing arrogant and cocky. "So what do you need me for? You're not getting much done with me locked in this cell."

"You know what I need."

"Actually I don't." I get close to his face, trying to see more of it. "Who are you?"

He turns, disappearing from my sight. I curse down the hall at him. A pain in my chest, causes me to sit down. It spreads through my body, sending tears down my dirty face. "Bastard." I whisper. Another pain spreads through my body.

Footsteps echo through the hallway and I await another enemy for yet, another torture session. But the footsteps were practically silent, they were those of an Elf. My heart flutters at the thought of it being Luthias and him finding me so soon. But my stomach dropped as it was not him that entered the hall.

The Elf is much taller than Luthias, his face paler and less happy. His grey eyes are rimmed with orange and he smiles. He crosses his arms in front of him and then bows quickly.

"I am Navarre."

I pull at a loose string on my torn dress. My eyes dart to my golden armor that has been sitting on the other side of my cell for days, taunting me, telling me to find a way out. "You seem too polite to torture me."

"Torture? Is that what you think we are doing?"

I nod my head, staring at his empty eyes.

"You're still standing." He pauses, waiting for my answer but I give none. "That's what I thought." He steps closer to my cell and he wraps his arms around the bars. "We are not here to harm you. I am here to help you. And in return you will help me."

"Depends."

"I believe that you are not the one that my master is looking for. Your looks do not match her description and you do not know what my master is talking about, so you will be mine until I convince him that you are not her."

I sigh in relief. I don't know who this Elf is, but they just might be able to save me from here and get the target of me actually being the Pathway off of my back.

"Now, what is your real name?" He smiles kindly.

"Aletie Elis."

"It is nice to meet you Aletie. Like I said I am Navarre." He unlocks the cell door, taking my arm gently and leading me to the end of the hall. It opens up to a room brighter than the dungeons. I squint, my head pounding by the sudden light.

"What gives you the power to do this?" I ask Navarre, staring up at his greyish hair.

"I have a high title in this kingdom."

"And that is?"

He glances back at me, his hand still wrapped lightly on my arm. "I have many titles. I am a Lord and a Councilman. A prince you could call me."

"A prince?"

He again meets my blue eyes. "My father is my master. I think you can put the pieces together."

"Well, he doesn't seem like a good father if you must call him your master. You shouldn't be his servant."

"Everyone is his servant here. Even you." We exit out of the hall and out into the open air. The smell of the sea is overwhelming and Navarre warns me to watch my step as we cross over an expanse of large, black rocks.

The wind fills me with new air, not like the heavy smoke that fills the dungeons. Navarre let's go of my arm as he reaches into his cloak's pocket, pulling out a key and unlocking the door to a stone tower. But when we walk inside, the area is large and open.

"I don't care much for the dark unlike the others that live here." He explains as I glance around at how bright the room is. "There are two other servants that will help you clean up around here and they will show you your room."

"Will I get my stuff back?"

"It is already in your room."

"And will I leave soon?"

"As soon as I can get you out."

I speak quietly. Trying to play the part of the innocent one. "Hopefully soon. I want to go home." I do want to go home. I know they have presumed me dead already, but I am hoping that Luthias had gotten my message that I tried so hard to conceive. It drained my strength for a while, the spell harder to make than I thought. Healing magic was all that ran through my bloodline, but this spell allowed healers to speak with each other across the battlefield.

"Aletie." Navarre calls from the fireplace, a metal rod in his hand. He places it in the flames, waiting for it to turn red and golden before taking it out and grabbing my arm. I try to pull away, but he places the rod onto my arm, the design burning into my skin. I hiss in pain. And when he lets go of my arm, I quickly back away, slipping onto the floor. I look down at my arm, the designs twisting into an Elven knot.

"I am sorry. I didn't mean to hurt you. It's just precautions. It's to let us know that you are not the one we are looking for."

I nod my head, staring back down at my arm. This is just leading me to a better path. They won't think I am the Pathway if they have already checked me off as not the one.

I rise to my feet, looking around the room. "You need new clothes. I can't stand to look at you." He pointed me towards a different room. "Take your time, you don't start work till tomorrow."

He closes the door behind me, the air steamy and hot, making my dirty clothes stick to my skin. A few baths are hidden behind doors and I enter the one farthest away from the entrance from which I came in.

I am hesitant at first and I watch the first door for shadows and I listen for footsteps. My whole body shakes and I realize that even though my captures had been giving me food, I have been refusing to eat it. I've been torturing myself.

I collapse onto the floor, my strength breaking and giving up. All I can see is black boots as I am picked up from the floor. My mind goes blank and I can't process anything but voices shine through, breaking through the blackness of my mind.

"I have to take her back. She can't stay here."

Chapter 20

And when I wake up, my eyes heavy from sleep, I find myself in Lindalin. Blue eyes gaze down at me, filled with worry. The Elf sighs in relief.

"When I heard you were in Lindalin I came as soon as I could." Luthias sits back down, taking my hand in his. "What's this?" He turns my arm around, looking at the scar.

"I was in Nadian. Navain beat me. His servant took me in and marked me. He said that this was to let him know that I wasn't who they were looking for."

"And I suppose they are looking for the Pathway."

"They don't think I am her. It seems that luck is on our side Luthias. This gives us an advantage." I sit up, my stomach rumbling and I reach over to the plate of food at my bedside.

"How did I get here?" I ask Luthias while I place my spoon in a bowl of soup.

"An Elf brought you here. A male with greyish hair and orange eyes."

"That's him. That's Navain's servant."

Luthias looks puzzled. "Why would Navain's servant help you when Navain is the one looking for you? How did he not realize that it wasn't you?"

"Navain seemed pretty sure that it was me, but the servant seemed convinced that I wasn't."

Luthias sits on my bedside and he looks across the room. "He didn't take your armor or anything of value. He brought it all back here with you."

I follow Luthias' eyes, finding my armor upon a stand. I look to the other table. Three gleaming swords lay on the table, surrounded by a dark blue cloth. Swords of the dead that will now be given to three loved ones. I guess I found the right place to be at the right time for I would have had to travel to Lindalin anyways. Silvyr's family lives here and I promised myself that I would speak with his wife.

***

I was in Lindalin. The home of Azariah and Faolan, my grandparents. The land used to be open to all, but now towering walls surround the land, keeping any foul beast and evil being out of the forest. The trees grew tall and silver and the creatures that are kept here are practically tamed. They know nothing of death and only see you as a friend.

The Elves here are very calm and quiet and the forest seemed to hum with music, as if the trees themselves were singing sweet, calming lullabies.

Luthias allows me to change and then returns when I am done. He pushes back a piece of my golden hair, placing a silver sword in my hand. The blade had been cleaned, the shining, blue, elvish knots lace through the blade.

I am lead to a table set out with food and gleaming dishes. A couple sits at one end of the table and a female at the other end. The lone Elf stares blankly at the surrounding trees. I must choose who I give this sword to. Silvyr's parents or his wife. His parents stare at me, their eyes not even filled with sorrow.

The world of Elves has changed, children were practically worshiped in the past Ages. How could a parent not love their child?

"I assume you have been given the news." I speak to them. "Silvyr wanted me to deliver a message to one of you. Which one of you are his wife?"

I know before I had to ask. Her black hair and blue eyes turned up brightly as I asked for her title as his wife. She slowly stood up, brushing her skirts down as she nears me.

"I hate to meet at such hard times, but I promised Silvyr that I am always here to help. There is more to his message, but I do think that we should speak in private." I look to his parents who stare at us. "My condolences to you and your family." I say to the uncaring parents before I leave up the stairs with the girl following behind me.

Her blue dress drags across from my green one. Her eyes stare at the floor, knowing every turn and step of the stairs. "I'm LaRue." I speak.

She seems shy and I half expect her not to answer. "I'm Elora." She picks up her skirts, stepping onto the platform connected to the trees. The window opened up, the river winding around the birch trees and the blue lights hanging from long branches.

"Why do these parents show hatred for their child?"

"I am not sure. They never loved him and now they never will. There was no reason for them to hate him, he did everything they wanted."

"He said you were with child."

Elora places her hands on her stomach. "I know what he has told you to say, but how am I supposed to love another when my heart has always been his?" Her voice seems hollow and haunting. Like no emotion can escape from her heart but sorrow and defeat.

I place the silver blade in her hands and she grips the handle tightly. For a moment I thought she was going to fall and I was prepared to catch her, but her eyes glimmered for a moment.

"He was a guard of my grandmother's, was he not?"

"It was a great day when he was granted the position of the Lady's guard."

"And do you have a position anywhere?" She had hands of a seamstress, but I doubt that she was one. She seemed too fragile and delicate to do anything. Even just talking to her made me think she was going to shatter at any time.

"I am a healer's apprentice."

"And do you like it here?"

She pauses afraid that someone might reprimand her if she said the wrong thing. "I do not want to be here anymore, yet at the same time I do." I give her a look to go on. "I feel so lonely here. But this is still my home, I was born and raised here."

"If at any time you feel like you want to leave, speak to my grandmother and she will send you to where you want to be. You are more than welcome to stay in Lithien or even Ambrose."

"Thank you LaRue."

She walks away, the sword still clutched in her small hands. I wait for her to walk down the stairs, before I sigh, letting the tears flow down my face. All there is left is empty hopes. I could feel the sorrow radiating off of Elora. The glow of her eyes were dimmed and her smile wasn't at its brightest.

I turn around, jumping as the pale white figure of my grandmother walks towards me.

"Why don't you come and eat LaRue?" It was a command not an option. She takes my hand, leading me down the hallway of trees. "Don't fret over the things you can't change my granddaughter. It is the path that was chosen for them." She speaks softly. "You are just like your mother, thinking that everything's your fault, or that you can change the past."

"And no matter how hard I try, I can't." I finish her sentence.

She smiles down at me, her white teeth gleaming. She then looks down at my feet. "You know you would be more comfortable not wearing shoes." I look down at her feet and then back to my boots.

"Grandmother, you know how much I love my boots."

"You always have." She laughs. "I hear that your armor was very popular on the battlefield."

"I am sure it was." I cover my mouth as I laugh.

***

The large table was set with silver utensils and white dishes, the men and woman at the table rose to their feet as I entered the room. They each bow their head, as I am seated next to Luthias. They seemed to only be allowed to sit back down when I pushed in my chair and was finally seated. Azariah and Faolan stand, smiling at us all.

"My granddaughter has returned and paid our kingdom a lovely visit. May the stars watch over her and the Electa shine bright protecting her."

Glasses are raised and then set back down. A few Elves exchange glances my way, looking at my healing bruises around my neck. They still haven't gone away. The Elves that were staring at me, quickly looked towards my grandmother. Their shocked faces told me that she had spoken to them through their minds. Azariah loved to do that so often. I try stifling my laugh, but it's no use.

I find Lindalin to be quite boring. Nothing ever happens here and everyone is so calm. All they talk about is boring stuff like how they learned to knit a thousand years ago.

I lean my head against my propped up hand, waiting for something interesting to happen. Suddenly, Tasar runs in, a fiddle in his hand and he starts to play, his hand holding the bow, sliding it over the strings until a tune started to come out.

I push out my chair, picking up my skirts and standing next to Tasar as my feet move in rhythm with his fiddle. I take Luthias' hands, moving him across the forest floor. Out of my eye I can see Faolan standing up, clapping to the upbeat tempo. My boots clack against the stone floor, as I spin around. It fills me with joy to be able to laugh. Tasar begins to sing, dancing around me with his string instrument.

The day shined bright, brighter than the sun.
As the blue sky gleamed through the shadow of day.
That is when I saw you.

Your voice bright and clear, sending the darkness away.
Only the stars knew how much she was loved!
She danced and twirled in the light of the waning sun.

Many came from lands away, to see the young lady.
She continued to dance, but for only one.
One that she loved and dreamed of.
Warm air filled the glade as the sun set,
She danced to the one she loved.

Up the hill and down to the river,
She went, not stopping till she reached the boy
She had grown to love.

When the sun sets and the stars come out.
The bells ring and the fiddles string.
Up the hill and down to the river,
She went, not stopping till she reached the boy

She had grown to love.

He turned to me waiting for me to sing as he still continued to play his fiddle. I grab Luthias' hands pulling him near me.

Many came from lands away, to see the young lady.
She continued to dance, but for only one.
One that she loved and dreamed of.
Warm air filled the glade as the sun set,
She danced to the one she loved.

Up the hill and down to the river,
She went, not stopping till she reached the boy
She had grown to love.

When the sun sets and the stars come out.
The bells ring and the fiddles string.
Up the hill and down to the river,
She went, not stopping till she reached the boy
She had grown to love.

I stop, laughing as Luthias trips over his shoes. Faolan claps his hands, gliding over to us. "It is nice to hear songs like these in this Elven kingdom. It's a change." He dismisses the dinner, sending us all away.

Tasar sets his fiddle down, his long brown hair is tied back in a ponytail. No matter what, a smile is always upon his face. "Why did you have the urge to do that in front of a dinner?" I snicker.

"Because, I can do whatever I want when I want. And you looked a little bored."

"Just a little?"

He laughs and we walk up the stairs to our rooms. The blue lights seemed to be dimming as the sun set. Stars shone through the clouds and thunder rumbles nearby. Lightning flashes in the distance towards the Black Lands. Luthias jumps, grabbing my hand. For some reason my anxiety picks up, worry bubbling up inside of me. The sky gets dark and the once warm air turns cold.

Pain shoots up through my body, but I ignore it, not wanting to worry Luthias. Rain starts to pour and we walk under the canopy. The thunder gets louder and closer. The leaves blow and they crinkle past our feet, the sky darkening. We continue on our way to our room, the thunder shaking the tree tops, sending leaves to the ground far below.

We pass by two guards, their faces lighting up as the lightning sparks. Tasar stares at them suspiciously as they walk over the bridge. They turn the corner, disappearing from our sight. Tasar stops and we wait for him.

"What's wrong Tasar?" I yell over the howling wind.

"The guards. They didn't have Lindalin's emblem on their uniforms."

"I don't think that it matters." Luthias says, more to me than to Tasar.

"It does. My Grandmother keeps everything orderly. She has the emblem stitched on every guard's uniform. And there is a reason why."

I move towards the two "guards" with Tasar right behind me. Quietly, we followed them. They spoke softly, too quiet for us to hear anything they were saying. The lightning flashed again and they looked behind at us. Luthias pulls us both away before they can look at us.

"You are going to get in so much trouble." He growls.

"So you do agree that they are not real guards."

"I didn't say anything about not believing you."

He tries to pull me away, but I yank my hand free. "You can come if you are so worried about me." He sighs, following us.

"Look at their boots." Tasar points out. "They're not from here."

"They're from Lithien."

They open a door leading into another hall. The hall is lined with more doors and seemed like it was living quarters for the maids and servants. At the third door on the right they stopped, one guard placed an ear to the door, listening for any sounds. The other pulls out a long blade from their side.

"Luthias, we need to stop them." I urge him.

Without hearing an answer from him, I make my way down the hall towards them. Tasar pulls out a long dagger, handing me his other. The guards walk through the doorway and we sneak up on them through the dim light. I place my blade across one of the guard's' neck and they freeze when the cold metal touches them.

"I wouldn't go any further if I were you."

He drops his sword and it clatters to the ground, a figure gets up from the bed and lights a candle. The room lights up, the shadows of the candle dancing across the wall. Tasar has the other guard up against the wall, a blade at his neck and a knife at his stomach, ready to spill his blood.

The resident of the room sits up, their nightgown glowing in the candle light. Elora's black hair casted shadows around her face and she stopped moving, looking at the five Elves that now stand in her room.

"What's going on?" She softly asked.

"It seems that you have an assassin." I push the blade closer the man's neck.

"They were...were trying to kill me?" She stutters.

The man struggles to move under my blade and I hold him tighter. "Why don't you ask him yourself?"

"I'll go retrieve your grandmother LaRue." Luthias says already existing the small room.

Elora proceeds to light the other candles around her room, she glares to the two guards. My grandmother comes in, a white cloak draped across her shoulders. Four guards are in tow behind her and they take the two assassins away, binding their hands.

"Send them to the throne room. I have many questions for them to answer." She commands. She places a hand on Elora's cheek. "I am so sorry, that you were put in harm's way. If you need anything please do tell me. I feel so responsible that my kingdom was unsafe and truly I don't know how this happened."

"I would like some tea at the moment." Her hands shake as Azariah smiles.

"That can be easily done." Before Azariah leaves to fetch Elora's tea, she places a hand on my shoulder. "Thank you."

Tasar decides to stay with Elora until my grandmother comes back. Luthias and I walk down the hall and into the throne room. The Elves were not from any of the three Elven kingdoms around here. They tried to frame the two kingdoms.

"What are your names?" Azariah asks them when she returns. Her blue eyes seemed to pierce into the two Elves.

"I am Holden and this is Arto."

"Where are you from?"

"We are not from anywhere."

"And why were you here to kill Elora Eadan?"

"We were given money to kill her. The person who wanted her killed didn't give us a name."

"So you followed their orders?"

"We had too. We were lucky he payed us. He said he would have killed us."

"He? What did he look like?"

"He was cloaked and dark. You couldn't see any of his face."

"He had scars across his face!" The other Elf butted in.

I look to Luthias, before I join in on the conversation. "I have met him before. While I was in Nadien he was there. He said he needed me for something? To find something?"

"This is very important information." Azariah ponders. "Holden and Arto, you can be sent free if you prove yourselves worthy enough."

The two Elves bow their head in thanks. Two guards take them away, the throne room growing quiet. "I want you to leave, take Elora away."

"That is her decision." I growl.

"I can see more than you Laerune!" She yells, her voice echoing through my mind, *"Her future is dark."*

"It will be darker if you don't let her make her own choices!"

I walk away, turning from my grandmother's tight grip. She lifts her head as if in warning. I turn down the hall until I find myself in Elora's hallway. I knock on the door, hoping that she wasn't asleep, or that I had woken her again.

"Hello LaRue." She manages to smile. Tasar still sits with her at the small table, a tea set spread against the wooden surface. Silvyr's sword takes up almost half the table, its long blade shining as the lightning strikes nearby. "Would you like some tea?" I nod my head as she leads me to the table.

She pours the silver kettle, the tea steaming into the tiny little cup. I watch her carefully as she sits down, crossing her legs. She acts as if an assassin didn't come into her room a little bit ago.

"My grandmother wants you to leave." I speak quickly. "It is your decision though...if you want to or not."

"Like I had told you before. I am not ready yet. Give me time and then I will leave."

"She deems it wise to leave. Something dark is in your future."

"Give me until the Adara and then I will leave. It will give me time. But wherever you go, I will follow."

"Then that is it. We made a compromise. My grandmother will feel a bit better."

I sip the hot tea as Tasar and Elora continue to talk about how great Silvyr was. Tears occasionally were shared between the three of us. Knowing him only for about one day made it worse. All the memories Elora shared seemed outnumbered compared to the few words I have shared with him myself.

Elora told us about when they had gotten married on the bridge by the tallest tree in Lindalin. As she talked a smile ran across her face, the memories had brought joy to her and her eyes regained that glow that was once gone. Elora continued with more stories about her life with Silvyr until the whole teapot was empty of its contents.

Chapter 21

I walked back to my room alone, thinking about how Luthias felt when I had gone missing from the battlefield that day. I opened the silver door of our room, the candles all lit and the moon shining through the open window. The sweet smell of rain lofted through the window, filling the room with crisp air. Luthias sits at the table, a book in his hand. The golden title across the leather book read: *The Dreamer of the Petals.*

He set the book down, standing from his seat and then walking to where I stood in the open doorway. He embraces me, placing his head in the crook of my neck.

He did something unexpected. He cried. It wasn't tears of joy, not even close. They were tears of fright. His hands grew tighter and I held him closer. His hand went up to my hair, running his fingers through it. His other hand was placed against my back.

"I'm scared LaRue. I'm scared that you are going to be taken away from me. I don't want anybody else to die." He cries. "I can't take it anymore."

"Luthias I'm not going to whisper sweet nothings to you. I am scared too and...And-" I couldn't finish my sentences. I didn't even want to think of losing him. The Electa has already seemed to send threats to destroy everything I love. I don't want to make them too angry and have them hurt him. Everything I do is for others, especially Luthias.

He walks towards the window, trying to calm himself down. "Why are you scared to cry?" I ask him.

"Males are supposed to be brave."

"Don't give me that answer." I whine. "Men are brave if they can cry. You have emotions and feelings for others and yourself. That is okay." He shakes his head no. "Yes, you must listen to me. Don't be scared to cry, it is brave and I look highly upon the men that do."

I wipe a tear from his right eye. A smile lifts at the corner of his mouth. I take his hand, looking towards the disappearing storm. The moon shines through the misty air, and the trees calm in the dying wind.

***

The next morning, the horses are brought out of the stables, tacked and ready. I strap my saddle bag onto Venetta, swinging my leg over her side. Luthias does the same with Tasar in tow. He had almost spent the whole night with Elora. She had been scared to be by herself that night.

***

As we crossed over the bridge into Ambrose, the sun shines across the misting waterfalls. Rainbows dance across the water as the people of Ambrose welcome us back. My brothers had arrived a few days ago with Amar and Chalsarda and they greeted us with bright smiles.

"Good to see you alive." Eldar and Eldrin speak in unison.

"Didn't think I would make it, did you?"

"It was iffy." They laugh together.

I bow my head as I walk inside, birds sit outside on the wooden beams of the building. The statues inside seem to point me down the hallway to Avon's room. The door was cracked and I open the door without knocking. Avon sits and stares out his window, his room's floor covered with clothes and the table littered with paper.

"Hello." I say softly. He doesn't answer. "Avon-"

"He's gone isn't he?"

I nod my head, looking away from him. His blue eyes are glossy and bright with tears. He looks back at the window, the birds singing sweet songs during a dark time. He brushes his dark hair out of his face. Avon stands up, looking up at my eyes. He stares at the sword in my hands.

"Caldon wanted you to have it."

"You know he was my only friend that cared." He spoke harshly, taking the sword from my hands.

"I cared Avon. I truly did! I couldn't drop my dreams and hopes just for you!"

"You didn't have to! You could've at least talked to me!"

"And do you think that I wanted to wander the woods at night looking for you! You knew the enemies that hunted for me! I was lucky that I could go outside during the day time!" I yell.

"Who did you think told you to fight for what you love? Who was it that filled your imagination with adventures to distant lands? Who gave you the story of Gracen?"

Gracen was a story of a girl who fought her way through everything. It was my inspiration for the longest time. It was never my father who had given me book after book when I was sick. It was Avon who left them on the table outside of my room.

He hid away because he had to, others were frightened by him. Other Elves thought he was harmful, thinking that if they stood close to him they would catch a disease.

"I'm sorry," I whisper.

"Why couldn't you love me?"

"Because you were just like me. We hid from the people who dislike us, we find comfort in fictional things. We love too much, and we're stubborn!"

"And you fell in love. You fell in love with someone who can put up with your stubbornness, because you can't put up with anyone else." He laughs. "Thank you for bringing a piece of him back, it means a lot to me."

"I'm sorry, but I have to go and deliver one more thing." He bows his head. "And I suggest that you clean up someday."

I exist the room, walking down the hallway. The sun shines through the open area, my boots clicking against the colored stone floor. Red and gold flags hang from the ceiling, adding color to the dark room. The room opens up to a balcony, a stone bench overlooking the valley.

I sit next to Linder, my father's new assistant. "He always loved visiting you."

I lightly place the small sword in his hands. His blue robes overlap mine. The silver circlet around his head shined in the afternoon sun. It had been a gift from me, when I was finally told when his birthday was. He hugs me, the sword still in his hands.

"I tried so hard to protect him Linder." I cry.

"I know, I know."

We take a moment to put ourselves back together, admiring the trees swaying in the wind. He takes my hand, helping me up from the stone bench. I brush my skirts down, looking up at Linder."

"How have you been feeling?" He asks.

"Sometimes the pain comes back, but I try to ignore it."

"You are strong Laerune. So very strong."

I wrap my arm around Linder's as he leads me to the dining hall, dinner had been set up early and the golden plates wrapped around the large table. I sit down next to Luthias, his golden robes bright. I drink out of the golden goblet to my right, the warm drink running down my sore throat.

Avon had finally accompanied us to dinner and he sat across from me. He filled his plate with food and maids brought in more plates of steaming vegetables. The smell lofted from the kitchen, filling the room. Music was played in the corner, making everyone talk above the loud music. It was just a normal dinner except, my brothers are here.

"So LaRue, tell us about yourself." They spoke at the same time.

"What do you want to know?" I smile.

"What's your favorite color?" Eldrin smiled.

"Really brother that's all you can think of?" Eldar adds.

I laugh. "I like green and sometimes purple." I look down at my green and purple gown, the sleeves almost reaching to the floor. "I see that you also like the color green."

They look at each other laughing. "This is true little sister. But I do believe we have different uses for the color green. Green blends us into our surroundings, making us easily hidden."

"We like blue better than green, is what Eldrin is trying to say."

"Do you both like the same things?"

"No...We have different hobbies." They ponder for a moment. "I like fighting, where Eldar likes his studies more."

"We are kind of like one person, each complementing each other."

"Making us one good fighter." Eldrin laughs.

The maids disappear along with the musicians, whose music dwindles with them. I see my father speaking to Dehlin. Dehlin shakes his golden head, probably giving my father his council. My father stands, setting down the napkin that was laid out across his lap.

"You have all played a part in my daughter's life. And I have lied to many of you. This meeting is for me to tell you as much of the truth as I can."

We all look at each other confused. There are guards surrounding every doorway and the information that is going to be shared can't be shared outside of this room.

"Laerune what I have told you your whole life is a lie. I told you that during the Second Age, year 2509, in the month of October, you were born. I told you that your mother died in childbirth and that you had never met her. Only few of you know the real truth."

I look around at everyone, wondering what the truth is. My father's eyes flicker to mine, his eyes glossy and on the verge of tears.

"Laerune Aduail, you were born during on the same day that you have always known. But your mother is alive. We just don't know where she is." Father looks away from my eyes. "We suspect she is residing with the Gods."

"There was a prophecy that was written near the First Age. Dehlin, would you hand her the scroll?"

The brittle paper was handed to me from across the table. I slowly unroll it, the yellow paper, water stained and wrinkled in some places.

"Please read it out loud, LaRue," Dehlin speaks.

It reads:

When two Elves create a fourth child of
Full Saleth and Narrod,
The Prophecy will begin.
Of the Silver Queen and the Golden Lord.
She shall be the Pathway.
War cannot cease until the wrong has
Been righted
And the balance restored.
Princess of the stars and sun so she shall be called.

The rightful queen to a hidden kingdom.
She would banish the evil,
Bringing back the light that was once lost to us.
Last of the Fae, bearer of magic.
She shall be the Pathway.

"What does any of this mean?" Luthias asks. "Queen of a hidden kingdom? Last of the Fae, bearer of magic?"

"We do not know much. Any documents of the Fae were burned years ago."

"And what about this nonsense with the Electa?" Sentier asks.

"They do not agree with this prophecy. There is already many evils in search of her, wanting to use her or destroy her. We didn't want the Electa's powers mixed in with this."

Avon sets down his fork. "But how do we all play a part in this? I know we all have been a part of LaRue's life, but there seems to be something that you're not saying."

Linder pulls out a silver box, setting it in front of my father. My father opens it, pulling out a glowing jewel. It's amber color, lighting up the room. He holds it by a chain as the colors dance across the wall. It slightly resembled the jewel that Sentier's wife used to wear.

"This is an ancient jewel, older than Laquilasse itself. It will be split into pieces, one for each of you. If one of you die, the light will dim and you will feel some of the pain. LaRue is a large target, and I want all of you to stick together. If you take up this task, it will follow you forever."

"What is the task?" Chalsarda asks.

"That whatever happens, you will protect LaRue-"

"Father, you can't make them do that."

He ignores me, continuing on with his speech. "And when she takes the throne to this hidden kingdom, you will become her court. And you will take a blood oath if she chooses. You won't be just her friends, but her family. You will die for each other, always protecting her, even if she doesn't want it. And when the light is returned, you may break the oath, but only then." He pauses for a moment, letting all the information sink in. "Who will take this oath?"

I close my eyes, not wanting to hear the first voice echo through the room. "I will." Luthias stands.

He is followed by Avon, my brothers and sister, and Dehlin. I continue to close my eyes, hearing every familiar voice in the room say those two words.

"Laerune, let me see your hand." My father speaks. I show him my hand and he lightly grabs it. He places the amber stone in my hand. "Luthias you were the first to volunteer, so you will hold her hand." He clasps my hand, the stone lying in between our palms. My father has the rest of the volunteers place a hand over ours. "Repeat after me. Until death takes me or the light restored I will always hold to my oath. I will protect Laerune Aduial even if it leads me to death or utter despair. Nor will I harm any of her court, unless she is in harm. I will become her court, her family, and will share her pain as she will share mine. My oath shall not be broken or death will take me."

The voices echo around the room. Each saying that they will protect me and each other. When they move their hands away, the amber jewel sits in pieces in my hand.

"Now each of you will take a piece." The pieces disappear from my hand, all but one, which will be mine. I clutch my hand, the amber jewel warm in my palm.

Chapter 22

My friends and family disappear, leaving me alone in the dining hall. I bow my head, tears falling from my face. This was one of the last things that I wanted to happen. I don't want people dying for me. My friends and family choosing to protect my life over theirs is the last thing I would want to happen.

"This is their choice LaRue. You are not forcing them." Luthias comforts me. I turn around in my chair, facing him. "Why don't you take a day for yourself? I won't be back till later."

"Where are you going?"

"I must speak to some of the guards. They will be helping us with our return journey home."

He leaves and I walk up to my old room, taking a book off the bookshelf and pulling the blanket off the bed. I wrap it around my shoulders, walking outside. I lay down the blanket, plopping myself onto it. I open up the book, starting to read.

I soon fall asleep, the afternoon sun shining down on me. I hear Luthias after an hour or so. I pretend to be asleep as he sits down on the blanket. Laughter builds up in my chest and I try to hold it in, but Luthias grabs at my waist, starting to tickle me.

"Stop," I giggle.

"Why would I do that?"

He leans across me, his chest up against mine. I catch my breath, still laughing. He stares at my eyes and I can't help but smile. He leans closer, his eyes glancing at my lips. With his kiss, all my grief and sorrow seemed to disappear.

"I don't like to see you unhappy LaRue. When you don't smile, it's like the sun doesn't shine." I give him a cheesy smile, showing all my teeth. "Not like that." He laughs. He kisses me again and I blush. "Like that."

Thunder rumbles and the sky darkens. I close my eyes, forcing myself to show no emotion in my face from the pain that bursts through my body. I fold the blanket around the book and the rain starts to pour. Luthias just stares at me, worry filling his eyes. He embraces me, the warm rain dripping down my face.

"The cloaked man you were talking about...he's causing you pain. Isn't he?" I simply nod my head. "Why don't you tell us these things LaRue? We might be able to help."

"I don't want to worry anybody." The thunder booms and lightning streaks across the sky. "Maybe we should go back in." I tell him.

"This is no ordinary storm. They have been happening almost every night since I left Lithien."

Luthias takes my hand as we walk inside. Our clothes drip on the stone floor and I look back at the mess we are making. I slip and Luthias grabs my waist before I can even touch the ground. He turns me around and I place my hands on his chest. I kiss him, but somebody clears their throat, interrupting us. The amber jewels around my brother's necks are already made into a necklace.

"Father wishes to speak with you. And Luthias is welcome to come with you."

"Thank you." I walk past them and towards the hall leading to my father's study.

I walk down the stairs carefully, each step silent. I knock on the door and my father opens it. He smiles, leading us to two seats that are placed before his desk.

"I just want to make sure that you are okay LaRue. I know you are angry that people gave an oath to you."

"I am father. I am very angry. I've been trying not to get my friends mixed in with my troubles. I don't want anybody getting hurt."

"I understand, but this was their decision."

"Father, why did you have to lie to me?"

"I did it to protect you-"

"Protect me? Maybe if you would've told me, we could've figured this out sooner. We could've spent years translating the prophecy. That would be an adventure in itself. But no, you let me sit here dreaming about all the adventures that I wanted to go on, and you know what happened! I became rebellious and left! This place was a prison for me." Guilt builds up in my chest as the words came out of my mouth. My father's eyes grow glossy and my hands cover my face in disgrace. "I am so sorry father...I didn't mean any of that."

"It's fine, just leave. Don't come back, for all that I care. You don't want to be here anyways."

Luthias helps me up from the chair, and I bury my face in his hair as he practically carries me out of the room. I yell from the hallway as my father closes the door. I say sorry over and over in Elvish.

"LaRue, shh. He just needs time to be alone. He didn't mean anything that he said and neither did you." I cry into his shoulder.

"He was the one to always be there for me." Pain shoots through my body and up into my heart. I lean all my weight into Luthias and he lies me down on the floor. I feel like I am endlessly falling into darkness. All I can see is a blurry image of Luthias as he holds his own chest in pain. *I will become her court, her family, and will share her pain as she will share mine.*

My breathing gets uneven and fast. As if I had fallen, I jolt awake. My eyes open and I feel like I am going to scream. Luthias covers my mouth, and I heavily breathe through my nose.

"Shh, just stay calm."

I close my eyes, tears falling down my cold face. Luthias slowly lifts his hand away from my mouth. I reached for his hand, placing it against my face. I savor his warm touch against my cold face.

"He was there. He knows about the oath. Navain knows who I am."

"Did he say anything?"

"He plans on killing all of us."

"How does he plan on doing that?" Luthias says almost with a laugh.

"This is not a joke, he is stronger than we think." I stop, laying back down. "My father...where is he?"

"He will be back, he is just checking on the others."

"Others? Are they okay?"

"They are perfectly fine."

The image of the cloaked man, seems etched in my mind. The scars across his face were more frightening than they had been before. He was starting to mention what he wanted me to find, but I woke up before he could say anything.

Familiar gold robes rush over to me. He takes my hands in his, holding them tightly.

"I'm sorry father."

He smiles, kneeling down on the floor. "I am sorry LaRue." He looks in Luthias' direction. "Luthias, could you go check on Linder, he is having more trouble than the others."

"Yes, my Lord."

He exits the room and my father walks me to a bench in the hall. He pulls a blanket off the edge of it. He places it over me and then sits on the edge of the small bench by my feet. "This blanket...it was your mother's. She had made it before she left her home in Lindalin."

"Can you tell me more about her?" I sound like a small child begging for another serving of dessert.

"Of course I can. It has been a while since I have talked about her. She would slap me upon the head if she knew that I didn't tell you about her." He laughs and I can't help but smile at him. "She told me how she imagined that she would often spend nights with you, reading books and pointing out what stars were what. She told me to make sure that you were always warm and loved."

"You should rest." Luthias' voice echoes through the now quiet hall.

My father helps me up from the bench. "Goodnight." He kisses my forehead, walking me down the hall some ways.

I grab Luthias' hand, as we walk down the hallway. I couldn't help but replay the blurry image of him in pain over and over in my head. *I will become her court, her family, and will share her pain as she will share mine.*

When we enter my old room, I grab a book of my shelf, sitting down at my desk. Luthias quickly grabs it from my hands, putting it neatly back on the shelf. "Not this time LaRue. You need rest. You haven't really had any time to sit and rest since the war."

I don't fight against him. He is right. I tried my best not to sleep while I was in Nadien, I didn't want to let my guard down.

I lay down next to him, pulling the blankets up to my neck. I look out the window and at the silhouette of the swaying trees. The wind comes in through the balcony doors, sending chills down my face. The distant sound of singing drifts me off to sleep.

Chapter 23

The morning sun rises and shines through the white curtains, pulled in on the windows. I sit up rubbing my eyes.

"Good morning." Luthias smiles. The rain and thunder passed and the sun rose high above the trees. "Maybe I should take your books away more often. It puts you in a better mood."

"You wouldn't," I smirk.

"Oh, I would."

He runs out of the room and I chase him down the stairs. When I turn the corner, the sun blinds my vision. I take another turn, stopping to make sure I went the right way. "You got a head start, that's unfair." I whine.

He peeks his head out from around a corner and laughs. As I turn another corner, I bump into Linder. I turn around, "I'm sorry!" He looks at my nightgown and shakes his head. I look around for Luthias and I walk a few steps forward. He pulls me to him from his hiding spot.

"I got you."

"Wasn't it me that was chasing *you*?"

"Yes, but I got you first." Before I can disagree, he pulls me into a kiss and then laughs.

"Why are you laughing at me?"

"Because a group of Elves just past and they found your nightgown to be quite entertaining."

"Maybe I should change."

***

After changing, we return to our original destination of the dining hall. My family and soon to be court, waits for us. More of waiting for an explanation to why we are late. Some of them start to laugh and Linder decides to give the explanation.

"They were playing a game of tag."

"Tag? I thought that was just a mere child game?" Eryn ponders.

"And she is supposed to be a queen someday?" My brothers tease.

I look to my father. "What is going on tonight?" I had noticed the different Elves from different kingdoms arriving today.

"Time must have slipped your mind. Tonight is the Feast of Adara."

***

Outside, butterflies float around in the treetops and horses whinnied in the background. Many Elves are outside setting up for the first of three great feasts. Lanterns are being hung and tables are set up.

This feast is very important, it lets us celebrate where we all came from and how our race started. What Elves love best is the light of the stars. We will celebrate the Electa, the ones who created us and the stars. Adara is our overall creator.

"Welcome to Ambrose." I bow to a woman from Lindalin.

She smiles, bowing back. She continued to walk, a basket wrapped around her hands. She set it on the table, pulling the objects out and neatly placing them on the table. The statues around Ambrose, seem to come alive, with all the light and festivities around.

"Ah, Lady LaRue." Lucia, a servant, bows to me. He was one of many to take the oath. "Would you like to help set up the tables?" He had three baskets in his hands and they seemed to be a handful for him.

"Of course I will." I take a basket from him and we walk together to a table. Two woman unfold a table cloth and it floats onto the table. I set the basket onto the table, unlatching the side. I pull out silver and gold plates and silverware. The spoons are shaped like leaves and the handle made out of wood, covered in delicate golden flowers.

I take my time setting them out neat and precise along the table. At the bottom of the basket was a set of green napkins. I folded them, setting them on the glass plates. I watch as gardeners prune vines that had wrapped around statues and I admire the one that looks like my mother.

She held a book with one hand and the other held the skirts of her dress. She seemed to be dancing. My father always said that she loved dancing and singing. She would often travel to secluded areas to gain inspiration for her music. And father had worried for her safety, like always.

Lucia and I, pulled out more chairs to put around the table. He then handed me a matchstick to light the many candles that were set around the tables. The table that was used to set out the food, was already filled with cakes and sweets.

"Lucia, why did you take the oath?" I asked him as he wiped down a clear goblet with his rag.

"You have helped me so much and it is my turn to help you. You have been such a strong and independent woman ever since you were little. Well, you weren't quite yet a woman, but that isn't what I am talking about right now." He rushes. "I could look up to you as a queen. It has been a long time since I could last say that. Evil still takes residence in Laquilasse and I believe that you are the one to end it. As the prophecy says, *war cannot cease until the wrong has been righted and the balance restored.*" He continues to clean the goblets.

I finish helping Lucia set the tables and when I am done he sends me on my way to get ready. "A queen must look her best." He jokes. I walk towards a small courtyard where my father usually holds councils.

"LaRue?" Luthias asks on the other side of the doorway. "Are you alright?"

"I am fine. Just remembering the past."

"The past? What's in the past?"

"Many things lie in the past. Things I wish not to forget."

He walks into the courtyard, sitting down in Lithien's representing chair. He rubs his hands against the hand rest of the seat. "It only seems like yesterday. I can still see you hiding behind that pillar."

"I had begged my father to let me go to that council. I was allowed to all the other ones."

"He knew you would leave. I too wouldn't of let you come."

"Why?" I walk around the circular table set up in the middle of the courtyard.

"I wouldn't have wanted you to see the death that we saw, or the ruin of the kingdoms we entered. I don't want to think about what would've happened when we reached our destination."

Many years ago a quest was at hand. A kingdom's heir had gone missing and the higher kingdoms went out to search for this young child.

He stands up, taking my hand. The amber jewel around his neck seems to shine brighter than usual. My hand goes to my own. I don't remember putting it on. He takes my other hand, standing on the other side of the stone table. He smiles, kissing my hand and then rubbing his thumb over my knuckles.

"Etta is looking for you," He whispers.

"She is always looking for me."

I let go of his hands, walking out of the courtyard. Etta stomps down the stairs, her hands on her hips. "I have been looking for you everywhere. Ugh, I knew I shouldn't have trusted Luthias to find you. He was probably off dancing with you, or whatever you younglings do."

"Younglings?"

"Yes, younglings, that's what I meant."

I laugh as she drags me up the stairs to my room. She sits me down in a chair that she pulled from my desk. She quickly messes with my hair, deciding whether or not she has to brush it. "I don't understand how you get so many tangles in only a few minutes." She grabs my brush off of my vanity, pulling the snarls out. I pull away quickly. "LaRue, this gets done faster if you don't act like a child."

"You're treating me like a child Etta. Why can't I do it myself? I have been for a very long time."

"I believe you can and have been doing it, but I just miss doing this every day when you were little. And you wonder why I took the oath." She laughs. "A queen always needs her lady in waiting."

"I'm not just a queen. And I am not even one yet."

"You will be." She smiles, pulling pieces of my hair back and clipping it with a silver jewel. I rub the amber stone around my neck. "Your dress is in the washroom."

I open the wooden door to the washroom and the dress hangs up by the window, billowing in the wind. I pull it off of its hanger, slipping it on over my head. Its white silk sleeves reach the bottom of the skirt. The bodice was sparkled in white and silver diamonds.

"How does it look?" I spin in a circle in front of Etta.

"Beautiful, as always."

She adds a few more pieces of silver jewels to my hair and then rushes me out the door. As I walk down the stairs, a familiar smile greets me. "LaRue, it seems that you have gotten older in just a few minutes," Ovaine, my studies teacher complimented. His own silver robes glowed in the dim light that shined through the hallway. His dark hair made his pale skin darker than mine. I brush a piece of my hair behind my pointed ear with a smile.

"You always give the best compliments."

"I try," He chuckles. "I sure hope you are excited for tonight, it seems like years since we last had a Feast of Adara."

"I was sick the last time and I did not get to attend."

"It had been a very boring year without you. We missed your singing and dancing."

"What about my snarky remarks about the wine?"

"We even missed that," Ovaine laughs again.

His arm links around mine as we descend the stairs. Music begins to fill the hall leading to the courtyard. The sun starts to set, giving the moon a chance to shine. The stars start to glimmer and I look up at the brightest star. It had always been a sign of hope for me.

I look ahead of me at the many guests surrounding the tables that Lucia and I had set up a little bit ago. I search for Luthias in the crowd, but it is no use. There is too many people.

"It was an honor to escort you, Lady LaRue." Ovaine bows, leaving me alone.

I continue to search, but he hugs me from behind, making me jump. Luthias kisses my cheek and I turn around to look at him. His eyes shine bright, just as bright as the stars. "You look elegant this night Laerune."

"Thank you. You look very handsome."

He laughs, taking my hand and pulling me towards the table set with food. He puts a plate in my hand, suggesting what I should try. We sit down at the long table, sitting next to our fathers. I take a bite of a cake, the sweetness filling my mouth.

I glance at the children that sit at the end of the table, they all look suspiciously at the wine that had been placed before them. One of them is brave enough to try it and their face scrunches together at the sour taste.

"Do you remember when that was us?" I ask Luthias.

"I'm pretty sure that was more you."

"Don't lie Luthias, it was both of you," Sentier laughs. He reaches for his own glass of wine, drinking it.

I still had a problem with the taste and the maids had learned that they should fill my glass with something else. They had learned the hard way, when they had to help me up to my room after drinking too much at one of my father's dinners.

My father stands and everyone becomes quiet. "Our three kingdoms come together for one night in Ambrose and then the next will take place in Lindalin and then Lithien. We have two guests from our allying kingdom of Everford. Welcome King Bainen and my lovely daughter Eryn." He smiles. "We are here to celebrate the creators of our lives and where we have come from. For Adara and our Gods, our creator and our creator of the stars."

We begin to dine, picking up our forks, spoons, and knives. The smell of the food and flowers drift around the courtyard. The table is filled with laughter as the food begins to disappear. Luthias takes my hand, smiling at me. His smile is full of mischief.

"What are you planning to do?" I smile back at him.

"What have we started almost every year?"

We stand up from our chairs and I kick off my shoes, they land somewhere in a nearby shrub. We dance along the grass as others join us. The musicians play their music louder and happier. Luthias grabs my waist and my other hand as he spins around the girls dressed in silver gowns.

I laugh as he attempts to dip me, my long hair touching the green grass. "Where did you learn how to do that?" I ask as he pulls me back up, continuing to dance.

"Tasar taught me."

I laugh at the thought of Tasar and Luthias dancing together. I look over at Tasar as he watches from the food table. His plate is piled high with cakes and cookies. He surely did not follow Elven traditions. A little Elven girl pulls at his robes and she asks him something. He sets down his plate, taking the little girl's hand. He smiles as the young girl giggles. She steps on his boots as he walks around, dancing with her.

"Look." I turn my head to show Luthias what I am looking at.

"That little girl has been following him everywhere today. Tasar has been so sweet to her. I even watched him at the dining table as he passed an extra cookie to her from under the table."

"He's not as mean and tough as he says he is."

He looks up at us, his face bright and shining in light of the stars. We smile back as the music beat gets faster. My dress twirls with me, as we move in between the Elves. A bell rings, stopping us from dancing. The next part of the feast had to be one of my favorites.

All the Elves gather in a circle, some sitting, some standing, and others lying on the ground. We were to tell a story or sing a song. It was a way for new tales to grow and old ones to reappear. They were then able to be spread through the land, shared and told throughout Laquilasse.

"Laerune, why don't you start us out?" Ovaine asks with a smile.

I smile back, glad to be chosen first. My stories were different. They were only just the beginning and I would leave the rest for others to come up with and tell to their friends. Few came back around, different and longer, each variation was unique.

"In a world with happiness and darkness with animals and creatures you couldn't imagine. Where fire and water surround the Earth in a pleasant way. With fights and gold, an adventure is always among you. Creatures like Almo, the Guardian Wolf, can give fortune and love. But someone with powers of darkness can give you death, if you turn the wrong way. Be careful in this world of adventure and cherish what is close to you.

On the day the very first solar eclipse happened, a girl named Willow was born. Guardians, witches, wizards, and many other magical creatures came to the land. Not knowing what

Willow was going to become in the near future, they dared not fall to their knees for the young princess.

Almo, the Guardian Wolf, was the namer of all creatures. He was chosen to do his job by his father Milu. Almo walked into the kingdom proudly and bravely. The crib was carved with all the good creatures in their world. The nymphs must have did it as a gift. Almo looks into the crib and sees Willow's eyes. Not red like the fire, but green like the nature around them. Her hair blonde, like the wheat grass in the northern pastures. Almo knew what she was capable of when she grew older, so he gave her a gift. A gift of life, love, and braveness.

The castle started to crumble and the guards pull out their weapons. They try to kill the demons of Darkwood. Kala, the dark queen, sliced through people like water. Willow's mother set Willow next to Almo.

"Take her," she said with tears in her eyes.

Almo gave a nod and ran away, leaving the people slaughtered by darkness. Almo ran until he reached his den. The den came out into a large castle with other wolves around. Everybody there stopped to see what Almo brought back. He usually brought gifts for the young pups, but this time, a friend."

The Elves applause, smiles written across their faces. Luthias smiles at me, his face bright in the moonlight. His red hair was the same color as the fire nearby. His eyes were as bright as the river that runs through Lithien.

The stories and songs continue, each different, telling a thousand different stories. As soon as the last Elf finished, we all took our separate ways. Some went back to their rooms and others stayed, continuing with stories and songs around the fire that had been lit outside.

I follow Luthias, as he walks up the paths of Ambrose. We enter the forest, following an old, worn path. "Where are we going?" I ask him.

"You'll see." He looks back at me, entwining his hand with mine.

We enter a meadow in the middle of the forest. The stars shone perfectly through the treetops. A blanket was set up in the middle of the meadow and a basket was set near it. Luthias sits down on the blanket, opening the basket. He sets out two glasses and pulls out a bottle.

"I know you don't like wine, but you should really try it. It is one of my father's best bottles."

"If you insist." I joke. He pours it into the glass, the red liquid swirling in the goblet. I put the glass to my mouth, sipping it slightly. It tastes different, it tastes sweet. "This isn't real wine." I tell him.

"It is real. Just made with a lot of...extra good stuff."

"So it's watered down is what you are trying to say."

"Exactly, but not really."

"You're confusing me."

"That's kind of the point." He lays down on his back, folding his arms behind his head. He stares up at the stars, the brightest one shine down upon us. "I have looked at this one star for my whole life and there seems to be a mystery about it."

"Is it odd that I have thought the same thing?"

I lay down next to him, gazing at the star. The warm air fills the meadow and little fireflies blink around. I can hear the waterfalls of Ambrose rush over the rocks and crickets chirp their sad songs.

"Eryn told me that Sibylla had taken a Saryniti and threw it into the stars so it would be impossible for Navain to retrieve it. I always thought that was why that one star shined the brightest."

"You think it is a Saryniti?"

The Saryniti had been crafted during the First Age by an Elf. He had put the brightest things into the three jewels. Navain had taken them, wanting their light, but he somehow managed to lose them. It is said that they are a part of the sky, sea, and earth now.

"I do. It may be just my imagination, but my heart says that I speak the truth."

I turn to look at him, his mind seems to ponder at the thought of the star being a Saryniti. He searches the sky for any answers.

"Do you think Navain will ever find the Saryniti?" He asks.

"I hope not. It would be a nightmare if he did." I have already had those nightmares.

"LaRue?" He turns towards me. "Why do you love me?"

"Do you have to question my love?"

"No, that's not what I mean. I mean what qualities do you like?"

"I love them all. Your outgoing personality, your never ending hope, your ocean eyes."

It was true, I loved everything about him. There wasn't a single thing that I disliked. He seemed to be acting different over the past couple weeks since I returned from the "*dead.*" He seemed more compassionate, showing more emotion. Maybe it was because his father and he had made amends. They haven't been the closest since Luvon's death.

"How is your father?" I ask him.

"He is doing better. We haven't talked much." *Then they hadn't made amends.* "He worries about you LaRue. He was pulled into another grief stricken state after we thought you had died."

"I'm sorry."

"Why are you saying sorry? None of this is your fault."

"But I feel like it is. All this stupid prophecy and oath stuff. I don't want anybody to risk their lives for just one person. Anybody else could be queen of this hidden kingdom or keep the peace in Laquilasse. Anybody can do that!"

A crunch sounds through the meadow. And we reach for our concealed daggers pulling them out. A white stag walks into the meadow. Its coat shines in the starlight and it stares at us, before it leaves back into the thick forest.

"That has to be a sign of something. It has happened before." Luthias stares into the forest.

It had happened before. It had happened when I was weak and everyone thought I was going to die. I like to leave those thoughts in the past.

"We should head back." Luthias suggests.

"No, can we stay?" I ask quietly.

"Yes." He smiles. "I didn't want to leave, I just want you to be safe and happy."

"You don't have to worry so much Luthias. I know I have been hurt a lot over the past years, but I can take care of myself."

"I know you can take care of yourself perfectly fine."

"Then what's the problem. You have been acting different."

He sighs, taking my hands in his. "I don't want to lose you. I have said this many times before, but I truly know how much you mean to me now. I won't be able to live if you are gone. I am trying to cherish every moment we have together, because we never know when it will be our last."

"Don't say that." I breathe. "We are going to be alive for eternity. We will not perish, our undying love with not diminish." I wrap my arms around his shoulders, placing my head in the crook of his shoulder. "We will never succumb into death. I will refuse death."

He holds me tighter. "I do hope you are right LaRue."

"I am." I try to sound confident, but it comes out sounding weaker than I thought. "You just have to stay strong." It's ironic how we tell others to stay strong, yet we can't even do it ourselves.

I lay down onto the blanket, Luthias' arm wrapped protectively around my waist. All we have to do is stare into each other's eyes and we can tell exactly what we are trying to say. My eyes gloss over, changing the surrounding area into a battlefield. I look down at my hands, three shining jewels lie in my palm. I turn around, taking in my surroundings. I spot Luthias' red hair and I run towards him, my excitement overwhelming. I run into his warm embrace and I whisper in his ear that I had found something. Pain shoots through my back and the vision ends. I try to ignore it, not wanting to know what my future has instore for me.

Luthias kisses my forehead. "LaRue." He whispers.

"Yes?"

"I love you."

I smile. "I love you too."

Chapter 24

The sun shines through the trees and I rub my eyes, yawning. I look around me, Luthias missing from my side. I start to panic, rushing to my feet to search for him.

"Luthias?" I call for him. "Luthias!" I turn around and jump. "Luthias Faen, you can't do that to me," I say while shoving my hands forward to collide with his chest.

"I was just messing around." He whined. I start to walk away, leaving the meadow. "I'm sorry LaRue, I didn't mean to scare you."

"I know."

"Then why are you leaving?"

"I'm hungry."

He laughs, following me out of the forest and back into the courtyards of Ambrose. The early rising Elves sit at a small table. We join them, filling food onto our plates. We would be leaving this afternoon for the feast in Lindalin.

"LaRue, your birthday is coming up." Luthias reminds me.

"It is."

"What would you like?"

"I have everything I could ever wish for." I will actually have friends to spend time with on that day, unlike the other years where I spent it alone.

***

After breakfast, I return to my room, packing the few possessions that I had brought with me. "That's not all you're bringing, is it?" Etta asks, entering the room.

I sigh. "What do you want me to bring Etta? You can choose what I wear this time."

She pulls a few gowns from my closet and dresser. And she even packs a few pairs of pants and tunics. I smile as she does so.

"Are you coming with Etta?" I did really miss having her around.

She nods her head, buckling my saddle bag closed. She hands me my bag and I walk out to the stables. Venetta neighs a hello and I stroke her black nose. I grab her saddle off of the wall, swinging it over her side and strapping it under her belly. I slip the reins around her neck and she nods her head, ready to start her trip.

"We're almost done Venetta," I grin.

I buckle my bag to the black and gold saddle, and I pull on her reins to exit the stables. She follows me out to the bridge where Luthias and the others wait patiently. I smile at them as I mount Venetta. The small bridge only fits one person at a time and I look down at the rushing river. Mist streams up from the chasm below and rainbows sparkle through the water.

Oka, follows behind Venetta, her tongue hanging from her jaws.

I look back at my home, I am leaving it once again. The golden wood of the buildings and the green trees that stood watch over my home seemed to reach out to me, trying to call me back. I look forward, wondering what I should gift to Luthias on his upcoming birthday. Our birthdays are only a couple weeks apart.

***

We reach Lindalin as the night falls across the land. Blue lights began to light up the forest. The Elves welcome Azariah and Faolan back.

I haven't got to spend much time with my grandfather and sometimes I think he doesn't want to. Like I am not real to him.

Azariah takes my hand leading me to the hallway. Faolan follows behind her, quiet as usual. She hands me a silver key with a sweet smile. "Faolan, why don't you take our Aduail to her mother's old room?"

It seems that Azariah has read my mind once again. As we awkwardly walk down the hallway, I twist the key in my hands.

"Do you have a problem with me?" I ask a little rudely.

"No, I don't."

"Then why won't you talk to me?"

"I'm scared to."

"Why?"

"Because you look exactly like Andwin and I don't want to lose you too."

"Well not talking to me isn't going to keep me safe." I whine.

He turns towards me, stopping in the hallway. "In some ways it does. There is information you shouldn't know yet. I have given my council to your father many times and he would not listen. You're too young in my eyes for this evil to be brought upon you. My daughter was even too young."

"How about tea tomorrow. Then we can talk more, get to know each other better."

"I would like that."

I nod my head and we continue to walk down the hallway. A silver painted tree stood out on the wooden door and I placed the key in the lock. It clicks as I twist it. The door opens and wind blows through an open window. Brown leaves cover the floor, crinkling past my feet.

"You can have anything in here." Faolan disappears and I slowly enter the room.

Books are stacked on the desk and I reach down to pick up a fallen one off of the floor. A picture falls out of the book and onto the dirty, wood flooring. I pick it up, the paper yellowed and water stained. It is a drawing of my mother and Azariah. Azariah is staring at my mother as she smiles at the artist who drew them. Even in black and white ink her eyes shined bright.

I place the picture on the table, smiling at it. I don't have many pictures to record my life and I may have to find an artist soon. I walk towards the closet, the doors half open. The gowns hang half off of their hangers and I neatly place them back. Dust specks float across the room, shining in the candle light.

I look under the bed, boxes strewn around in the blackness. I slide a wooden chest out and I unlock the hatch, lifting up the heavy lid. I cough as dust flies out, escaping from its dungeon. There is paper and jewels mixed in with a few daggers and a book. A knock echoes off of the door, causing me to jump and knock the lid off of the chest. It falls and I pull my hands away quickly.

I rise to my feet, brushing dust off of my gown. My hands shake as I open the door.

I sigh. "Luthias you scared me."

"I'm sorry, I didn't me to frighten you." His sideways smirk shines. "It's late you know. You should come to bed." I nod my head, locking the door behind me. As we walk to our room, Luthias asks me a few questions. "Have you found anything interesting in your mother's room?"

"I have, actually. There is lots of papers and books I will have to sort through. And lots of unusual jewels and pictures."

"What do you want for your birthday?" He smirks, changing the subject rather quickly.

"I don't know Luthias. I am not lacking anything."

"I know you aren't lacking, but do you know how hard it is to find a gift for you?"

"Actually yes, your birthday is coming up as well."

As we enter our room, I plop down onto the bed, Luthias doing the same next to me. I close my eyes, scrunching my nose together. "What is that look for?"

"I forgot something in Nadien."

"What did you forget?"

"A dress that was in my bag. I can see it in my head, right where it was left."

"And that's a bad thing?"

"If they do find out who I really am, they will now know where I am from."

"Lithien stitching." He whispers, realizing the danger of leaving a simple dress. "Let's not worry about it now. I doubt that they will pull a connection from that."

I roll over onto my side, placing my head on my hands. Navarre seemed smart. *Did he really know that I wasn't the person he was looking for?*

***

The sun rises, beginning a new day. I get up, changing into a new set of clothes. I brush my hair out, braiding it to the side. "Luthias!" I call from another room. "It's time to get up."

"I am up." He pokes his head through the doorway.

We walk down to the throne room, passing many different guests. Azariah and Faolan speak in angered voices and I stop in the doorway, pulling Luthias away with me.

"Laerune Aduial." Azariah calls back to me.

"Yes?" I cringe.

"Why are you leaving?"

"I didn't want to bother you. I know how important your council meetings are."

"That hasn't stopped you before."

I don't know how many meetings I have snuck into or interrupted. I just know there has been a lot of them. I have always been rebellious that way, especially when I was little. "Now, what did you want to tell me?"

"Oh, umm, nothing. I just wanted to say hello."

She looks at me suspiciously. And she had every right to. I have been debating on whether or not I should tell her about my visions. They have been appearing more often. And each one is more frightening than the last. I try to walk away, but Azariah places a hand on my shoulder.

"What is it?"

"I...I don't want to talk about it...yet." I nervously speak.

She bows her head and returns to her chair. "Luthias." She calls to him. "May I speak to you alone?" He smiles and steps closer to her.

I disappear from the room, practically running through the halls. I don't know why I cannot speak about my problems. It has gotten to the point where I can't even tell Luthias some things. I fumble for the key, fetching it out of my pocket and sliding it into the lock.

The door swings open and I run in, slamming the door behind me. I lay onto the bed, my tears soaking the blue velvet blanket. Why can't these visions go away? My father always used to say it was a gift, but it is truly a curse. I would rather have my future unknown to me then to be told out in a series of nightmares.

I stand up, grabbing the side of the bookshelf for support. I pull off a book and it falls to the ground. I flip through the book, stopping at a page with paper sticking out. I slide it out of the book. My father's name is etched on the top and a lady's handwriting is scribbled across the aged paper.

My dear Elender,

Do not worry, this is a letter of good news, not bad. I have seen our daughter, our fourth child. My mother has been very kind and has given me a glimpse of her future. She will fall in love with a very handsome Elf. He is of tall stature and raven hair. I have seen him as a caring and kind young man, perfectly fit for our unborn child. He will protect our petite golden child.

And our daughter, oh her golden hair. Her eyes shine bright with interest and curiosity. Yet there is a trick in our unborn daughter. She will be a prophecy. A very important one. You have read this prophecy before, many times actually. Go back and read The Greatness and Darkness of the First Age and the Beginnings. *You will understand soon.*

We will talk more when I return. Elbonare is watching and there is much to be told personally, not in a letter. I love you my dear and promise me to not worry.

Why was this letter never sent nor given? It was well written before my birth date. And my mother knew of Avon. *He was destined to marry me?* And in my mother's letter she talked about me as if I was weak and needed protecting.

"Our petite golden child, hmph." I cross my arms. "If mother could see me now. Fighting in wars and making my way to be a queen. And marrying who I truly love." I smile to myself, crumpling the letter in my fist. I throw it across the room.

I stand up, locking up the room and walking down the stairs in search of Luthias.

I climb up the branches of a tree and I search down the path. I see him, walking with his bow strapped across his shoulder, he seems ready to go somewhere. As he walks under the tree, I lock my legs around the branch, swinging upside down in front of him. My hair dangles in his face and he parts it, revealing his gleaming smile.

"Where have you been?' I swing down from the tree.

"Looking for you." He chuckles.

"Oh, I was in my mother's room."

"Find anything interesting today?"

"No." I lie. I search his eyes for some sort of answers. "You're leaving?" I say shocked.

He nods, taking my hand. “Azariah wishes for me to retrieve something from Lithien.”

“And that is?”

“I can’t tell you.”

I pause in the pathway of trees. “When will you return?”

“I will be back by your birthday. Faolan set the feast date for two weeks and your birthday is the day before.”

“Be safe.” He lets go of my hands, leaving me alone. I watch as he walks away, disappearing into the forest. “Goodbye.” I whisper to myself.

***

I decide to return to my mother’s room, a broom in my hand as I walk up the many stairs. I run into a small figure and I look up to the sweet eyes of Elora. “Hello Elora, it is nice to see you.”

“It is nice to see you as well.” She looks at the broom in my hand. “What is the broom for?”

“I am cleaning my mother’s old room.”

“Can I come with?” Without an answer she leads me up the stairs, knowing exactly where I am going. She waits as I unlock the door. Books fall off of the bookshelf unexpectedly and Elora jumps. “How do you spend time in here alone? I rather be cursed.”

She picks up the fallen books, dusting them off with her apron. I pick up the leaves, tossing them out the window. I watch as they float down, flying in the wind. I move the paper and books off of the table, wiping down the table with a cloth. Elora pulls books of off the dusty shelf, she stacks them on the floor, dusting each one with her blue skirt.

She squeals as she steps back, knocking over a pile of books she had stacked earlier. I bend down to help her restack them, setting four similar books together. They shine, a blue light filling the room. The four books come together as one, an elaborate Elven symbol twists around the cover and metal vines lock it shut.

Elora looks at me shocked. “What just happened?” She asks, staring back at the book.

“I think I just discovered something my mother didn’t want anyone to know.” I pick the book up carefully, placing it under my arm. “Will you come with me to find my father?” I run down the stairs, not bothering to check to see if Elora is behind me. I bump into Linder and he holds my shoulders.

“Where are you going in such a rush?”

“I need to find my father.”

“He is in a meeting.”

“Where is it being held at?”

“Near the river, but they need not be disturbed.”

He is calling after me as I run down the path to the lake. This book seemed important, too important to wait. Something took over me, causing me to rush. A large pavilion stands tall near the river and I see my father. I barge in, the Elves stare at me, shocked by my sudden appearance. My father, Sentier, and my grandparents weren't the only ones there. Many Elves sat in chairs and some paced back and forth.

My father shuts his eyes in embarrassment. “Laerune how many times have I told you that if you are not invited, then you do not come? I would've thought you had learned your lesson by now.”

“Father it is very important.” I set the book down on the table and the Elves step back in fright.

“Where did you get this?” An unknown Elf turns to me.

“I...I found it.”

“You just found it?”

“Well, yes. But, what is it?” I ask the Elf with the caramel brown hair. He moves closer to the book that I placed on the silver table. He carefully reaches out for it, but then quickly decided against it. “Will anyone answer my questions?”

“We truly don’t know what this is, but the energy that comes off of it...it’s not good.”

“Well if you can’t tell me anything else, then I will take the book and leave.”

I pick the book up, but it sends pain through my body. I try to ignore it as I walk out of the pavilion. I hold the book close to my chest and I try to keep myself standing straight. I decide to open the book, the dark language was scribbled onto the paper. It was written in a spell or prophecy form.

I don’t wander far before the pain shot through my body again. This time was worse, much worse. It blurred my vision and I could feel blood drip down my nose. I wipe it away as it is followed by blood running down my neck. The warm liquid drips down from my ears and I drop the book. It lands onto the ground with a thud. I fall to my knees and then onto my side.

Elora calls my name, sitting next to me. She picks my head up, setting it in her lap. "LaRue? Look at me LaRue." She tries to get a response from me, but I can't seem to answer. Everything goes black from there and I suddenly wish that Luthias was by my side. I cry out as another rush of pain shocks through me, leaving me paralyzed and not even able to open my eyes.

Chapter 25

My thoughts wander endlessly, walking through never ending halls and memories. My thoughts are drawn to Ambrose. I walk around a pillar holding up one of the many walls in Ambrose. I find a younger version of myself, speaking in an angered tone to my father.

"Father!" The younger version of me whines. "Please let me go."

My father takes his finger and begins to try to wipe dirt off of my face.

"Look at yourself. You can't even keep clean Laerune Aduial. Why should I let you go?"

"I want to go somewhere new father! Please. I haven't been to Lithien before. I know you are going with that great King. Can I please, please come with?"

"And what would a little girl like you do with Kings." My father laughs at younger me.

Little me follows after him, determined to make my father change his mind. "I will do great things with Kings one day Father. Just you wait and see." Little me crosses her arms and fixes her hair and dress before my father turns around.

"For the last time Laerune. No." He leaves the hall, leaving me behind to mumble about all the things I don't get to do. I take a step forward already knowing what little me will do. She rushes angrily into the forest, her little legs carrying her far. Her golden, curly hair blows behind her as she searches her way through the tall Oak trees.

Little me looks back, as if she knows that I am watching her. Judging her. I want to call out to stop her, but my voice is useless in memories. She trips, cutting her hand on the edge of a glass window on a pile of ruins.

A horse snorts, its hooves slowing to a stop. Blood covers the younger version of me and she begins to cry. Panicking because she has never seen her own blood until that very moment.

"What is your name?"

Little me looks up, trying to back away as she sees the crown upon the Elve's head. His crown matched the summer season and it was adorned with little, red flowers. He was tall and looked strong-willed. His face was serious and intimidating. It was a normal look to Sentier, but I saw kindness in his eyes. And so, little me stood to her feet, clutching her hands.

She stands tall and proud, remembering what she said to her father. *I will do great things with Kings one day.*

"I am Laerune Aduial, daughter of Elender and Aveneth, Lady of Ambrose." She bows.

"I am impressed by such a young lady. So many titles." He chuckles. "I am King Sentier, son of Emisen and Gracen." He places his hand over his heart, bowing his head. "Let me help you."

He grabs the back of younger me's dress and without effort places me in front of him upon his horse. He searches through his saddle bag, finding a bandage that he wraps around her hand. Little me looks next to Sentier. Two young boys on white mares smile at me.

The youngest who looks closer to my age smiles the brightest. His reddish hair is halfway pulled back in a braid and he wears a circlet that looked to be made out of tree branches. His eyes are a piercing blue.

I quickly turned away, not wanting him to know I was staring at him. My cheeks burned with a crimson color from embarrassment. "I'll take you back home, Lady of Ambrose."

"Thank you, King Sentier."

He chuckles and then grabs the reigns of his golden mare. I follow next to his side wanting to reach out and touch younger me and tell her that she had just met the love of her life.

"How does it feel to ride upon a King's mare?" Sentier questions little me.

"It is a great honor, your majesty."

His laugh is deep. "Such politeness. My sons should learn from you!" He places the reigns in my hands and lets younger me steer. I look up, smiling at how little and proud I was to be sitting with a King.

Sentier reaches the courtyard and he dismounts his mare, his cloak flowing over his shoulder. He picks little me up, setting me down softly upon the ground. He takes my hand, bringing it to his lips.

"It is an honor to meet you Lady Laerune Aduial of Ambrose."

"And you, King Sentier of Lithien." She curtseys.

Younger me walks towards me as if knowing that I am there. I place a hand on her shoulder as her blue, bright eyes meet with Luthias'. Luthias swings his leg over his mare and stands tall with his brother Luvon at his side. The both bow, placing their hands over their hearts.

"These are my sons." Sentier turns towards them. "Luvon and Luthias."

They both wear a light, shiny, blue cloak, the color of Lithien. Their tunics are laced with silver and glistening jewels clasp their cloaks together.

I turn around to find my father rushing towards little me and his guest. Elender bows. "I see that you have met my daughter."

"I did not know that you had a second daughter Elender. You hardly send me letters anymore."

"We will speak of that soon." Elender looks down at little me. "Why don't you show Luvon and Luthias to their rooms?"

"Yes, father." I bow my head and he smiles, winking.

Little LaRue grins at the young Elves behind her. I place my hand on the back of Luthias, making him walk forward, knowing that he had been very nervous and shy. His mother was still alive back then and life was at its best for them.

Elender had sent for Sentier and his sons to see if they would be a good match for my sister and me.

"So Laerune?" Luvon asks. "What do you do around here for fun?" Luvon was a teen during this memory. A sly, curious Elf, who was the perfect example of a ladies man.

"Well, I can't do much. My father is very, very protective and really cares about my studies. But, I like to sneak out and explore the woods."

"You sneak out LaRue? Wouldn't you get in trouble for that?" Luthias seems shocked.

"LaRue?" Little me questions.

"I am sorry." Luthias lowers his head. "I didn't mean to call you that."

Little Laerune turns around and smiles. "I like it. I like it a lot."

Luthias steps forward. "You don't mind? I thought it sounded nice." His face goes red. "I like Laerune, but LaRue fits too. I am not trying to change your name-"

"Don't ramble little brother." Luvon pushes Luthias' shoulder.

I open the door to a room in the guest hall, showing them in. Servants had already brought their trunks in, setting them near each bed. Luthias pulls a sword from his trunk.

"You sword fight?" Luthias nods his head as I speak. "Can you teach me?"

My mind suddenly goes dark, the memories fading away into nothing. A black hole, filled with light. A sight that confuses my eyes and my brain.

My mare trotted through the forest, the land changing every mile I hit. My mind wanders to LaRue, wondering how she is doing. My mind often wanders to her and her bright, beautiful eyes. I could stare at them for eternity.

Every day I had to remind myself that she is actually my wife and that she would be mine forever if the Gods allowed it. And these past weeks I have been determined to find her the greatest gift. Azariel had given me ideas, so that was very helpful. *But, what do you get for someone who is over one hundred years old?*

Lithien is practically empty, only a few Elves wandering the halls, mostly guards keeping our kingdom protected. I enter the jewel room, the gold and silver shining like the sun and the moon. I search through them, finding the one that Azariel was speaking of. I hold it to the flame, admiring how it reflected the light.

I shove it into my bag, slinging it over my shoulder as I walk back outside and to my horse. I set back out onto the path back to Lindalin, but as I soon find out, Orcs block my path. I dare not fight them alone, so I turn back, taking the long way through Nolan's borders in his land of Ebin.

***

I have almost passed Nolan's borders when a scout spots me. I sigh, pulling out my daggers. The scout had ran away, most likely to send a warning to his king.

Just as I had thought, the horn echoed through the field as Nolan's guards trekked over the hill. More and more followed what I thought was the last troop. Nolan did not want to lose another fight.

"I meant no harm. I was only passing through."

"I have heard that excuse before." Nolan laughs, his dark armor glistening in the sun. "But I think that today will end just a bit different. At least I don't have to clean your blood off of my floor."

His men laugh along with him and he nods at one of his biggest guards. The mace in his hand waits to taste victory and I swing my daggers in my hand, waiting for him to make the first move.

Pain shoots through my chest and I touch the warm amber jewel around my neck. The large guard swings his mace, nearly knocking off my head. "Dammit LaRue! You have to feel pain at this exact moment." I growl. The pain shoots through me again, this time much worse. Blood drips from my nose and the guard knocks me over.

He places one foot onto my arm and the other on my ribs. They slowly crack from the weight and I feel my rib snap along with the bone in my arm. I try to bite back the pain, but the scream builds up in my throat, threatening to break free.

An arrow shoots above my head, landing into the chest of the large guard. His body lands on top of me and I try to push it away. Every breath is another shot of pain. Blood continues to drip down my nose and then starts in my ears. *What kind of trouble have you gotten yourself into LaRue?*

"Too much." I can almost imagine her answer back.

I couldn't get up, the pain ran through my body with every move I make. I forced myself to turn my head, searching for who had shot the arrow. I see a long, brown bow fire another arrow through the woods. Her red hair peeked out through the lush greenness. A spear was thrown from beside Chalsarda and they revealed themselves from their hiding spot.

The arrows continued to be fired at Nolan's guards. Nolan and his black armor disappeared from the fight. *Coward.* I am thankful that Amar and Chalsarda had followed me. The last arrow is shot and the guard drops to the ground with a thud. Blood drips from Amar's nose and he wipes it away with an already blood covered hand. Chalsarda on the other hand, had spread it across her face when she wiped it with the back of her hand.

Amar picks me up, setting me up onto his horse. "What happened?" He yells. "I have never seen you so weak." I shoot an angered glance at him and he calms down. "Why did we all just succumb to pain? There was no reason to feel it."

"Don't you remember? By Electa's sake! You took that oath just as I did! We will feel her pain as she will feel ours!"

Chalsarda cursed. "We left her in Lindalin. We're not supposed to leave her side. We promised to protect her. What if something happened?"

"Can we stop talking and get back." I growl.

"You know it may take a while to get back. Two days at the least. Orcs are roaming the woods and we are in no shape to fight. Especially you."

We have to take different paths, and some end up as dead ends as we searched for our way to Lindalin. "I think we are lost." Amar growls at Chalsarda.

"I know where we are going." Chalsarda snarls back.

"We just need to turn right." I tell them. "We would've been down the normal path if you listened to me an hour ago. I may be broken, but my mind isn't."

We continue down the treed path, listening for unwelcome creatures. We stop, the horses pin down their ears, knowing what roams the woods. The Dark language of the Orcs screech through the woods. I lift up my hand weakly, motioning to turn around.

Chalsarda's horse bolts, leaving Amar and I alone in the woods. The Orcs stomp through the woods, blood covered daggers in their hands. *Could this day get any worse?*

"Ah, look what we found here. Elven scum." He spits.

"Leave and your lives will be spared," I say, trying to scare them off.

"We just want information. And if you don't give us what we want, we know how easy it will be to defeat you both. We all watched what happened between you and the men." The Orc smiles.

I swing my leg around the horse, stepping off the side. As my feet hit the ground, the impact rings through my ribs and my arm. "Luthias what are you doing?" Amar questions angrily. He jumps down from his horse, pulling out his sword. I reach for my dagger, unsheathing it from my quiver.

With one hit from the Orc, I fall. If I was to die, I would at least try to fight. The Orc grabs my face, lifting it up to meet his. Amar had already tried to interfere, but failed. The Orcs held his hands behind his back.

"Now, tell me where to find the Elven girl."

"There is many Elven girls." I smirk.

"I am talking about the Prophecy. They call her the Pathway, Princess of the stars and sun."

I tilt my head in his hand. "How do you know this?" An Orc pulls out a paper, blood is splattered across the yellowed pages.

"We read it."

"You can't even read!" Amar insults them. The Orc holding him covers his face with his large grey hand.

"Tell me where she is."

"Describe her to me. Refresh my memory."

"Just read it for yourself." He growls. The paper is put in front of me and I skim through it, already knowing it by heart.

"Hmm, I don't think you would want her to banish evil and bring back the light, do you?"

I look to my right, a flash of red hair rushes through the forest. As I turn my head back to the Orc, I get a blow to the jaw. Blood drips from my mouth and I smile. "How positive are you that you will gain a victory today?"

"I am more than positive."

"I think you may have to rethink that." Chalsarda shoots an arrow into the Orc and I pick up my dagger, attempting to fight. I am not much help to them, but right now every ounce of energy counts at this moment. Amar kicks the Orc that is holding him and I swing my leg around, knocking over another Orc. I shove my dagger into him and he twitches on the forest floor.

As the last of the Orcs are killed, Amar helps me back onto my horse. The pain is more intense and through the power of the oath, they are starting to feel it. "By Electa's sake. How much pain are you in?"

"A lot more than you."

"And everyone that took the oath can feel that?"

"Yes, even LaRue."

"That sounds more like a curse to me." Amar replies, pulling his hood up and over his face. He jumps back onto his own horse. "We should get going, the sun is setting."

Chalsarda doesn't move. "We should rest here tonight. I don't want to be searching through the woods for another enemy."

"But-" I whine.

"Chalsarda is right. LaRue will be fine, right now we need to be focusing on you."

"Fine, then help me off my horse." Amar helps me walk over to a large pine tree, its branches will easily conceal us for the night. Chalsarda lies down my cloak and I sit down. They tie up the horses right next to us. "Chalsarda, could you go into my saddle bag and grab the extra cloak?"

She pulls it out, examining it. "This looks a little small for you...and it's purple?" She throws it at me.

"It's LaRue's."

"You miss her, don't you?"

"I am worried about her. The pain I felt this morning was like nothing else I have ever experienced."

She sits down next to me. "I can't tell you that she will be okay, but I truly hope that she is. She has her brother's to keep her safe right now."

LaRue's sweet smell radiated off of her cloak, it is a mix of lavender and parchment paper. There is a mix of apples and the fresh smell of the forest. Chalsarda pats my shoulder and then lies down next to me. I can see Amar pace back and forth, a bow in his hand ready to aim at any enemy that decides to enter the glade. I lay down, my ribs sighing in relief as I finally rest.

The sun rose yellow over the trees, the dead bodies of the Orcs we killed yesterday are scattered across the forest floor. Chalsarda trips over an Orc and Amar laughs, helping her up. I stand up, soreness taking over my body.

"We need to get him back soon Chalsarda." I can hear them speak to each other. "If it heals wrong, he might never be able to move right again."

"You know I can hear you!" I scowl. I walk over to my horse, trying to get on by myself. Amar rushes over, lifting me up onto the saddle. "Can we get going now?"

They mount their horses and I ride in front of them. I make sure that I am the one to tell them the directions. I follow down the path, the familiar forest of Lindalin getting closer. I can soon see the blue lights hanging in the trees and Elves welcome us back, they then help me to the healers. I grab onto a young Elf's shoulder, as he helps me walk to the healers.

Chapter 26

I open one eye, expecting to see Luthias beside me, but Eldrin takes his place. He holds my hand and I open my other eye, getting a full look at him. I watch as he cries, not noticing that I have woken up.

"You better not be crying over me."

He looks up shocked, quickly wrapping his hands around me. He continues to cry as I wrap my arms around him. His smile seems to brighten up the room and he looks at a strand of my hair.

"It's back to its golden color!" He exclaims.

"It changed?"

"Yes, it was silver, slowly turning into white. We were afraid you were never going to wake up."

"Where's the book?" I ponder. It was Navain's book and he did not like that I had it. He still wants to see how much pain I can go through and I have accepted my suspicions on who he is. The cloaked man in the Orc's dungeons is Navain, there is no denying that. It has seemed that he has been following me around my whole life, but now he is strong enough to hurt me.

"I think Elora has it."

"Can she bring it to me?"

"I think it should be locked away LaRue. It holds so much dark power and we don't want you to get hurt again. I didn't know what was happening when I felt your pain, all I know is that I don't want to feel it again."

It then hit me that Navain had said something about Luthias. Worry fills me, sending tears with it. "Where's Luthias? Is he okay? Did he return from Lithien?" I know what he is going to say even before he says it. I sit up, swinging my legs over the side of the bed to get up.

I feel wobbly and weak. It hurts to breath and pain flows through my arm. I attempt to walk towards the door, but Eldrin ends up holding me up. "Please. I need to find him."

"He will be found, but you can't do it yourself. You're not strong enough."

"Then at least let me get out of this room. I feel trapped."

He takes my hand, slowly helping me walk to the stairs. The steps would be the hardest part, with gravity wishing to pull me down.

"Just one step at a time LaRue."

"What? You expect me to take two?"

It seems like hours before we make it to the bottom of the stairs. I am out of breath and I sit down on the last step. Horses trot in and a body is limply sitting upon the horse in front of Amar. *He can't be dead. He can't be.* I try standing up, but I quickly fall.

"Eldrin help me." I plead.

I then see Luthias' head lift up, the light still in his eyes. I sigh, my shoulders being lifted of an unseen weight. Amar helps him from his horse and a healer takes him away.

"Give them time LaRue. Let them heal him without any distractions."

I would be a distraction, to both of them. I can't help but feel that all this is my fault. If the oath hadn't been taken then nobody would have felt the pain that I caused upon myself.

I let Eldrin give him twenty minutes before I get too anxious. I stand up a little too quickly and almost fall if it wasn't for my brother's strong arms keeping me up. We rush over to the healers and I practically barge into the room. Luthias is shirtless and a bandage is wrapped around his ribs and his arm.

He holds up his good hand, stopping me from serenading him with kisses and hugs. So I slowly walk to his bedside and sit down in the chair. He says nothing, does nothing but stare.

"What the hell did you do LaRue?" He is angry, *very angry.*

"What do you mean?"

"Why did you feel so much pain? I know you were sick. They told me you were unresponsive until today when I had come back."

You will be her court, her family and you will feel her pain, as she will feel yours. "I opened a book."

"You opened a book?"

"A dark magic book. It belonged to Navain."

He curses and then goes silent. “Are you okay?”

“I feel sick, but I’m fine. And you? I felt the pain that you had gone through, even though I wasn't conscious.”

“Just a few broken ribs, sternum, my arm will take a couple of days to heal.”

He bends across, hissing as he reaches for the table and for his bag. He pulls out my purple cloak and hands it out to me.

“I thought you would want this.”

“Thank you.”

He lies back down, resting his head against the pillow. He pats the side of the bed and I lift up the blanket, snuggling in next to him. “Orcs are still looking for you.” He runs his hand over my branded wrist.

I close my eyes. “Hello Laerune.” The cloaked man speaks. “You have spoken with my son recently, didn’t you.” He lifts a piece of my golden hair in his pale, scarred hand. “His servant treated you well in Nadien, didn’t he?”

“They were fair.”

“The servant. He likes you.” The cloaked man walks around me. “But his path isn't as long as yours.”

The servant, Navarre, stands before me. His hands are crossed and a dark cloak covers him. I move forward towards him, ripping the cloak from his face. “You know what to do Laerune.” The pale, cloaked figure tells me.

My hands grip his face and I stare into his orange and grey eyes. “I serve the Queen.” Navarre speaks proudly. “My death is a sacrifice to her.” I twist his neck, hearing it crack.

I jolt awake, Luthias sound asleep beside me, his hand placed over his bandaged chest. I run a finger over his cheek and I then rise from the bed, moving silently towards the door.

I grab the candle on the desk, placing my hand in front of it so the wind doesn't blow the flame out. A shiver goes up my spine as my feet touch the cold forest floor. My steps are slight, as if I am a spirit wandering the forest in white.

I pause, searching the trees, trying to find the stars and their bright, cold glow. None shine, only the light of the moon casting its rays upon the silver leaves of the trees. I drop to my knees, placing my hand over my heart and stomach.

"Electa hear my prayer. You have allowed me to see all that I will do wrong. But, I do not see how I turn out to be so cruel and morbid. Electa, please guide me along the right path to stop me from the nightmares you have allowed me to see. Please set me back on the path of the right direction. Anngel."

Chapter 27

It takes two days for Luthias to heal enough to actually walk, his Elven blood still strong with his healing abilities. The first thing he insists he does is to give his thanks to Amar and Chalsarda. Without them he wouldn't be alive.

They stand on the bridge, talking to each other about what seem to be something important.

"We both want to say thank you. I wouldn't be here without you. If there is anything I can do for both of you, yet my debt will never be repaired for the tasks you have done, please do say what it is."

"We are friends, we do not want payment, only thanks and friendship." Amar tells us.

Luthias nods his head. "Now, will you tell me of the great news?"

Chalsarda only holds up her hand, a shining ring around her finger. She winks, brushing her red hair to the side of her face. "Will you accept our invitation?"

"Of course we do."

We walk to the breakfast table and my court stands as I enter the room. I sit down, allowing them to sit as well. Eldrin sits next to Elora and I watch as he passes a plate of food in her direction. My whole court seems very happy today, but one does not. Avon is quiet, keeping to himself. He doesn't smile or lift his head to look at us.

"Avon are you okay?" I ask.

He finally looks up, tears falling from his face. He gets up, running from the table. My court becomes silent and they wait for me to do something. I stand up to go after him, but Tasar stops me.

"I will talk to him. Just sit."

Tasar leaves the table and I slowly sit down. The breakfast table changes and my eyes adjust to the new lighting.

The sun reflects across the ocean water, and the sails of a boat billow in the wind. I pick up my skirts, boarding onto the large ship. The Elven symbol for the sea is stitched onto the sails and I speak to the captain of the ship.

"Is the home of the Electa beautiful?"

"Don't be scared Lady LaRue. You will be welcomed and cared for."

I proceed to board onto the large ship, the wind blowing through my loose hair. The sun starts to set and I look overboard at the changing sea. My tears drip down my face, mixing with the salty ocean water.

I jump when the vision ends. My court watches as I look around at my surroundings. I can't go across the sea. I don't want to go to the Electa's Home.

"The Electa, it's calling me."

My father looks at me apologetically, his eyes filled with sorrow. "You must answer to their call Laerune. The Electa-"

"I know what the Electa wants!" I refuse to look at him. He walks over to me, lifting my head with his hands. Tears fall down my face and onto war scarred hands. "I spoke with the Gods last night. Asking them to set me back on the right path."

I leave in another direction away from my court. I plop myself onto the grassy ground, plucking at the soft green grass. Luthias finally comes and he sits down next to me. He does nothing, says nothing, but stare up at the birds that fly by.

"I don't want to go, but the things I have done will not help anyone in the future."

"Any choice you make LaRue, I will be next to you the whole time."

"But, I know you don't want to leave Laquilasse. And you don't have to, I am not going to allow you to give up everything just for me."

"But LaRue, you are everything."

A long silence comes over us and after a while I break it. "How's Avon?"

"I don't know. He and Tasar haven't returned." I don't answer. "You know he still loves you very much. He holds onto hope."

"A lost hope. He holds on just like everyone else. I'm hopeless."

"You are not hopeless."

He leans in to kiss me, but Linder clears his throat to make his presence known. "My Lady, my Lord. There will be a council with the High Elves of Laquilasse."

We follow Linder to the pavilion and I feel slightly embarrassed that my eyes are still red from crying. There are very few faces that are familiar. It seems that the Elves that traveled from the distant lands decided to stay. A very tall, skinny Elf with white hair introduces himself first.

"I am Katar, Lord of the Earth Elves."

"It is nice to meet you Katar. I am-"

He stops me from taking. "We all know who you are. You are the Prophecy."

"Does the Electa still hold to this Prophecy?"

"They are not the ones that created it."

"Then who did?" I raise my voice.

"Laerune!" My father reprimands me.

Azariel walks over to me. "My dear, calm down. We are having this council to decide what to do."

"I have decided my fate and it will stay that way."

"You can and will."

She's lying and I give her the look, telling her that I know. "I know that the Electa does not want me here, so I am returning to them. So, if you don't want me to leave you better put up a pretty good fight."

Katar walks into the middle of the council, beginning his speech. "She is our Pathway and we have spent years trying to figure out what she is a pathway to. Peace or destruction. For many years we had thought destruction but, hoped for peace. And now, finally we have found our peace."

"Peace? Do we really have peace?" Most of them nod their heads in agreement. "Then tell me why Luthias was attacked by Nolan's guards just four days ago. Tell me why we just fought in a war. Tell me why they took me to their dungeons and I was tortured by a cloaked figure. Tell me why Navain has returned."

They talk in hushed voices and Luthias looks at me, shaking his head. "Navain has not returned." Katar growls.

"You have not felt the pain from him then." I get closer to his face. "I think I would know that Navain has returned when I have felt his hands lock around my neck. Or that I have endured endless torture from him in the ruins of Nadian. Do not think that I am a liar!" I walk around the pavilion. "And I wouldn't act this way in front of your future queen." I smirk.

"Don't be so arrogant. You will never be queen." An unknown Elf growls. My court did not like his attitude and multiple swords are pointed at his face, Luthias' included. Also an array of daggers and blades were held up from Avon and Tasar.

"I will still be Queen to some."

"Laerune." Another Elf grabs my shoulder and I quickly pull away. "We want to keep you safe and your court. I agree that we do not have peace, but we do need to keep our Pathway safe. If you agree to another war on Nolan's kingdom, then that will be done. I agree that you should do as the Electa has told you. Do you accept your fate?"

"I accept it."

Luthias turns to me, tears falling from his eyes. "No LaRue, you can't. You can't leave!" Even after all the things he had said to me, he never thought I would actually go through with this. I ignore his pleas for me to change my mind.

"Nolan could have alliances with Navain and his band of Orcs. We should not hesitate to rage war against him. It will be one less problem to take care of."

The unknown Elf walks towards me. "We would want you to sail away before this battle begins."

"I will leave a day before."

"Then it has been decided. LaRue will sail away a day before we enter battle."

The council is dismissed and Luthias follows me from the pavilion. "I'm sorry Luthias. It's what the Electa wants me to do. If you saw the nightmares and visions I have had you would understand."

"Then after this war, I will sail to you. I can't imagine even a month without you."

"Nor can I."

Tears run down his face and I finally understand the worse pain he has felt. He is scared to lose the ones he loves. He had already lost his mother and brother and he had promised himself that he would not lose another.

"I love you Luthias." He holds me tight, refusing to let go. "I don't want to go. I don't. I want to run through the woods, see the stars. I want to climb to the tops of trees and watch the sun set. Not to be climbing the mountain peaks of the crashing waves. I want to dance in the rain and watch the snow fall like jewels from the sky. I still want to see the rolling hills and climb the tallest mountain to see if can reach up and touch the stars. But I don't want to harm anyone."

"LaRue, tomorrow is your birthday and we must forget about what is to come and celebrate your life. Promise me you will forget for at least one day."

"I promise."

Chapter 28

Luthias shakes me awake and I grab for my dagger that sits on the bedside table.

"What is it?" I worry. I then see that it is nothing. "What time is it?"

"A little before midnight."

"Midnight? Why so early?"

"Almost midnight means almost your birthday." He throws some clothes at me, making me change into something other than my nightgown. As I walk into the the other room to grab my cloak, I notice a piece of paper set on the table.

I pick it up and it reads: *Accept not the false teachings of the Electa, and enjoy another year closer to the Void.*

Typical. Navain has sent yet another promise of my death. I crumple up the paper, throwing it into the wastebasket. We walk down the halls, they are too silent and I am afraid that every noise I make will wake the Elves locked up in their rooms for the night.

Branches and leaves break under my feet and Luthias keeps his head facing forward. A blue glow shines from the forest, brighter than any of the lights hung up in the treetops. I feel almost entranced with it.

"You still haven't-" Luthias puts his hand over my mouth. He then looks behind a tree, his eyes searching for something.

I then see it. A group of Elves enter into the meadow, each one wrapped in a blue light. "This is for you. They have done it every year on this exact date."

"But, where are they from?"

"I do not know. I have never gotten close enough to find out."

I look back at the Elves, they have started to sing and dance. Their blue light gets brighter with every note they sing and every step they dance. One Elf stood outside of their circle, he seemed to be monitoring them all carefully. He holds a silver shield that seemed to mirror the silver stars perfectly. He grips a long spear in his other hand. He seems familiar.

"Who is that?" I ask Luthias.

"I do believe that is Tervaughn."

"I thought he died?"

"It did. Some residents of Lindalin say they have seen his shadow roaming around on this one night every year."

"But, why tonight?"

"I have thought about that for many years. But, the prophecy seems to hold some answers. Others want to help you Laerune even when their spirits can't fully appear." I look back at the Elves. "I discovered this when Tasar and I traveled to Lindalin many years ago. I was exploring the woods and it happened to be your birth date. I was curious so I kept on coming back, seeing if they would return that very night every year."

"Can I talk to them?" I ask, sneaking over to the next tree.

"I have always watched them from afar, but I do think it would be different if you conversed with them."

I make my way to the nearest tree bordering the meadow. I watch as a small Elf pulls at the hands of Tervaughn, trying to make him join her in a dance. He refuses, stiffening as I enter the glade. They all stop singing and dancing, their blue light slowly dimming. I back up a little, showing that I don't mean any harm.

"Hello Laerune Aduial." The small girl cheerfully speaks. "You have finally come! We have waited years for you to one day notice us and join us for a dance." She laughs jokingly. She notices my fright and takes my hands in hers. "Don't be scared, I was only joking. But, we have waited years for you."

Her voice is soothing, like a river rushing against rocks. She pulls on my hands, leading me towards the middle of the circle. Her white curls bounce as she walks and her violet eyes shine just as bright as the light that is wrapped around her.

"I am Tolendeil, daughter of, well, I don't really know. Tervaughn I guess." She giggles.

I look back at Luthias as she pulls me closer to the middle of the clearing. Tolendeil also looks back at us.

"Oh, Luthias! You are a very good Elf. You treat our Princess of the Stars and Sun very well."

He laughs, he has done too much for me and I can never repay him for the happiness he has given me. "I think she takes care of me more."

Tervaughn then clears his throat, signaling Tolendeil to let go of my hand. His presence sends shivers down my spine. When I was little I had sung many songs about him. He was my father's best friend and I heard much about him because of it.

"How are you still alive?"

"I am not. My spirit stays tied to this land through two things. You and my adopted daughter. The Electa said that I could stay until the two of you have found what you are looking for, or in your case LaRue, the information you have needed for many years."

"And that is?"

"You must make your own decisions Aduial. What you do with this information is mainly up to you. Laquilasse is in great danger. Navain has returned and is searching the land for what was taken from him."

"The Saryniti." Luthias and I both whisper, too scared to say it too loudly.

"Yes, he is looking for them and he won't stop until they are found. He wants you to help him find them."

"Why can't he do it himself? Or his Orc minions?"

"He is not strong enough. You saw his form in the Dungeons of Nadien. He is wrapped in darkness to make himself stronger, but for now he cannot move far without losing his strength. He has escaped the Void and power is slowly returning to him."

"But why does he want me to find the Saryniti?"

"You can freely touch them where he cannot."

"Be he touched them for many years. Why can't he touch them now?"

"He became accustomed to it in the First Age. Now that he has returned to Laquilasse he has...restarted, you could say. He does not know where to look first for they are spread out across our world, fathoms apart." Tervaughn looks away. "If someone unworthy of the jewels touches them, their hands will be burned and not even the greatest Elven healers will be able to fix it."

"You can't leave Laquilasse!" Tolendiel voices her opinion.

"Tolendiel that is her decision." She sits down on the ground, folding her arms around her chest like a pouting child. "Two fates come from two paths. I think you know that very well Laerune."

I nod my head. "I do very much. It can change your whole life." Tolendiel looks to Tervaughn in yearning. Her violet eyes full of wanting.

The Elves that were singing and dancing before continue, their music upbeat and lively. Tolendiel grabs my hands, spinning me around until I seem enveloped in their blue light. She pushes me to Luthias and he spins me in a circle. Our dances seemed to be our own, coming up with each step together. Our minds connected to be one for each dance.

The music only slowed when a ray of sun shined through the trees. The Elves scampered off into the woods like deer. They were like forest animals changed into Elves for one night and then suddenly, as the sun's first light shines through the trees, they turn back into the quick forest creatures. Tervaughn disappeared with them, but Tolendiel stayed.

"Do you think I can come with?" She asks us, a small glimmer shines in the corner of her eye.

"Of course." I smile.

As we walked back to Lindalin, Tolendiel skips the whole way like a child. She spins and dances across the path, her head tilted up at the bright blue sky and the canopy of trees above her.

Luthias takes my hand, rubbing his thumb across my knuckles. "Happy birthday LaRue." I lean my head against his strong shoulder. His blue eyes shine bright like jewels, as if they were replaced with them.

"Can I meet your friends? I have never had friends. How should I act around them?"

"Just act like yourself." I grin. "I am going to change into something a little more festive. Do you want to come with me Tolendiel? I could find you something new to wear."

He eyes again brighten up. "You could do that for me?" She messed with the hem of her tattered skirt.

"I could easily do that."

Even though she is much, much older than me, she only seems like a child. Innocent from the ruin of evil and I do think Tervaughn has tried very hard for it to stay that way.

"I am going to go see my father." Luthias says. "There is a few things I have to do before breakfast."

I smile as he walks away, Tolendiel waits for me as I turn towards the steps. She seems to ask me another question with every step we take. A lot of them involved Luthias.

I open the door and Tolendiel gasps. "Is this your room?"

"It is only my guest room. I live in Lithien." A blue dress lays on my bed and a small piece of paper lies on top of it.

It reads: *I have only seen one person wear this and I hope I can see another. –Sentier*

The dress is stitched with gold and blue. Elk dot the bottom of the skirt and the sleeves are like gloves on my arms. The silk slips through my hands easily. I move towards my closet, trying to find something for Tolendeil, other than her tattered white skirt, which is now covered in dirt.

I find a plain silver one that matches her white hair perfectly. I lay it in her arms and she carefully carries it to the bathroom to get changed. I have to take a moment to stare at the blue dress that Sentier had given to me. It matches the gown that Luthias' mother is dressed in the art hall.

I slip the dress over my head, the sleeves carefully forming around my hand. I stand in front of the mirror, admiring how the blue fabric makes my eyes brighter. Tolendeil spins out of the room, her eyes shining like grey mist. She then gasps, reaching her hands out as if she wanted to touch something beautiful, but could not.

"Your beauty shines within, but also on the outside LaRue."

"Thank you." I turn back to the mirror, taking one more glance at myself.

We walk down the stairs to the dining room. The laughter and smiles makes the room bright with happiness. They all stop talking to see that I have entered the room. Luthias looks shocked, but then smiles.

"Happy Birthday LaRue." They all cheer.

Birthdays were not common, but when others know that someone keeps track of the years, they are more than happy to celebrate a birthday.

I sit down next to Luthias and he pushes my chair in. Tolendeil sits down shyly at the end of the table, her silver eyes are filled with worry. My court smiles at her, casting her frown away. "I am Tolendeil, daughter of Tervaughn." She speaks proudly. They all welcome her, each introducing themselves.

Across from me sits Avon and I am glad to see him today. Yesterday he had disappeared from the table and Tasar went to find him. He looks much happier today. Avon's blue eyes shine in the morning light. He lifts up his fork filled with a mixture of food, he stares at me as he lifts it up to his mouth. He misses and it drops onto his cloak. I giggle as his face turns a beet red color.

"Thank you Sentier, for allowing me to wear this dress."

"I must say it does look lovely on you. As you might have figured out it was my wife's. I have waited for the next heiress of Lithien to wear it for it has been passed down for many generations."

I bow my head, accepting his great gift. It must have been hard for him at first to give up something like that. He rarely pulled out things of his wife's. He kept them under lock and key for many years.

***

After breakfast we meet up under the pavilion. The pavilion is decorated with yellow and blue flowers that twist around the latticework of the walls. We sit in a circle and each guest has a different sized package wrapped up in silver paper in their laps.

I have never had a birthday like this. In Ambrose, there was usually a dinner and Eryn would give me a small gift, but nothing like this. This was nice, but I truly miss the family dinner, but I guess this is my family now.

Amar and Chalsarda hand me their package first. I carefully unfold the paper, scared to break the beautiful wrappings. A knife made out of three different colored metals lie in the silver packaging.

"We took Vestan's, Silvyr's, and Caldon's knives and forged them into one," Amar says.

"We thought it would be a good way to remember them," Chalsarda adds.

"Thank you so much. It means a lot to me."

The knife shines in the sun and I set it next to my chair. The blade is sharp and will surely make a mark into an enemy.

The next gift is from Tasar and he doesn't even bother to wrap it. He tosses it in my direction. The small vial is filled with bright green leaves. Athelas leaves are used in many Elven healing tasks.

"I thought you might need this the next time you stab yourself." He jokes.

I thank him with a small giggle. He has always been the one to make jokes, it's living with the Dwarves for many years that has made him different. Linder hands me his gift politely. I brush my hand against the package, trying to feel what it is.

"Are you really adding another book to my collection?" I laugh.

"Not quite."

I unwrap it, the cover of the book is wrapped in a blue velvet sheath and I open it up to see the title. There is nothing there, it's blank. I look up to him in questioning.

"I think it is time to write your own story."

"What would I write about?"

"Maybe your life?" He smiles.

"Hmm, what would the title be?" I ponder for a moment. "The Tales of LaRue." The words roll off of my tongue like they have been waiting to be said for years. My family smiles at me and I think about how the book would start.

Members of my other courts give me small gifts like jewelry and books. Each gift is something special and different. My father smiles when it is his turn to give me my gift. Instead of the silver wrappings, this one is covered in gold. I open the box that sits in my lap.

The inside is velvet and a silver and gold circlet lies inside. The crown is covered in little jeweled flowers and every direction you turn the crown, it shines a different color. “Thank you father.”

“You know a queen always needs a crown.”

“I am not queen yet.”

“In our eyes you are.”

Even if I was sailing across the sea I guess I was still a queen in their eyes. I am still bonded to them through the oath. *The oath?* How would this oath still work when I was gone, away from all of them? I push the thought to the back of my mind. Luthias told me not to worry today.

There is four guests missing and I noticed that during breakfast. My brothers and sister, along with Elora, had gone to Everford. It seemed important and they said that they would not return until we had arrived back in Lithien.

Avon reaches over to me, setting a silver box in my hand. I open up the jeweled box and a folded up paper lies inside. It is the title sheet of the book Gracen. It was my favorite to read when I was younger, but I had lost it.

“It’s all that is left. But, I figured it’s something.”

“Thank you Avon.”

The last gift left is from Luthias. And he smiles suspiciously. He hands me a new sheath of arrows, something that I wanted, but never really said that I needed it.
“I...umm...stepped on one of your old ones before we left to Lindalin.” He confesses.

“So that’s why there was one missing.”

He blushes and then reaches behind his chair for his second gift. He opens up a box to me, the jewelry shines bright, almost blinding. I look up to him, the smile on his face is contagious.

“It can’t be.” I whisper.

“Elbonare’s Prize, created by the Dwarves and given to the Elves as a peace offering. But, war has raged and the necklace was fought over and then lost. But, my ancestors had found it and kept it hidden for many years, locked away in the darkness. I want it to shine again. And upon the right owner.”

Luthias places it around me, the jewels glowing around my neck.

“I love you.”

"I love you too LaRue."

His eyes shine with accomplishment. He had picked an amazing gift and all by himself. He usually had help from others, but I just knew that he had this planned all along.

"Luthias, Laerune." My grandmother speaks. "Would you come with me please?"

I thank my court for the amazing gifts and then Luthias and I turn to follow Azariel. She is quiet as we walk down stone stairs and into a courtyard. A pool stands in the middle, its base carved with leaves and vines.

"This is my gift to the both of you."

She motions for me to go first with Luthias standing next to me. I cautiously walk up to it. I have heard about what this mirror may show. The past, present, or future. I did not want to see the future. I have had enough of that in my visions and nightmares.

I look over into the water, my hands gripping the side on its base. I look up at Azariel quickly and then back down the the pool. The water ripples, its image changing. I let out a sigh of relief as it shows the past. The pool forms into the garden in Ambrose.

I laugh at Luthias. "I would never in my long life learn how to play the harp." He helps me up, leading me to the gardens. My father said that my mother had loved the gardens in Ambrose the best. And ever since, he always kept them clean and clipped, down to the smallest Evening Primrose. I watch Luthias admire the Foxglove and the Tulips and I laugh.

"Why are you laughing?" He whines.

"Because, even though you are a male, you still admire the beauty of flowers. And I love that."

"I am going to take that as a compliment." He fingers with a Snapdragon. "What is your favorite flower?"

"Daffodils." I say, moving to the yellow and orange flowers. "What is yours?"

"Blue Bells."

He plucks one from the bush in which they grew. He hands it to me and I hand him a Daffodil. "See, one for each of us."

"You know I plan to keep this forever."
"As do I."

The next image turns into the archery range, the wildflowers growing behind it and the trees standing tall.

When we get to the archery range other Elves turn to look at us. Their eyes have a judgmental glare to them and I start to back away. My breathing becomes uneven, but a strong hand on my shoulder calms me down.

"It's all right. Don't worry about them." Luthias tells me.

I nod my head and he hands me the bow. I strap the quiver of arrows across my back. I look down at the target, the Elves still staring at me. My hands shake as I begin to attempt to pull back the bow. I pull it halfway, before my arms give up, releasing the arrow. The golden arrow lands with a thud in the dirt and the younger Elves try to hide their snickered laughs. Luthias turns to them, glaring. I notice Avon near the end of the targets with his daggers. He watches carefully as I again knock in another arrow. I start to pull the bow back, my arms starting to shake about a quarter of the way there.

"Pull it back!" A familiar voice growls. I look back at Dehlin, who has been my trainer over the past years. "I said pull it back." I have never seen him angry like this. "Pull it back or everyone is going to laugh at you. Do you want that?"

I look back, breathing in deeply. Pull it back LaRue, pull it back. *My arms burn by the time I get it pulled halfway back.* Pull it! *With the last of my energy, I pull it back, the bow creaking in the process.* Now hold it. *I aim down the target, releasing the arrow. My cheek burns from the arrow sliding against it and I can feel the slightest trickle of blood roll down my cheek.*

I follow through, looking at the target. The Elves stand astonished, they didn't think I could do it. But three smiled at me. Luthias, Dehlin, and Avon. I look back at the target, the arrow protruding from directly the center of the target. You did it and you made them proud. *Made them proud? I do not think the voice in my head meant Luthias and Dehlin.* No, the Electa. *The voice in my head answered back.*

The Electa are the Gods and Goddesses that watch over our lands and people. Is this part of the Pathway nonsense that my father was talking about? It is no nonsense. It is a great honor being the gift from the Electa. *I ignore it,, thinking that it is just my mind making up thoughts.*

"I think that's enough for one day." Dehlin leads me away from the crowd of Elves that stare at me and my golden arrow.

He wipes the blood from my cheek with a smile. "Your father is going to be so proud."

The images end and I look up to my grandmother, trying to gather the emotion that they felt with those two different images. One showed me as just a girl admiring flowers with a boy and the other showed me how strong I could be at a time of weakness. And together, those two personalities made me.

"I hope this is good for both of you. Answers will come when they choose to." Azariel disappears and I take Luthias' hand. We walk to the lake, dangling our legs off the side of the bridge.

"How is your birthday going?" He asks.

"It is amazing. Thank you Luthias."

"Hmm, over 100 years old. That's a long time to know somebody."

"But a short time to fall in love."

Chapter 29

We talk most of the day until we are called down for dinner. It had become dark and the blue lights were lit like usual. Elves had already started to sing and dance. I am immediately pulled into their circle to join in with their festivities.

After a while of dancing, I make my way to the table filled with food. It's not long before I am pulled back into the dancing.

"Don't your feet hurt?" Luthias asks while looking at my boots.

"Yes. They have grown uncomfortable over the past weeks." I kick off my shoes, not bothering where they land.

The festivities continue until the first light of day shines upon the woods. When the Elves decided to retire, Luthias picks me up, just like our wedding night. He carries me up to our room, laying me down on the bed. As soon as we lie down, we are fast asleep.

The next morning, Luthias and I help set up the next feast. Everyone seemed to walk around slowly, tired from the night before. I don't feel any older, or younger. Mature would be the word to describe how I feel. I feel like I can do anything and make my own choices.

Tables and chairs are set up by nightfall, small talk is exchanged as we take our seat. It is less exciting than the festival we had at Ambrose. I sit at the table, my chin propped up by my hand. Lindalin is very simple when it comes to things like this. They like to keep everything calm, not even wine is passed out to the table.

Sentier seems to be feeling the effect of not having wine more than the others. I always see him with a glass in his hand. In the cellars of Lithien, there is bottle after bottle of different wines. There are even some that haven't been opened since the First Age.

I escape from the boring feast, sneaking past the guards that stand watch. I walk up the stairs in search of the small room that I had found earlier this morning. It seems to be a meeting room and a small couch is pushed up against a window. I plop down on the couch, grabbing the book I had placed here earlier.

The book is the one that Linder gave to me yesterday. I haven't written in it yet and I do wish to do that tonight. I light some candles around the room and the shadows flicker on the walls. Another book is set on the desk by the door. I don't remember that being there earlier. I walk up to it, flipping through its pages.

The door clicks open and Sentier stands shocked in the doorway. He sighs when he notices that it is me. "You have taken my spot." He says with a smile.

"I'm sorry, I just had to get away."

"It's boring isn't it?" He opens up a drawer in the desk, pulling out two glasses and a bottle of wine. "Do you want some?"

"Umm...yes I do." He pours the purple liquid into the glass goblet, handing it over to me. "I see that you have come here more than me."

"That is true. I like to get away."

"Then you understand and will let me stay."

He laughs, nodding his head. Sentier sits down in a chair, sipping his wine. I move back to my couch, keeping the glass in my hand. It is silent for a moment and I look out the window trying to avoid the awkwardness.

"You know Luthias won't be able to follow you to the land of the Gods."

"I have suspected that."

"There is only one ship at this time. And you have to be asked by the Electa themselves to be able to go

"And he must stay here to fight. They need him here." I pause, trying to think about life without him is impossible. "You will keep him safe. Make him understand why I had to leave."

"I will try my best." He grabs his book, opening to his marked page. I drown the glass of wine and he looks up to laugh at me. "You are supposed to enjoy it, taste it."

I look back out at the window. The stars shine through the canopy of trees, covering us in a blanket of light. I open to the first page of the book. I stare at the blank page, picking up my ink quill. *The Tales of LaRue.*

The next morning, I wake up in my guest room next to Luthias. I don't remember coming back. He smiles at me. "Are you excited to return home?"

I sigh. "Yes. Can we leave now?"

"Everything is all packed, you just have to get dressed."

I jump out of bed, slipping on a tunic and pants. I practically run down the stairs to my horse and Luthias follows after me. Tolendeil joins us and she smiles brightly as we leave the golden wood behind. She is a bit nervous at first, but as we tell her more about home she seems to calm down.

The day after we return will be Luthias' birthday and the Feast of Adara. I try to think of gift ideas, but none seem to come to me. I am too excited about returning home.

***

As the gate draws near, I gallop Venetta to the stables. The stable boys nicely take her and Luthias and I run to our room. Home is one of the most important things to us. Home and each other. We unpack our things, placing them in their rightful places.

"My father has summoned me LaRue. I will be back in about an hour or two." Before he leaves he kisses my cheek.

I had asked Sentier to spend the day with him, so I could find Luthias a gift. It is probably a good thing for them to do because they rarely get to spend time together. It might make their bond stronger.

I leave Tolendeil to explore the castle as I make my way to the armory. I had an idea and hopefully it will work. Luthias never really had a special sword like most royalty had. His long sword didn't even have a name.

I half expected the man I had talked to before I was married would be here working. But I asked another sword maker where that man was and said that he had past. It was not the information I had expected to be given and my mind blurs at what his name is.

The heat leaps around the room and fires shine bright in almost every corner. "Are you looking for anything?" The blacksmith asks.

"Yes, do you by any chance think you can forge a sword for me?"

"I can do almost anything LaRue." I pull out the folded piece of paper and I hand it to him. He unfolds it, looking at every detail. He nods his head in agreement. "Did you draw this?"

"Yes. Now the question is, can it be done by tomorrow."

He smiles, sticking the paper into his black apron. "It can be done." I leave at that good note. It wasn't long before I was called back to the armory. The blade of the sword sat across the table, still red from being pulled out from the fire.

"Do you want anything written across it?" The Elf asks. I look over at the handle that is ready to be put together with the blade.

"King to the Hidden Kingdom." If I was Queen he was King. He would rule that kingdom now, especially if I am leaving. With a sharp tool he carves the Elven runes in carefully. I watch as he puts the handle to the blade. The handle shines bright with blue and green jewels just like Luthias' eyes.

The Elf hands me the sword, its metal still hot, but it is strong as dragon scales. It's long, fit for a tall Elf like Luthias.

I exist the armory, searching the halls for Tolendeil. I find her in the kitchen, leaning over the table to steal a cookie while the cook has her back turned. I watch as she takes three more before the cook again turns around.

"Tolendeil." I call. It seems that even though she is much, much older than me, she still has the sense of a young child. She jumps off the stool, taking a bite of one of the cookies she had taken. "Have you explored anywhere else?" I ask her.

"Can you show me my room?" She pleads.

I grin. "Of course." She wraps my arm around her's and pleads me to walk faster to her room. "There's not going to be much in your room Tolendeil. That will be your job to collect and buy things for your room. Clothes will be provided for you and I think you have a fitting next week."

"Really!" Tolendeil jumps around.

"Calm down. Sentier likes it quiet. Especially down this hall."

The statues glow in the sun and many have been added to the hall since the war and they now stand beside Lauralaethee and Luvon. I pause, Tolendeil still pulling on my arm.

"Come on LaRue."

I raise my hand, telling her to stop and be quite. Sentier had my friends honored here, even though they had not been from Lithien. I touch the stone face of Vestan, running a hand over Silvyr's arm, and then I give a slight nod to Caldon. I wish they were still here, that I was able to speak with them and get to know them more.

They each hold a sword, a replica of their own that I gave to the people who desired them and needed that one last object from their deceased loved one.

"Do you know them?" Tolendeil asks.

"I know many in this hall."

"Are they still alive?"

"No. They have passed."

She bows her head. "I am sorry."

I smile at her, continuing down the hall and to her room. "This is yours and you can do with it as you please. Sentier only asks that you aren't too loud and you keep things clean."

I bow, turning out of the doorway. 'LaRue," She calls and I pause. "Are you really, truly leaving?"

"I believe so, Tolendeil."

I close the door behind her, not wanting to talk about leaving again. It just has to happen. I pause. Remembering one of my visions of pushing the white haired girl off of the cliff. It was Tolendeil. I don't know why I would harm her, I wouldn't even dare threaten her.

I continue to walk down the corridor, feeling lonelier with every step I take.

***

A great feast is held the next day to honor Luthias and the last Feast of Adara. I am able to pull Luthias away from the party to give him his gift, but he seems slightly distracted.

"Happy Birthday Luthias." I say as I pull the sword from out of my cloak. With a smile he takes it from my hands. He pulls it out of its sheath and he admires the jeweled handle. He tests it out with a couple of swings, before he slides it back into the sheath.

"King to the Hidden Kingdom?"

"If I am Queen, what does that make you?" I laugh.

"I suppose a king." He embraces me. "Thank you LaRue."

I smile, breathing in his familiar scent of peppermint, oak leaves and the slightest bit of vanilla. I breathe his name, a tear slips down my cheek and onto his shoulder. If I leave like I said I would, I would never get to be by his side again. I am better off dead, but I made a promise to go to the Electa.

"You may be a Queen, but you will always be my stars and sun."

I interrupt him, my mind wandering quickly. "If the Electa didn't write the prophecy, then who did?"

"LaRue-"

"What year was it written?"

"The First Age."

"I said year."

He sighs. "1489. Two great kings had written it, wanting the future of their kingdoms safe. It wasn't till the second age around your birthday when it was found. It still holds true to you though. It always has and it always will. That's the way they intended it to be."

"I just wish that I could do something more. The Electa has showed me my future and I am not pleased about it, so they are advising me to leave. I don't want to hurt anyone."

"I understand. I truly do LaRue. And I'll be right here and by your side the whole entire time. I promise."

My heart pounds knowing that he is wrong. Knowing that we may never see each other again.

Chapter 30

The next few days passed and were gone, the Feasts of Adara are over. I have been spending my time helping Chalsarda with her wedding; she had been a panic for the last day. I sit in a chair as a maid pins her dress together.

"Are you sure it looks nice? Do you think Amar will like it?"

"He will love it Chalsarda. There is no need to worry."

"But I am worrying." She squirms.

The maid looks up to her as she hems the bottom of the dress. "If you move you're going to get pricked by a needle." Needles dotted the sides of the dress and around the hem.

"I can't believe I am wearing a dress and a white one at that! Ouch!" She yelps. "That needle hurt!"

"I told you not to move."

I cover my mouth to stifle a giggle. She glares at me, crossing her arms. She again goes into panic mode. "What kind of flowers did you pick?"

"You said you wanted a surprise."

"I do, but I don't."

"I am not going to tell you."

"Are they red? I do love red. Oh! What about yellow or purple? You know I love those colors."

"I have it all under control." I had all her flowers ready and made into a bouquet. They were all the colors she had asked about.

Chalsarda turned to look in the mirror and she just about cried, but she wiped away the tears quickly before I could even see them. "I am getting married tomorrow. Can you believe it?"

"It seems surreal doesn't it?"

***

The next day Chalsarda paced back and forth in her room. Her white dress barely touched the stone floor. I place a silver jewel in her hair. "You will be fine." She smiles, looking into the mirror for the last time. "And for your surprise." I had her the bouquet of flowers.

"Thank you, you got them perfect."

"I picked them myself."

I take her hand as we walk down to the garden. The leaves are slowly turning from green to gold. Her hand clutches mine in a death grip and I look down at her boots, a dagger gleams on the inside.

"Do you really need a weapon?"

"Yes, I feel more secure."

I laugh as we stop at the garden entrance. There are very few guests and I see Chalsarda searching for Amar. "He is there, don't worry. Now, keep your head up and stand tall."

"Are you leaving?"

"Yes, you can't walk down the aisle with me."

I walk away, taking the long way through the gardens. I stand next to Luthias as the music begins. The harpists flutter their fingers over the strings creating a beautiful melody. Amar waits patiently, this is one of the first times he hasn't worn a cloak to cover his head.

His breath caught in his throat as Chalsarda walked down the stone path. She smiled brightly, keeping her eyes interlocked with Amar's. As she took hands with Amar, a rope is wrapped around their hands, keeping them together for the vows.

The vows are spoken quietly between them, not wanting others to hear their confessions of love to each other. Their kiss ties it together, a bond that cannot be broken. They left after, spending the rest of the day together

***

Over the past few days, soldiers were preparing for war against Nolan for he had sent a messenger and proved what we have all thought. So many Elves are ready to fight and I am leaving them all even before it begins. Guilt runs through me like a rushing river. I would rather die beside them, then sail to the Electa. I wish I could spend more time with Luthias, but he is always getting pulled away from me.

She slept with her hands around her head like a pillow. Her curly hair is scattered in every direction. LaRue always had curly hair and was one of the only Elves to have this strange quality.

Many Elves have straight hair or even a few simple curls. But her golden hair was one ringlet after the other. I loved it and often found myself playing with it when I got the chance.

I pull the blanket over her body and kiss her forehead. “I will be back.” I said quietly.

“Where are you going?” She slowly opened her blue eyes.

“I have to scout the boundaries with the guards.”

She grabbed my hand before I could even look at the door. “Be safe.”

“I will.”

I get up after he leaves, I find myself wandering the halls, not knowing what to do while he is gone. As the tears fall from my face a hand is placed on my shoulder. Tolendeil frowns. “What is wrong LaRue?”

“I am never going to see him again.”

“LaRue, must you go?”

“I already told the council that I would. They won’t change their minds after I have agreed with them.”

“Luthias will never forgive himself for letting you go. And you wouldn’t forgive yourself.”

I leave, going back into my room. I sit at my desk, finishing some of the last lines of my book. It is dark when Luthias returns.

“Is there something I don’t know LaRue.”

“No. Why were you gone for so long?” I ask, changing the subject.

“The guards wanted me to stay longer than expected.”

I get up from the desk, getting into bed. He lies beside me, pulling the blanket over us. He wraps his arms around my waist and I start to feel more relaxed.

I close my eyes, but I find myself stuck, unable to move. I only watch as Navain brings my siblings in one at a time, torturing them, harming them. They cry out for me to help, yelling at me to stand up. Navain hands me a knife, but I wake up before I am able to do anything.

My nightmares are at the worst this night. Just about every hour I wake screaming or crying. Luthias holds me until I fall back asleep again. The next time I wake up, I am screaming for my brothers and sister.

They had not return from Everford and I have been worried about them. They had also brought Elora with them who has been with child. Again Luthias comforts me, calming me down.

"They came back tonight LaRue. It's all right," He coos. "It's all right."

We stayed up till morning, his comforting words spoken often. Luthias opens the balcony windows, letting the light shine in. He then moves to the closet and pulls out a tunic and pants.

"Get ready to go."

"Go where?"

"Hunting. You don't mind, do you?"

"No, but can I see my siblings first. You said that they had arrived last night."

"I was planning on that." He laughs.

I slip into my leather armor and grab my bow before I exit the room. As I walk outside, my brothers and sister wait for me. They laugh about something that I cannot hear. I then see Elora, a small bundle is wrapped in her arms. Eryn turns towards me, embracing me.

"We are so sorry that we missed your birthday. Both of you."

"Its fine, I am just glad that you are all back safely."

"I have a gift for both of you." She pulls out a package wrapped in brown paper for each of us. "It's not much, but it's something." Eryn smiles as we unwrap the gifts. "I know how much you both complain about your boots and you both just love dancing so much."

The shoes are forest green and will match most of our clothes. "Thank you Eryn." We both say. Eldrin and Eldar each hand us a small box.

"They're rune stones. If you're ever lost or a choice undecided, just give them a toss and they will tell you."

I smile in thanks. "I am sorry LaRue. I don't have a gift." Elora explains.

"It doesn't matter. All that matters is that I have one of my best friends back!" I hug her carefully, trying not to squish the baby in her arms. "Now who is this?" I say in a sweet voice.

"LaRue I would like you to meet my daughter. Her name is Silevel."

"She is beautiful." I say, looking at her silver eyes that are just like her father's.

"I tried to make her name like Silvyr's. If she was a boy that would have been her name."

Elora stares down at her beautiful baby girl, Silevel already has silver hair like her father. She bounces the girl softly in her arms, staring at her like she is the only thing in her world.

Luthias and I continue with our plan of hunting. We sit on a rock ledge by the river. We watch as the birds pass their songs to each other, floating down to rest in the Oak trees around us.

After a few hours of sitting a deer comes into view. Luthias aims his bow down at it, preparing to make his deadly shot. I place a hand on his bow, stopping him from letting his arrow loose.

"Luthias we do not shoot this one." The white stag comes into a better view, its coat like winter snow. He stares at us, nodding his head like he usually does and then leaves.

"We should head back."

"I agree." As we walk back to the castle, I ask Luthias about the plans for war. "When do you plan to march to Nolan's borders?"

"Maybe in a week or so. We are still gathering extra forces."

"I have talked to Avon and Tolendeil and they said they will ride with me to the ship."

"That makes me feel a bit better. I do wish I could ride there with you." Luthias grabs my hands and spins me around in a circle, right into his arms. "Have I ever told you how in love I am with you?"

"A million times."

"And I will say it a million more."

His soft lips touch mine and we then continue down the corridor. As we walk down the hall, voices echo, their angered voices bounce off of the walls.

"We must ride to war! Nolan has somehow found out, he marches closer to the forest as we speak."

"Then we have a traitor amongst us, find them immediately."

"I am giving you my council, will you not take it?"

It is silent for a moment. "How long till they reach my courtyard?"

"Three days, two, maybe even one. One cannot tell."

"Prepare Laerune's horse, she will leave at sundown. And find her a worthy escort, not some lousy traitor!" Glass shatters as Sentier turns the corner with the guard next to him. "I'm sorry." Is all he says as he continues down the hall.

Leaving today! That only leaves me a few hours to say goodbye, to spend my last moments with Luthias and my court. I walk into the dining hall, not able to make eye contact with anyone, especially Luthias.

"I am leaving tonight." I finally look up at my court and friends.

"You're leaving tonight!" Tolendeil stands up in anger.

"Please sit down." I speak calmly.

"You're leaving? To where?" Elora asks.

"I am sailing to the Electa. A council was held to decide if I should go or not and I agreed."

"But...but why?" Eldrin stutters, tears falling from his eyes.

"They want to keep me safe. I want to keep all of you safe."

"You can't go!" He yells, storming out of the room.

Eldar and I follow him and we find him sitting in the hallway, his knees pulled up to his chest. "Eldrin. Listen to me." He looks up, wiping his eyes with his sleeve. "I am sorry. If I don't do this I fear that the Electa will hurt all of you."

"How can you leave Luthias? Does he know that there isn't another ship?"

"No he does not know. I am scared to tell him. Maybe it will be better if he doesn't know."

Eldrin doesn't reply. "I am going to miss you."

"I am going to miss you too. Both of you." Eldrin and Eldar both envelope me in a hug. "You will protect him. Make him understand."

"We will."

I walk back to my room and Luthias, Chalsarda, Elora, Eryn, and Tolendeil sit quietly in my room. They don't know what to say, especially Luthias. The light had disappeared from his eyes and he stares down at the floor.

I open my saddle bag, stuffing clothes and miscellaneous object into it. I grab sentimental things, like journals and books, my mother's crown, and gifts from my friends. I slide my sword and dagger into my belt, strapping my bow and arrows over my shoulder. I shove my rune stones into my pocket along with my vile of Athelas leaves.

I look at them, their eyes filled with sadness as I turn my head to look at the nearly setting sun. The colors mix with gold and purple. Tears slip down my face and also theirs. They follow me as I walk outside and into the courtyard. Avon and Tolendeil have already mounted their horses, waiting for me to say my last goodbyes.

I walk over to Amar and Chalsarda, their hands interlocked. "I wish you the best in luck in all that is to come. I will miss you both dearly." *I want to make this quick.*

"Thank you for everything."

I then move over to Elora, the baby girl still in her arms. "You are a great friend. And I hope you enjoy being a mother, because I know you will be a great one." She doesn't say anything else, she just hugs me.

"Eldrin, Eldar, I must say you are the best brothers I could ever ask for. Even if it was just a short while. I love you both."

I then turn to Eryn, her blue eyes fill with tears. "I love you." She cries. "I am sorry I couldn't be there more for you."

"Don't say that. You will always be here for me. Always. I will miss you my beautiful sister."

"I will miss you too."

She slips a piece of paper into my pocket and I smile at her. The next goodbyes will be the hardest. I turn to Sentier, he quickly wipes the tears away, trying to hide that he actually felt emotion.

"Make amends with your son. He is going to need you more than ever. And don't be scared to show emotion," I whisper

"I will."

I tightly embrace him and he is shocked at first, but he then wraps his arms around me, placing his head on top of mine. "You are and will always be like a daughter to me."

"And you a father." I look up at him, smiling.

I move to my father, his face strong and his head held up high. "My beautiful daughter." He smiles, his blue eyes turning glossy.

"I tried father." I cry.

"You tried what?"

"I tried being someone you would be proud of; most importantly, I tried being someone I would be proud of."

"I am beyond proud of you. You have overcome the worst, you have even cheated death, my daughter!" He laughs. He lifts up my head, so my eyes meet his. "Now, keep your head up and stand tall. A new adventure is ahead of you, are you ready to take it?"

"I will try."

"Give your mother my love." He kisses my forehead. "I love you."

"I love you too, father."

Now, the last and hardest goodbye. Luthias pulls me into his arms, refusing to let go. He breathes in deeply. "After all the times I have had to say goodbye to you, this has to be the worst."

"I know." His scent fills my nose and I bury my face in his blonde hair. "I love you Luthias."

"I love you LaRue."

"You have made my life amazing. You made every day worth living and I regret none of it. You have saved my life so many times and I thank you for that."

"And by many, you mean many!"

"Yes many! And my life seems complete as it will ever be and I haven't had to go through anything alone. You have taught me so much in life and most importantly, you gave me the greatest adventure I could ever ask for." The tears stream down my face endlessly. A never ending rainstorm woken up from the roar of thunder and the flash of lightning.

"No Laerune Aduial, you gave me the most important adventure. It has been better than anything I could ever ask for. But, I don't understand why you are saying such meaningful things when I will see you again? I will be a month at the least." I quickly kiss him before Sentier picks me up, setting me up onto my horse. "There isn't another ship, is there?" I shake my head and Sentier slaps the back of my horse, causing it to run down the stone path.

"I love you." I cry.

I turn my head to look back, Luthias is on his knees crying. It hurts my heart to see him in this much pain. Avon and Tolendeil ride ahead and I turn back for one last time. Sentier and Amar are pulling Luthias back inside the castle. His pained cries echo through the forest and it makes my heart clench in my chest. Eldrin looks back at me, tears in his sorrowful eyes.

I cry into Venetta's mane and the sun finally sets behind the mountains. I lift my head up at the sky, hoping to see the stars, but they are veiled. I take in my surroundings for it will be my last time in Laquilasse.

"My Prince, they have arrived." I pull on my golden armor that was the twin set to LaRue's. I sheath my sword at my side, letting the last tears fall before I put myself back together.

A horn blows, guards run to the gates and I nock an arrow into my bow. "There's Orcs as well my Prince." A guard tells me. I shove the doors open, beginning the war. I have no hope to live, no fear of death. I slice through my enemies with anger and sadness.

I search for Nolan, he had started this and I will finish it.

Nolan wears white armor to show the blood of his victims. I take one last look around my home. I see my family and friends stop, watching me as I walk towards Nolan.

"Luthias!" Amar calls, but I ignore him.

"You think you can win this Elf?"

"I may not win, but I can kill you."

"Then you will die with me!" He growls.

Nolan swings his blade towards my chest, but I block it with my blade. I take my next chance to swing, but I only rip the side of his white armor. Out of the corner of my eye I can see Amar trying to get to me. "Luthias!" He yells again. I turn back to Nolan, his sword sliding into my side. I do the same to him and his laugh catches in his throat.

"For Laerune Aduial." I whisper as I fall to my knees. I see Nolan look around the battlefield, blood dripping from his mouth, his eyes confused as he takes his last look at the word he has lost.

I pull the sword from my side, dropping it onto the ground. The stars spin above me and Amar comes into my view. He speaks, but his words silent.

The sun reflects across the ocean water and the sails of the boat billow in the wind. I pick up my skirts, boarding onto the large ship. The Elven symbol for the sea is stitched onto the sails and I speak to the captain of the ship.

"Is the island beautiful?"

"Don't be scared Lady Laerune. You will be welcomed and cared for."

I proceed to board onto the large ship, the wind blowing through my loose hair. The sun starts to set, it took us a day to get here. I look overboard at the changing sea. My tears drip down my face, mixing with the salty ocean water.

I place my hands in my pockets. I feel something familiar and I pull my hand out, revealing the rune stones that my brothers gave me.

If you're ever lost and don't know where to turn, these shall give you the answer.

"Do I leave across the sea?" I ask as I toss them up. I open my palm, each of them turned over to say no.

I shove the stones into my pocket, running off of the boat. The plank had been taken off and I jump across to the dock. I mount Venetta, starting the trek back to Lithien. I would not be left out of a fight. *Never again.*

"Friend, stay strong. Help is coming." Amar rushes.

"Amar I can't. There is no reason for me to live. She is gone. Never to return."

"What of your friends? Your father?"

"Being immortal doesn't mean you can't die."

Venetta jumps over fallen trees and skids down the paths of Lithien. Bodies become more common and I reach the courtyard. Blood rushes through the grooves of the stone and I search for familiar faces. I see Nolan, Luthias' sword through his stomach. *Why wouldn't he take his sword? Where is he?* I go through all the possibilities in my head, very few end with him alive.

"Luthias!" I yell out his name.

"My mother is calling for me Amar. I must go."

"It's not your mother Luthias! It's her! It's LaRue. She's here."

I shake my head. My memories of my mother become more vivid, as if color was added to them. Her smiling face shines above me, tears dripping down her face.

"You must stay my son. You cannot leave. I do miss you, but you can't end your adventure here." She places a hand on my cheek and then disappears without a goodbye and I frown.

I drop my weapons, running over to the fallen figure that Amar is crying over. Blood covers Luthias' face and body. The wound is fatal, yet I refuse to believe it.

"Mother?" He asks.

"No Luthias, it's me. It's LaRue."

He shakes his head. "No, she is gone, beyond the sea. I loved my mother very much." He looks beyond me, maybe his mother is really there. He then looks at me. "My greatest adventure is ending LaRue. Forgive me."

"This adventure can't end, it just started."

"I love you Laerune Aduial."

"I love you too, but you can't go." I hold him in my arms. The sight of his blood makes me shake. I quickly pull out the vile of Athelas leaves and I whisper the words of healing as I rub the leaves into his wound. His tears fall faster, the pain taking over him.

"Please Electa, with any of the power you have given to me, allow me to heal him. Please."

I can feel his pain through my body, it pounds through my head. My vision blurs and I wipe the blood that drips down from my mouth. A sharp pain pounds through my head again and I lie my head on his shoulder, falling asleep next to him. I am unable to open my eyes and it feels like years had passed in only seconds. I do not know if Luthias was alive, I didn't even know if I, myself, were alive.

Chapter 31

I open my heavy eyelids and the sun blinds me. My eyes start to adjust and I examine my surroundings. I am in my old room in Ambrose. I look to my left, Luthias is gone from his normal spot next to me. A wedding dress hangs by my door. It was not the dress from Luthias and I's wedding, but from the one I was supposed to wear from Avon's. *Was this all a dream? A nightmare?*

I start to cry and I yell for my father. He rushes into the room. "You're awake!"

"Father please, don't make me get married to Avon. I don't love him that way."

"LaRue, what are you talking about? You're not getting married."

"I'm not? Then why is my dress hanging up?"

"It was in your closet, but the maids cleaned your room and pulled it out. They forgot to put it away that is all."

"It wasn't just a dream?"

"Are you feeling well LaRue? I can call a healer."

"I am fine father."

He feels my forehead with the back of his hand. I look at my shining silver ring, it still shines like the stars, just like the day Luthias had given it to me. I then remember what had happened after the battle against Nolan. I try to decide what is my imagination and what it reality.

"Father, where is Luthias?"

"Laerune-"

"Where is Luthias?" I yell in anger. He can't be dead. I refuse to believe it. "Is he dead?"

"I don't know." He sadly answers.

I get up from my bed, grabbing my bag and slamming the door behind me. He is not dead. *He is not dead. He is not dead.* He is not dead. He has to be alive. *Alive. Alive. He is not dead.* Not dead.

About the Author

Sydney McNeill is a self-published author who lives in Gwinn, Michigan. She loves watching *The Lord of the Rings* and writing in her free time. After high school, her plans are to go to Northern Michigan University and become an English Professor. And hopefully have a dog in the future.

Made in the USA
Lexington, KY
20 December 2018